SMOKE AND SMOLDER

THE AZAR TRILOGY: BOOK ONE

GRACE MCGINTY

This book is dedicated to my mother, who loved the first story I wrote when I was five, and has loved every one I have written since. Thank you for your never ending encouragement and support.

All my love.

SMOKE AND SMOLDER

CHAPTER 1

Azar braced herself as the fire raged around her. This was the best part of her job; the smoke filling her lungs like sweet perfume, the heat from the flames stretching out to embrace her. She felt alive at times like this, when her true nature was a blessing not a curse, and the constant war she fought within held a truce for a brief moment.

She was a firefighter, but she was also Ifrit, a form of Djinn that was made of, you guessed it, fire. It flowed through her veins and along her skin. Not literally of course, she was only half Ifrit, the bastard creation of a fire Djinn, or genies as Westerners called them, and her Iranian mother. It was probably fortunate she was a half blood. She was pretty certain that Joe would freak out if her turnout gear suddenly combusted and she grew fiery bat wings and horns. Not to mention the goats feet.

Joe suddenly appeared from the smoke in front of her. Shit, she'd been standing still for too long.

"Az, what the hell are you doing?"

Well that's what he would have said if he wasn't busy examining her for injuries and electrocution entry points. What he actually did was give her the okay sign with his gloved hands. She returned the sign and got her head back in the game. The small residential building had caught on fire in one of the lower apartments. The fire was spreading rapidly, probably due to cost cutting measures by the construction firm.

There were a few tenants unaccounted for, and Azar hoped they were all out for dinner somewhere nice. She and Joe had been with the first responding truck, which meant it was their job to find the source of the fire and any potential victims. They swept through the burning apartment, calling out to anyone who might need help in the smoke-filled room. They made their way along the walls, away from the kitchen, where the fire had started.

As Azar walked along at a brisk pace, she sent out her consciousness to the fire. She would never be able to explain what talking to a fire felt like exactly, but it recognized her as one of its own kind. Fire didn't consume fire. It would ignore her as it greedily ate up everything in the room. It was its greed that told her if there was someone left in the area. The fire would continue to reach until it was devouring the life force of the unfortunate victim.

Her heart sank as she felt it lurch towards the wall, desperately trying to break through the flimsy barrier to the life on the other side. She searched the rest of this apartment quickly but methodically, then touched Joe's arm to get his attention. She indicated that she'd heard something in the next apartment. A lie, but a better option than telling the truth.

Sprinting to the next apartment as fast as they could while weighed down by their turnout gear, they swept through the rooms. Azar shouted with controlled desperation as they searched for signs of life. They searched the bedrooms, bathroom, kitchen and the living room with no sign of any victims.

Frustrated, she continued to look more thoroughly than protocol demanded. She knew there was someone here, and the fire had raced down the hall after them because it knew it too. They opened cupboards and closets but there was no sign of anyone. Joe motioned that they should move on, but Azar wanted to search again.

"Give me fifteen more seconds," she yelled back. The fire had eaten through the paper-thin walls and the whole living room was quickly going up in flames. Azar stopped and concentrated, sending out her own abilities, similar to those of the fire. Then she knew.

She sprinted towards the bathroom, wrenching open the cabinet door under the sink. A little boy about three or four was curled up around the pipe, tears streaming down his chubby little cheeks from fear and the smoke burning his eyes. Azar pried the child from the pipes and he clung tightly to her neck. Joe was behind her, already radioing in that they had a victim who would need medics. He turned and strode out of the apartment towards the exit.

As Azar reached the apartment door, a popping noise followed by a crack directly above her head made her jump back instinctively. A support beam crashed down between her and Joe, trapping her and the boy inside the apartment. The fire flared up angrily, the heat so intense that she worried the child's skin would burn. She saw the look of horror on Joe's face as he uselessly tried to shift the beam.

"Get out! We'll go out through the window!" she

yelled at him. Joe nodded; it had been drummed into them through training that standing there would only get someone killed and helps no one. He would call in a mayday and get a ladder around to the northside of the building, because that was protocol.

Azar turned her back against the flames to protect the boy from the fires heat. When she was sure Joe would be out of the building, she broke all the rules and took off her mask, putting the oxygen over the boy's face.

Her lungs welcomed the smoke like an old friend. It would take approximately six minutes for them to utilize their available resources and run the ladder up to the second story window. Azar predicted there was about four minutes before the entire apartment went up in flames. She ran to the farthest window from the fire to make sure she was clearly visible to her colleagues below. Breaking the window would make the fire roar to life as oxygen flooded in, feeding the fire; they would only smash it at the last minute.

She was going to have to starve the fire of oxygen to slow it down, and the only way to do that was to feed her own internal fire. She closed her eyes. She had the boy clutched close to her chest with the oxygen mask covering almost all of his little face and she kept him angled away from the fire that raged at their backs. Azar breathed deep, sucking the oxygen from the room.

The Ifrit in her rejoiced, the flames roiling under her skin, desperately trying to cover her body in spectacular flames. Her turnout gear kept the intense heat that emitted from her body from burning the child. The fire inside her grew until it hurt to contain.

Azar gritted her teeth as the flames in the room shrank back, retreating from its attack as it lost its food source. She wouldn't be able to extinguish it. To do that she would have to surrender completely to the Ifrit, causing huge flaming wings to spread out from her back and her body would be encased in fire. But she could hold it back for a few minutes, to give the boy a fighting chance. The fire couldn't burn her; it would just lick at her body like a lover's tongue.

Turning back to the window, she saw Lieutenant Ryan's head come up over the window sill and Azar remembered to cough so she appeared human. Ryan motioned her back as he smashed the glass with a small fire axe. The subdued fire roared back to life.

Azar quickly handed the boy off to Ryan. Securing her oxygen mask back on her face, she climbed through the window and followed Ryan down the ladder to the safety of the pavement. The fire flicked angrily out the window after her and she smiled to herself. She was its master. As she set her feet on the ground, and the outside team attacked the fire with the hose lines.

She was ushered over to the medics, who would fuss until they marvelled at her lack of injuries and cleared her for a return to duty. She was happy to see the boy in the arms of an extremely distraught woman. The woman spotted Azar above his sooty head and rushed over. Then she burst into a fresh bout of tears. Azar shifted uncomfortably from foot to foot. She was no good with overt displays of emotion.

"Thank you so much. I have five children and he was hiding-" the mother's voice cracked as she sobbed, "and I couldn't find him and I didn't know what to do. I thought I'd lost..." The rest of her words were incomprehensible over her sobs as she broke down into a fresh wave of tears. Azar patted the woman's shoulder awkwardly. She never knew what to do when someone started crying.

"I was just doing my job. Everything will be okay now." Azar used her most soothing voice.

In all honesty, everything probably wasn't going

to be okay. The woman didn't seem like the type of person who could afford insurance and she'd just lost everything except her children. But Azar knew she'd be fine. If her 125 years on this earth had taught her anything, it was that humans were resilient and resourceful. Far more so than her own kind, whose numbers dwindled century by century until their population was only in the thousands.

Joe's wife Linda volunteered with a charity that provided emergency housing and Azar made a mental note to get Joe to give the woman Linda's number before they left.

The mother was still crying and hugging her shocked children as Azar drifted away from the ambulance toward her Officer In Charge. Captain José Fuentes was in his early fifties and had more than his fair share of gray hair. The look he shot her would have withered an oak.

"Take off your air again, Nazemi, and I'll put you on suspension. Hell, I might even leave you up there for being so stupid." He pointed to the burning building which still had smoke pouring out of several windows.

Azar smiled. "Yes Sir," she said in a semi-apologetic tone. They both knew that if the need arose again, she'd do exactly the same thing. The chastisement was merely to release the tension of almost losing a man. Joe came over and wrapped an arm around her shoulders.

"You had me worried. I didn't know how I was going to tell Linda that you wouldn't be able to make her *Zereshk Polow* for dinner ever again." He smiled at her, relief evident in his eyes. *Zereshk Polow* was an Iranian dish her mother had taught her. It was one of the few dishes that Azar could actually cook with anything resembling edibility.

"I would have run straight for the hills if I was you." She nudged the crook of his shoulder with her head. "Speaking of Linda, could you give her number to the kid's mother? She seems pretty desperate."

Joe nodded, pulling out one of the cards he kept in the pocket of his coveralls for just this kind of occasion and strode over to talk to the boy's mother. He was tall, easily matching her six feet, and his stride ate up the pavement with a purposeful swagger only gifted to those with extreme confidence.

Captain Fuentes addressed her without taking his eyes off the operation in front of him. "The medics clear you for duty?"

She nodded.

"Good. Stop standing around and go help your Lieutenant put a secondary line to the charlie side."

And just like that, she went from conquering hero to dismissed subordinate. She smiled. This wasn't the industry for showboating; you got things done, saved lives and went home safe.

Hours later, the fire was finally extinguished and Azar helped Joe repack the equipment. The apartment building was a sooty, soggy mess and she felt a momentary twinge of sadness for the people that lived inside, especially those who'd just lost everything. It was always the same in these cases. The buildings were nothing more than demolition jobs once the fire was finished. Joe stood up from where he was rolling hose lines and looked over her shoulder.

"Uh oh, your favorite person has just arrived."

Azar stiffened. She knew Joe could only mean one person.

Keenan Reilly. What a snake.

He was an Arson Detective for the NYPD. Azar seriously disliked the pompous jackass. He was from the old school and believed the fire and police departments were a man's domain. A woman still belonged in the home, where she could be ignored and insulated from the big bad world.

Azar had first met him at the FDNY 233rd battalion Christmas party about five years ago, just after she'd started working at the firehouse. He'd been standing in a group of women, looking sexy as sin; all tall, dark and devilish. Joe had introduced them, and Keenan had smiled and asked whose wife she was. She'd smiled back politely and told him she was a firefighter, not someone's arm candy. He'd had the good grace to look abashed, but from that moment her mind had been made up about Keenan Reilly. He was a chauvinist and a playboy, and she tried to have as little interaction with him as possible.

But everytime they were in the same room, sexual tension sparked between them like an Ifrit in a fireworks factory. There had been several almost kisses, and even more stand up arguments at inter-departmental functions over the years.

The sexy snake in question strode over to Joe and shook his hand.

"Maconi, Nazemi." He reached out a hand to Azar and she took it, letting go as quickly as possible. Not because it was sweaty or disgusting, but because of the jolt of excitement that always hit her stomach whenever they touched. Azar had tried to convince herself that it was a physical manifestation of the disgust she felt toward the man, but she wasn't that delusional. It was the thrill of physical attraction.

Reilly was stunning.

Black Irish, with blue eyes and jet black hair, pale Irish skin like marble and a good five inches on her six feet height; he made her mouth water. It made it doubly disappointing that he was such a jackass.

Keenan turned to Azar. "Fuentes would like you to join us while I do the inspection of the crime scene."

Azar nodded and shucked off her turnout gear to put back in the truck. Joe's eyes glittered with mirth. He was getting a real kick out of the Nazemi/Reilly show. "Don't wait around. I'll walk home from here. Give my love to Linda," she said, giving him the bird when he waggled his eyebrows.

She trailed after Reilly as he strode towards the building, appreciating the view. She liked that his height exceeded her own. It was pretty difficult to find these days; next to most men she looked Amazonian. It was a pity that his good points stopped at his physical aesthetics.

They ducked under the police tape that crossed the front door of the first apartment. Someone had decreed the remaining structure safe, though Azar doubted it was particularly safe before the fire. They strode toward the ignition point in the kitchen.

Chief Fuentes was talking to Burt, a veteran Fire Marshal from way back. He was a nice guy, coming up to retirement, and she'd often seen him and his wife at FDNY functions. The fact that Reilly and someone from the Bureau of Fire Investigations were here meant there was something pretty bad going down. Reilly took control of the group.

"The fire started here, but I can't see any accelerant that would have caused such a fast growing blaze." He indicated a spot in the middle of the tiled kitchen floor, where a charred pattern had seared into the tiles surface. "Plus the burn pattern is odd. I'll get a sample to send to the lab, but this is the third strange arson case this month..." Keenan's voice faded out until it was merely a buzz in the back of her mind.

Azar stared down at the pattern. It was a design she recognized only too well. It was the pattern every Ifrit knew instinctively. It was the emblem of the Djinn.

There was a serious embarrassment to being a fiery

supernatural badass that could faint like a 1920's silver screen damsel.

When she came around, Keenan was staring down at her with what appeared to be concern.

I must have hit my head on the way down, Azar thought, shaking the remaining blackness from her vision. She must have thought too loudly because the look on Reilly's face went from one of concern to one of annoyance in an instant.

"I may have inhaled more of that smoke than I thought," she said weakly, forcing a cough. "I'll be fine. Please continue."

She pushed herself up, ignoring Reilly's outstretched hand. Chief Fuentes gave her a hard stare and she did her best not to quake in her department issued boots. Fuentes wasn't a big man, but he knew people and Azar could only pray that he didn't see straight through her bad theatrics. He wasn't above kicking her butt all the way back to the station house if he thought she cheated on her medical check. She shuddered to think what he would do if he knew the real reason behind her momentary attack of the vapors.

"You need to go home Nazemi, and don't bother coming in for your shift tomorrow either. Just stay home and relax. My wife watches 'Dirty Dancing' in her pajamas and eats ice cream when she's sick. Perhaps you should try it."

Azar tried not to laugh. The Chief's wife, Natalia, was a former Russian Ballet dancer, and if she was watching movies and eating ice cream on the couch then she was probably as close to death as a person could get.

"Sure, Sir. I'll do that, right after we finish up here. Sorry for interrupting, Reilly. What were you saying?"

Reilly was starting to look suspicious. He narrowed his eyes at her, but continued. "As I was saying, we've had three suspicious fires with no accelerants and unusual points of ignition. The Coney Island fire three months ago, a sorority house fire over at NYU district two months ago that killed two students, and then this one. I can't find any correlation between them except they all have the same ignition pattern. I was hoping you may have seen something like this before, Chief. Both Burt and I have reached a dead end."

Azar's vision went blurry again but she held it together. The blood rushed from her face and she could only hope that the other guys put it down to smoke inhalation. She'd heard about something exactly like this before and it wasn't good. "Crap!" she muttered under her breath.

"What was that?"

Azar involuntarily cleared her throat. Shit, wasn't that some kind of tell? *Pull it together,* she chastised herself. "I said crap. It seems like we have ourselves a serial arsonist, doesn't it?"

It was the Chief who answered.

"Yes, it does. I hope you catch this guy soon, Detective. The death toll is already two lives too high. It would have been three today if Nazemi hadn't found the boy. I'm glad the family who lived in this apartment were out."

Everyone nodded. Saving lives was the most important part of both of their jobs, and the whole service felt it when someone died on a call out.

They quickly finished up the walk through as the crime scene guys wandered in with their latex gloves, and started snapping photos and gathering evidence. As they walked past the apartment where Azar and Joe had found the kid, Reilly looked through the door at the shell of the room.

"You're lucky you got out of there alive. From what Joe reported to the Chief, he didn't seem to think that you'd have enough time to get out."

Azar shrugged and walked back towards the exit.

"Maybe I have a little bit of the luck of the Irish in me too." She gave him her most winning smile and hoped he'd just drop it.

Joe had been right. If their roles were reversed and Joe had been stuck in the apartment with the boy, they both would have died before the team could have gotten the ladder truck to the window.

As they left the building, the police were cordoning off the main entrance with police tape. Fuentes walked towards his First Response Vehicle. "Nazemi, do you need a lift back to the firehouse?"

"No thanks, Chief. My apartment is right around the corner and I carpooled to work with Joe today. I'll walk it."

Fuentes looked like he wanted to argue, but the stubborn set of her jaw must have dissuaded him. He merely nodded, got in the SUV and drove off. That was the most important thing about managing a group of people who risked their lives every day; you had to pick your battles.

Unfortunately, Keenan Reilly wasn't so easily dissuaded.

"I'll give you a lift home." He ordered and strode off toward his car.

Azar stuck her tongue out at his retreating back. Sure, it was juvenile, but who the hell did he think he was? She turned on her heel and walked off in the opposite direction. She didn't take orders from his overbearing ass.

She'd walked about fifty feet before Reilly's car pulled up next to her.

"Don't be stubborn, Azar. I will get out and put you in that seat myself if I have to," he said through the rolled down window. Azar stopped mostly out of surprise. Reilly had never used her first name. She didn't even think he knew it.

She leaned down and braced her arms on the door, giving Reilly her most withering stare.

"Firstly, that would be abduction or false imprisonment or some other kind of felony. Secondly, you obnoxious asshole, I don't want a ride from you. I'd rather stand on hot coals all day!" He didn't need to know that standing on hot coals was actually rather pleasant for her kind. She pushed off the car and did her best to walk away with a 'fuck you' posture.

Reilly's car just rolled up next to her again. "You know something about that fire. Get in the car or I'll tell my suspicions to Fuentes and my superiors."

Azar swore violently on the inside while maintaining a perfectly neutral face. At least she hoped it was neutral, or at least expressing the pure disdain she actually felt right now. She took a deep breath in and counted to ten. It was a technique that Joe had taught to his sons when they were feeling extra feral. Unfortunately, it didn't really help right now. She was furious as she wrenched open the door and leaned into the car.

"What the hell would I know about a serial arsonist? Are you trying to tell me that I light these fires, race back across town and then go out and fight them? I'm fast Reilly, but I'm not that fast." She took a deep, calming breath. "It's no secret that I don't like you. Actually, right now, I loathe you, but I can tell you that I take my job and the protection of life very seriously."

Deep breaths, Azar. Deep breaths, she chanted to herself so she didn't give into the urge to reach between the seats and punch him in his perfectly square jaw.

"But fine, if you want to give me a ride home bad, then let's do it. But you better make it fast, because I'm fairly sure my commitment to protecting life doesn't extend to you right now," Azar growled as she slid into the car and sat as far away from Reilly as she could. To her annoyance, he didn't even look a little bit perturbed by her outraged soliloquy.

She gave him her address and sat in the passenger seat silently cursing him in every language she knew. The silence grew heavier as they drove down the busy streets of Brownsville and when they got to the curb at the front of her apartment block, Azar leapt out of the car before it had finished rolling to a stop. She marched towards the security door and punched in the code. Someone pulled the door open for her and she looked back to see Reilly standing right behind her.

"I'll walk you up." His tone was as stubborn as his expression. Asshole. Fucking chauvinistic, sexy as hell, asshole.

"Whatever." Azar set a punishing pace up the stairs to her apartment on the fifth floor, hoping that his cushy detective job had made him soft. Unfortunately, she had no such luck; he matched her pace the whole way and wasn't even out of breath when they got to her floor. Azar ground her teeth in frustration. She needed to process what she'd learned today and then figure out what she was going to do about it. What she didn't need was an audience to her soul searching moment.

She stood outside her door and jammed her keys into the multiple locks. She turned to dismiss Reilly but he'd moved closer so her breasts were mere inches from his chest. She could feel the heat coming from his skin and her breath hitched a little. He smelled like soap and smoke; an intoxicating aroma if you are a half human/half Ifrit woman.

"I'm here now, so you can go." Her voice wavered as she tried to push words pass the lump in her throat. She went to turn away but one of his arms shot up to block her escape. His other arm landed on the opposite side of her, boxing her in between his strong, tanned forearms, the door and his body. He leaned forward, his face so close that she could feel his breath fanning out on her cheeks. She held his gaze, refusing to back down first.

"I want you to tell me what you know about the fires. You know something, Azar, so don't bother denying it. Your face is like an open book for the entire world to read."

She hoped he was reading the giant 'Fuck You' that was written across her face right now, and not the subheading that said 'Please Fuck Me' instead.

It was the second time he'd used her first name in his slight Irish accent, and it sound sexy as hell. The skin on her shoulder burned where his forearms brushed against it. Her breaths came in choppy bursts as her body strained towards his like a magnet.

Dammit, Azar. Remember he's a giant jerk, she repeated to herself.

"I don't know what the hell you are talking about. I think your cop instincts are on the fritz." The words came out raspier than she intended. His blue eyes had her mesmerized and her arms reached up to rest on his shoulders of their own accord.

"This is such a bad idea." He ground out the words as their mouths and bodies crashed together. Her arms wrapped around his neck and his hands grabbed hold of her hips, pulling her against him. His lips were firm against hers, as demanding as his questions. He ran his tongue along her bottom lip before pushing it into her mouth. Their tongues thrust against each other as she tangled her fingers in his hair, pulling his head away slightly so she could tug on his lower lip, biting it hard.

Reilly groaned, pressing her back against the door until their bodies were jammed together so tightly she could feel the hard outline of his erection. He grabbed hold of her ass and lifted her up so their hips met, their bodies fitting perfectly together. Azar groaned and wrapped her legs around his waist, holding him to her.

Azar was vaguely aware of them moving into the apartment, as she buried her face in his neck. He pushed her against the wall of the entrance hall. He tore off his shirt, and she ran her hands over every angle and plane of his torso so she could commit them to memory. It was going in the spank bank, that was for sure. Still resting her against the wall, Reilly dragged her shirt up and leaned down to take one of her lace covered nipples into his mouth. Azar groaned, the sensation shooting straight down to pool between her legs. She didn't know what it was about this brooding alpha asshole, but he made her wet. Even when they were fighting, there was a little part of her that wanted to fuck him as well. Usually she had great self control, but the sexual tension between them had been brewing for so long now, it was give into it or let it consume her.

"Fuck, Reilly," she moaned.

"Call me Keenan," he whispered back before gently nipping her hard nipple.

"Fuck, Keenan!"

He growled and turned, walking further into her apartment, moving them toward the couch. He laid her down on the soft leather and started unzipping his pants as she propped up her butt and wiggled out of her cargos. When she finished, she looked at the hard edges of Keenan's naked body and momentarily forgot her burning need. His pale skin made him look like a marble statue, except for his pink nipples and the black hair that dusted his chest and trailed down to his very impressive dick.

He ran a condom over it and Azar had no idea where or when he'd had time to retrieve one. He must have been a boy scout as a kid. Always be prepared. He dipped his fingers inside her, stroking her like someone had given him a cheat sheet to all her happy places.

"Fuck, you're amazing," she said breathlessly.

"You swear a lot," was all he mumbled as he knelt between her thighs.

"Only when I'm frustrated and right now you're driving me crazy." He smiled down at her, the warmth in his face making her breath catch.

"Let's see if we can fix that."

He grabbed one of her legs and put it over his shoulder, then leaned forward and kissed her. When he gently rubbed his erection against her, she thought she might combust. She pushed back against him, urging him while her fingers dug into his impossibly hard shoulders. Keenan finally slipped himself inside. A moan tore out of Azar, as she matched the slow rhythm of his thrusts that built in speed and ferocity until they were slamming together almost violently.

Her nails tore into his back and she pulled his body down to bite his shoulder. Keenan groaned, pounding into her and catching her moans with his mouth. Her heel wrapped around his hips, driving him harder and faster as the pressure built, his fingers pressing almost painfully into her hips. Her hands roamed over his body as his mouth licked and sucked at her breasts and neck. Azar felt the precipice coming and her moans got louder and louder until she screamed his name as she shattered; her body gripping him close as the waves of her orgasm washed over her.

Keenan roared, buried to the hilt inside her as he came with her. They rode the waves of bliss together until he collapsed on top of her; his body as slick as hers and his breathing equally as erratic. Simultaneous orgams? He really must have the luck of the Irish.

Azar shifted over to give him some room on her couch and he rolled off her. The silence in the room was almost deafening. She'd never been able to deal with awkward silences. The sun had set sometime during their feverish fucking, and she could hardly see Keenan's face.

"Well, that was unexpected. Who knew you had it in you, Reilly?" she chuckled, hoping to ease the tension. She almost sighed with relief when Keenan laughed too.

"Call me Keenan from now on, yeah?"

Azar was relieved that this situation wasn't going to get weird. Tomorrow she was going to pretend that it never happened. But tonight, the damage had been done so she was going to enjoy every moment.

"I don't know, Keenan. Now that I think about it, that time might have been a fluke. I mean, it had been a really long time for me, you know," she teased. Keenan gave a mock growl.

"A fluke? I'll show you a fluke, but first, let's find a bed. It's where I do all my best work." He smiled and winked, and she actually giggled. Giggled! A little bit of good sex and she turned into an airhead. She was sure that would be a key feature in tomor-row's inevitable cringe-worthy post mortem of the night.

She gave him a long, slow, burning kiss that made heat pool in her abdomen and she could feel him harden against her thigh. She let her hand run down and stroke his erection, feeling it jump at her touch. She grasped it in her hand and stroked up, his groan making her grin.

"Well, you definitely have stamina." She stroked a few more times until his groans were almost whimpers. "Not so fast big guy." She kissed him again and ran both hands up his chest. "I tell you what, I'll race you to bed and the first one there gets to choose the position!"

Azar jumped off the couch and raced down the hallway, Keenan's heavy footsteps right behind her. She'd almost reached the bed when two strong arms banded around her midsection. Azar laughed as he spun around and fell backwards onto the bed, still holding her tightly against his body, his manhood nestled against her ass. She stretched and switched on the lamp on her bedside table so she could see his beautiful body.

"I win. Now I get to choose," he whispered against her ear as he rolled her onto her stomach, his hard body pressed behind her. He levered himself up, pulling her to her knees, running his tongue down the line of her back, down to the base of her spine and stilled over her... oh shit.

"What the fuck is that?"

CHAPTER 2

O h shit, oh shit, oh shit. Her slave brand. The same six point sun symbol of the Djinn that was at the scene of the arsons. This one was going to be tough to explain.

"Azar, what the hell is this?" He sounded angry and betrayed.

"Would you believe it was just a really coincidental birthmark?" She smiled sheepishly, hoping that a little levity would help diffuse the situation.

"This isn't the time to be cute. I knew that you were hiding something. Did you sleep with me just to throw me off the trail?"

It was Azar's turn to feel angry now. "Are you implying that I'm some sort of slut for a psychotic serial arsonist and murderer? Because if that's what you meant, get the hell out of my bed and my apartment. If it's not what you meant and you would like me to explain, then keep your mouth shut and your insults to yourself."

She got out of bed and pulled on some sweats and a ratty T-shirt from the laundry hamper in the corner of her bedroom, too furious to be embarrassed by her nudity. "Get dressed. I'll meet you in the kitchen."

With that she stormed out of the room, closing the door softly even though she wanted to slam it like a teenager. Actually, what she wanted to do was set something on fire, but that would hardly fix the situation.

In the kitchen, she put some water and a teabag in a mug and used her abilities to heat the water. It was only a small outlet, but it helped to quell some of her boiling anger. Her fear was making the fire churn under her skin. She had to tell him what she really was, even though it could mean the end of her life as she knew it. There was a reason the Djinn were nothing more than fodder for Disney movies in the human world. Telling a human about the existence of the Djinn was considered treason and punishable by death. If this went badly, and Keenan told his superiors, she would have to run again.

Azar looked around her little apartment; it wasn't much, but it had been her safe haven for so many years. It didn't have a nice view, unless you liked looking at Mrs Lewkowski, in the apartment across the street, doing Zumba in bike shorts. Quite frankly, Azar was pretty impressed that she could still shake her hips like that without doing damage, because the woman had to be at least seventy.

It wasn't the aesthetics that made the little apartment her sanctuary. It was the things that Azar wouldn't be able to take with her that made it home. Like the dinette setting that Lieutenant Ryan had given her when she had first moved in and started at the firehouse. Or the huge framed photo of her running out of a burning building that the guys had gotten from a press photographer to give to her for her birthday. It was hung over a hole in the wall above the TV, where Joe had accidentally put a Wii remote through the wall when the guys had came around for a Whiskey and Wii night. It was the burn mark on the bench where Azar had tried to cook roast beef for Joe's family, and when it wasn't quite cooked enough, she tried to nuke it with her abilities and set the thing on fire instead. Leaving these memories behind would be heartbreaking. She would just have to have faith that Keenan would see the bigger picture.

Keenan emerged from the entrance hall. He was dressed again, his shirt undone because all the buttons had flown off in their haste. His face was grim and Azar didn't wait around for him to insult her again.

"It really is a birthmark. Well, sort of. It's actually probably more like a brand but I've had it since birth. And I really don't know who is lighting the fires but I know what is lighting the fires. It's a rogue Ifrit." There, it was out now, and there was no going back.

"What the hell is an Ifrit? Look, if you've gotten mixed up in some weird gang or cult, you can tell me and I can help." He obviously thought Azar was giving him bogus answers. She smiled, because it was actually kind of sweet, if somewhat misguided. It wasn't going to get any better either, Azar acknowledged with a sigh.

"No, an Ifrit is a kind of Djinn. Westerners call them Genies." It sounded crazy even to her ears. "An Ifrit is a fire Djinn and I think it's doing a fire pledge by burning the Djinn emblem onto all the representations of the Djinn. Fire pledges are kind of hard to explain." Ugh, this whole thing was hard to explain. She felt like she was speaking another language.

Keenan pulled out a stool from the breakfast bar and the look of concern on his face was not a good sign. Anger, incredulity or flat out disbelief she could understand and deal with. But concern wasn't a response she had ever encountered before when she told someone what she was.

"So a fire genie is pledging itself to something all over the city and burning things down." His eyes got soft, and he gentled his voice. "Azar, do you think you might be suffering from post-traumatic stress or something? Maybe you hit your head when you passed out?" He studied her face, probably looking for dilated pupils. Azar slapped her palm against her forehead and sighed. Damn these modern humans and their 'seeing is believing' motto.

She held out her hand, palm up, and focused her energy, balling her fire under the skin of her palm until it burst to the surface. A perfect little flame flickered in her palm. "I'm not crazy or suffering from PTSD. I'm Ifrit too."

Keenan shot off the stool and backed away across the room. His hand went to his gun automatically.

Azar just shook her head with exasperation. "Don't be ridiculous, Reilly. I am the same person you have known for years with a few cool party tricks that you didn't know about. As if I would ever hurt you, no matter how much you piss me off at times." Azar closed her hand and extinguished the little flame. "So now we've established I'm not insane, can we talk about the real issue here? I think this Ifrit is going to light three more fires." She sipped her tea. "Where are my manners, would you like some tea? Or I have a nice twenty-five year old scotch in the cupboard if that's more your style. Maybe it will help with the shock." Keenan edged back towards the counter top but remained standing, probably so he could make a quick escape.

"Scotch, please." His voice was flat.

"Good choice. I might have one too." She pulled two tumblers from the top cupboard. "I got this bottle from London when I was over there in 1983. It was a great time to be in London; the music scene was alive and there were lots of fires." Keenan threw back his drink in one mouthful and Azar tutted. "I'll give you that one because you've had a bit of a shock but I didn't keep it for over twenty-five years so you could throw it down the hatch like a frat boy." Azar poured him another one and motioned him into the living room. If they were going to have to talk the whole thing out like a touchy-feely couple in a therapist's office, then they may as well be comfortable while they did it.

"Okay, so I'll tell you a little about myself and then I'll tell you what I know about the Djinn and the Ifrit in particular, which isn't much I'm afraid." She grimaced as he swallowed the rest of his scotch in a single mouthful. Philistine.

Sighing, she began at the beginning. "I was born in Persia one hundred and twenty five years ago. My mother was a human and my father was a full Ifrit. That makes me a half blood. The Djinn do that sometimes, change form to get it on with a mortal woman; more often than not it's how the Djinn manage to reproduce. There are not many Djinn left.

"So giving birth to me basically killed my mother, but she had enough strength left to move us to Europe. My mother told me what I was, as a cautionary tale I guess. The same way you teach children not to stick a fork in the electrical socket, she taught me not to ignite. She also taught me to avoid the Djinn at all costs. She died in Spain when I was five and even at that age I was relieved not to have to watch her suffer any longer. I was put in an orphanage but never adopted. I guess people could tell I was different somehow even at that young of an age."

She could still imagine her mother after all this time. She didn't look much like her. Her mother had been a smallish woman, with bright brown eyes and long nut brown hair that she always braided into a long plait down her back. She had a beautiful laugh, and a smile that was full of straight, white teeth, which was rarer than it sounded back then. But she'd already been dying by the time Azar was old enough to commit her image to memory, so she never knew her when she wasn't wasting away. Azar smiled a sad smile; she always did when she thought about her mother.

"Anyway, they kicked me out of the orphanage at twenty; they only let me stay that long because I looked young for my age and no one really knew how old I was. It was probably the first time I was thankful for my heritage, because it let me keep a roof over my head for a couple of more years. When I left, I floated around Spain, working when I could and begging when I couldn't. I travelled around Europe, never staying in one spot too long in case I came to the attention of any of the local Djinn. I was in Ireland when World War One broke out and that's when I became a firefighter. There was a shortage of men to fight the fires so it was down to the local women. I mastered my skills during the bombings of London in World War Two though. But by the end of the forties, the Djinn were moving away from the Middle East and spreading into Europe. I decided to come to America in 1948 and I've been here ever since. Sometimes I go back, like in the eighties, but the States is where I intended to stay." Intended. Past tense. She just hoped she wouldn't have to run again.

Azar sat back on the couch and sipped her drink. It was actually kind of nice to tell someone her life story. She'd told so few people, and none in the last half century. And never a human. That was the ultimate sin, even she knew that.

They sat in silence. Before tonight, she'd relished the moments when Keenan wasn't opening his big opinionated mouth. But after everything that had happened, his silence was making her a little anxious. She watched him digest her story, the little lines between his brows creasing and relaxing at intervals.

Keenan finally nodded to himself and turned to her. "Okay."

Azar raised her eyebrows in surprise. "That's it? Just okay? No questions, no calling the men in white coats to send me to the funny farm?"

Keenan shook his head. "We'll get to that later.

Now I want to know everything you know about the arsonist."

She nodded. She was far more comfortable with the Keenan Reilly who was all work and no play. But when he decided to play, he really knew how to play. A vivid recollection of the feel of Keenan's hard chest pressed against her back had Azar's cheeks turning pink. She cleared the lump from her throat.

"I can only tell you what I know. I know the arsonist is a Djinn because the mark was there, the six point sun; a point for every race of the Djinn. I know it was an Ifrit in particular because they are the only Djinn who control fire like that. The other Djinn are generally quite fearful of fire, being creatures of air. Mostly air anyway. Fire consumes air. Rock beats scissors, so on and so forth." Keenan nodded again, not even laughing at her joke.

"If you have had nothing to do with the Djinn, why do you have that mark on your back?" Less suspicion tainted his voice, but it was still there.

Azar really couldn't blame him. In his position she'd be suspicious too. Hell, who was she kidding? If she was in his position, she would have politely excused herself to go to the bathroom and then escaped through the window.

"It's a slave mark. Every Djinn of full or half

blood is born with one. You are meant to do one hundred years of slavery upon your twenty fifth birthday and the mark is removed once you're done. It's the main reason I kept running for so long. I'm in no hurry to get conscripted into slavery and as far as I know, none of the ruling Council know I exist. I'd like to keep it that way." She'd heard stories about Djinn slavery from other supes. Females were usually sold into sexual slavery, the good looking ones anyway. The more unfortunate ones did hard labor for powerful supes or in very rare cases, very powerful mortals.

"What's the Djinn Council?" Keenan looked like he was desperate for a notepad and pen. Azar was thankful he didn't have one. Physical evidence didn't need to be floating around in the world. The written word was a powerful tool.

"The Djinn Council is the governing body of the Djinn. They manage the compulsory servitude and they punish the Djinn who break the covenants, such as revealing our true natures to unsanctioned humans." Azar grimaced. If the Council found out she was spilling millennia old secrets to a mortal, instant death would be the happy way out; for both her and Keenan. "That's why you can never speak about any of this outside these four walls. We'll both

be dead if you decide to open your big mouth."
Keenan looked skeptical but nodded.

Azar got a piece of paper and drew the six point
sun on it. It was a pattern that came naturally to her,
basically encoded in her DNA. She could probably
draw it blindfolded with her left hand.

"So the Djinn have six different races. Each has a
spot on the emblem and on the Djinn Council. Our
placement on the star is important because the race
opposite us is our natural contrast. Our fail-safe, I
guess. If one race tries to overrun the Council, the
contrasting race can put them down." I took a deep
breath. This next bit got a little complicated.

"The races that hold the top half of the sun are
the good Djinn. Okay, maybe good is not the right
word; we'll say benevolent Djinn. The lower half is
the malevolent Djinn. It's not really that black and
white. You can't say any individual is good and bad
by their race. There are plenty of shades of grey in
this scenario. All Djinn have free will, and it's even
less clear cut when you had the half bloods into the
mix. Halfies get some traits from their human side.

"Anyway, the benevolent races are the Jann, who
live in the desert mostly and create oases for those
they consider worthy. They also have quite a green
thumb, they can make violets grow in the Sahara if

they wish it. Then there's the Sila; they are an all female race and extremely smart, if a little wily. They are also big fans of lightning. They could strike you down with a bolt of lightning from halfway across the world on a clear day. The last of the benevolent races are the Marid, who are very old and powerful and have an affinity with water in all its forms, solid, liquid or gas. Some say they can control the sea, but if they do, they've kept that fact very much to themselves."

She downed the rest of her drink and placed the glass on the coffee table. She needed another one, or ten, to get the rest of this explanation out, but she didn't want to stop. She tucked her feet under her body, and continued.

"The Malevolent races are the Ghul, who contrast with the Jann. The Ghul are nasty cannibals who like to hang around graveyards and eat newly buried corpses. They also like to lick blood out of the living, through the soles of their feet. It's pretty damn weird. The Shaitan is the contrast of the Sila. The Shaitan are the worst form of Djinn. They are what mortals call Demons. They are to be avoided at all costs. Are you following Keenan?" Azar had been writing them into their positions on the Sun Symbol as they spoke, to give him a clearer idea. She'd make sure she burnt it later. Keenan nodded but his eyes had glazed over. Azar was tempted to stop but she was almost finished and didn't want to have this conversation again.

"Lastly, there is the Ifrit. We have fiery tempers, to say the least, and when we get all worked up we light up like a bonfire. We are the most destructive of the Djinn and probably the least forgiving, but I don't think we are as bad as the Shaitan or the Ghul. Like I said, these aren't hard and fast rules. We have free will and some bad ones choose to be good, like me, and vice versa."

She stood up and stretched, her eyes darting down to the man still studying the emblem in front of him. She was nervous, waiting for him to call her evil, or still get her committed to the funny farm or something. But he just kept studying that damn piece of paper until she thought she'd go mad. She clicked her fingers, and the piece of paper went up in flames like a tiny bonfire. Keenan pulled his fingers away quickly.

"So, that's the crash course in Djinn culture. If you don't have any more questions, you should go. I've had a long day." Keenan looked hesitant, still sitting on the couch. "Don't worry, I'm not going to do a middle of the night runner. Too many people depend on me to show up every day. Besides, it's not like you are going to tell anyone right? You'd sound stark raving mad." Azar laughed but Keenan didn't join in.

Finally, he stood and Azar got a good look at the long line of flesh gaping out at her through the front of his button up shirt.

"We need to talk about the arsonist and this fire pledge," he insisted. "We need to talk about what happened tonight."

Her heart pounding in her chest, she faked a yawn and pushed him down the hall towards the door. "We can talk about it tomorrow. There's nothing we can do about it now. Fuentes gave me the day off, so come over about lunch time." She gave him one last shove through the door and locked it.

Turning out the lights, Azar shuffled through the house and collapsed face down onto her bed.

CHAPTER 3

Azar slammed her hand on the alarm clock the next morning and got in the shower before she remembered that she didn't have to go to her shift. She rested her head against the tiles as the hot water pounded down on her body. Full blooded Ifrit didn't actually shower and she considered the ability to stand under the stinging spray one of the benefits of being a half blood.

The previous night's events kept going around and around inside her head, especially the sex. That's how screwed up her priorities were. She'd just told a human a millennia old secret that had the potential to get her killed if anyone ever found out, and she couldn't stop thinking about the hot sex she had with Keenan Reilly. She smacked her forehead against the tiles. She was such an idiot.

She opened her eyes and noticed a soap spot on the tile next to her nose. She pulled back and scrubbed at it with her finger. Then she noticed more. She turned off the shower, threw on her favorite pair of denim cutoffs that made her ass look great but were so indecent she never left the house in them, and a tank top that had more holes than fabric, and went to get her cleaning supplies. House-work was the one thing guaranteed to keep her mind off Keenan and his delicious body.

A knock at the door interrupted Azar's cleaning spree. She glanced at the clock on the wall and noticed it was noon. That would be Keenan and she wasn't even dressed yet. She'd cleaned so furiously that time had slipped away from her and now she was running late. On the plus side, the house sparkled so brightly that Keenan would have to wear his shades inside.

She pulled open the door and was satisfied when Keenan's eyes went straight to her long legs and then slowly devoured their way up her body. Let him see what he was missing. She cleared her throat and his eyes shot to hers. She turned and let him into her apartment, making sure he got a good view of her ass, putting a little more sway in her stride than was strictly necessary.

"I'm running late, sorry. Come in and I'll go get ready. Help yourself to the fridge." She yelled the last part from the bedroom as she sprinted over to her wardrobe. Pulling out a pair of tight black skinny jeans and another tight tank top from the rack, she quickly threw them on. She brushed out her dark hair and smudged on some lip gloss. She was blessed with a smooth olive complexion and thick dark eyelashes from her mother's Iranian heritage, which made her morning ritual a breeze. Pulling on a pair of combat boots to complete the look, she strolled out of the bedroom as if she had all the time in the world. There was no way she was going to let Keenan think she was rushing around for him.

Keenan was standing stiffly in the living room but his eyes kept darting to the couch. Azar smirked again. Obviously he couldn't get their moment of dirty sex out of his mind either. She clicked her fingers to get Keenan's attention.

"I thought we might go down to the sorority house and Coney Island to check out the other crime scenes. Maybe I can pick up something the CSU guys have missed."

She knew the sorority house and the part of Coney Island that had been burnt out would still be taped off to the public until they either wrapped up the investigation or the case went cold.

Azar picked up her keys. "But we are taking my car."

They caught the elevator from the fifth floor to the basement car park, and Keenan let out a small whistle when they stopped in front of her 1969 Ford Mustang Shelby GT500 in Candy Apple Red. It was her baby, and she stroked the roof as she walked to the driver's door.

"I bought her fresh off the lot. She's all original, right down to the stitching in the leather upholstery." She slid into the driver's seat and turned the key, grinning from ear to ear as the motor rumbled to life. "I know a great place to get lunch near Central Park. You might want to hang on."

Thirty hair-raising minutes later, she pulled into a car space close enough to Central Park, and Keenan was looking a little pale.

"You drive like a lunatic," he wheezed.

Azar just waved him off with a grin as she hopped out of the driver's seat. "There's this amazing hot dog stand in Central Park near the corner of East 67th street. The dogs there are to die for, and the relish is heavenly."

They'd parked a couple of blocks away but by New York standards, that wasn't even a short stroll. They stood at the crosswalk, and looked everywhere but at each other. Well, this was awkward. When the little green man finally heralded them across the road, it was a godsend. She didn't know what to say, how to make conversation that didn't revolve around mythical beings or wild sex.

They walked in silence, until she stopped in front of a hot dog cart. It had a big red and white striped umbrella and had been run by the same old guy for years. He was at least six inches shorter than Azar in height and almost six inches wider on both sides of his waist. But he always wore a genuinely large smile, as if he enjoyed meeting new people as much as he liked his own hotdogs. Azar's mouth watered as the fragrant steam around the cart assailed her senses. She stepped closer to the old man to order; he was a bit hard of hearing.

"Hi, can we have four dogs with the lot, please? Go heavy on your relish, it's spectacular," she shouted. The little guy smiled as he loaded up their hotdogs.

"I will tell my wife that. Every day she says, 'Antonio, when will you retire so I no longer have to make this sauce every day. Sometimes I sleep walk and wake up making this sauce.' But I tell my Rosa that the people love her relish. It makes the customers happy. We will sell hotdogs until we can afford to buy a condo in Florida or people no longer flock to my cart to taste her amazing relish." He finished squirting mustard and ketchup on each and Azar handed the man a twenty.

"Keep the change. Put it towards an early retirement to keep Rosa happy," Azar said, laughing as she took her hotdogs and Keenan took his. She wandered over to an uncrowded patch of grass in the sun and sat down, a hotdog in each hand. Keenan sat next to her, and licked at a dollop of mustard that had squirted onto his pinkie finger. I momentarily envied that finger.

Keenan took a bite of his hotdog and let out a little groan. "These are really good," he said, his mouth stuffed to capacity with half-masticated hotdog.

"I know." Azar smiled as she took a huge bite of her own. Maybe she should have ordered three. She didn't get to Central Park enough. "So Keenan, tell me a bit about yourself? It feels weird that I've seen you naked but don't know anything about you other than your name and occupation."

Keenan shrugged. "There's really not much to tell. I was born in Ireland and lived there until I was ten. We moved to Boston after my mother died. My Da thought a new start in a new country would help us all recover. I've got two sisters and a brother. That's about it." He shoved half a hotdog in his mouth and seemed to chew without difficulty. Azar thought his talents were wasted with the police force. He should be doing hotdog competitions at County Fairs for a living.

"I'm really sorry about your mother. I know what that's like." They sat in silence for a little while, watching people go by. Dead parents was a real conversation killer.

One of those big fancy dogs that are basically mixed breeds but with fancier names, like labradoodle or bullmastador, ran over to them and sniffed at Azar's lunch. She tore her hotdog in two, gave the dog half and shoveled the rest down herself.

A woman in running gear followed along behind the dog about twenty feet. She was in stretchy yoga pants and a sports bra and had her cellphone strapped to her upper arm.

"Bad boy Snookums, don't run off on Mommy!

What are you eating? You didn't give him meat did you? He's on a vegan diet!" The woman shot Azar a glare.

"No way! It was a falafel-dog, I swear. Does he have a medical condition where he can't eat meat?" Azar hoped she hadn't accidentally killed the dog by way of processed meat by-products, although it probably wasn't a bad way to go for a dog on a vegan diet.

"No, we just don't believe in slaughtering animals for food."

Azar opened her mouth to tell the woman that that was the stupidest thing she had ever heard but before she could get the first incredulous word out, the woman huffed, called the dog and ran off. Snookums the dog shot them one more pitiful look, and Keenan gave him the rest of his hotdog for the road. They both shook their heads after the poor animal.

"If I was that dog, I don't know what I'd be more upset about; the vegan diet or having to respond to Snookums every day," Keenan said seriously. She had to agree; at least one of those things should be classified as cruelty to animals.

Lunch now finished, she stood up and brushed grass off her butt. She watched wistfully as Keenan did the same. He had an ass made to dig your nails into and hold on for dear life.

After a quick discussion on the merits of catching the subway or parking in the NYU district, they decided it would be easier to ride the train to the sorority house, which was in the penthouse of one of the residence halls on Lafayette Street.

Keenan flashed his badge to get them through the station gates without having to buy a ticket. The train was reasonably quiet; just a couple of shift workers asleep with their faces squished against the window, a crazy guy talking to himself at the end of the carriage and some students with their music blaring through their headphones, obviously on their way to NYU too. Azar and Keenan remained standing, both holding onto the supports above their head.

"So, how did you end up in New York if you grew up in Boston?" Azar asked, her eyes focused on the darkness outside the window. She wasn't big on tunnels. Regardless of the fact that the chances of a tunnel collapsing on her train were slim, they still made her anxious. Making small talk with Keenan would help pass the time between stops.

"There are a lot of Irish expats in South Boston, so when we arrived it was like we hadn't even left

Dublin. You see so many people you know, or your Da knows, and before you know it, the old folks are sitting around talking about the old days with a Guinness. I just wanted something different, I guess. So I moved to New York and became a police officer. Besides, my family drive me crazy. I decided to move far enough away that they couldn't drop in, but close enough that I could be there if they needed me." A grin lit his face, and it made her heart beat wildly. When he smiled like that, she knew why she'd thrown caution to the wind and slept with a man who was almost a coworker. "You'd know what I mean if you'd had two older sisters. So bossy. Patrick went into the army just to escape their interfering ways." Keenan's tone was warm; they might annoy him but it was obvious that he loved his family very much. The doors opened on the Bleecker Street Station and they jumped off.

The NYU district was hectic. Groups of students milled around the sidewalks along with the everyday crowds. All the fresh faced freshman, out of home for the first time, added an air of excitement to the area. Azar and Keenan headed up Lafayette Street towards the building that had housed the sorority.

She knew they had reached the right place from the massive memorial in front of the building.

Pictures of the two girls who had died were surrounded by masses of flowers and candles, stuffed animals and letters of sorrow. The girls had been young, maybe nineteen or twenty, and their loss would have devastated a lot of people. Azar leaned over and touched the picture of one of the girls. She had dark brown laughing eyes in the picture, as if someone just out of the shot was doing something to make her laugh. The other girl was a blonde girl with short feather cut hair and a broad white smile. She looked like she could have been a model for Abercrombie and Fitch. It didn't matter who they were, the loss of their lives would have been no less tragic to Azar if they'd been homeless women on the street. No one deserved to die in that much pain, let alone anyone so young.

Keenan held her elbow and directed her into the building. "All the students have been rehoused as a precaution, but as soon as this investigation wraps up they'll come back and rebuild." He started climbing the stairs to the penthouse. "This building was housing one hundred and fifty students the night of the fire. The students reported that the fire alarms went off at around three in the morning, and all the levels evacuated. When they got down to the footpath they realized that it was the penthouse that was burning. By the time the fire trucks arrived almost everyone was out, except for the two deceased girls. The fire was contained on the top floor without doing much structural damage. The coroner said that the heat which incinerated the bodies was inconsistent with the amount of structural damage in the apartment. It led the coroner to believe that maybe the girls were physically set on fire but we could find no trace of accelerant on their clothing or bodies. The girls were deceased when the FDNY arrived."

The coroner was right. The kind of fire produced by the Ifrit was different to the average kind of fire. Ifrit fire followed the instructions of its master. If the Rogue had wanted to destroy as much life as possible, he would have directed the fire to focus on the life energy within its reach instead of burning the inanimate objects in each room.

Keenan continued down the hall. "The fire didn't look as if it had been started near the girl's room, but rather rushed unbelievably quickly towards them. They really didn't have a chance of escape."

They stood outside the penthouse entrance and Azar could see where the soot had tried to escape under the door. Keenan turned the knob and let the door swing open.

The inside was a sad, barren landscape of black and grey. Everything had been charred or burnt, and what had once been a beautiful apartment was now just a desolate shell. A spiral staircase came down on the left hand side of an open plan living/dining room with two hallways leading off down either side of the room.

"There were fourteen girls on these two floors, two to a room. Most got out through the fire escape on the other side of the building to where the fire started. Somehow our perp got through the security at the front of the building, up all the floors, into a locked apartment and then set a fire, disappeared out the same way and no one saw him at any point. Initially, we thought it had to be someone on the inside before we made the connection to the Coney Island fire." Keenan led her further into the main living area. "The fire was started on the landing above this staircase and spread from there. The two victims were in the furthest bedroom and couldn't get to the staircase or to the fire escape. They essentially burnt to death before the firemen had even rolled up the doors at the firehouse. The University ensures that the fire escapes are well maintained and it saved lives."

They gingerly walked up the spiral staircase, and

it creaked under their weight. At the top of the stairs, on the wall in front of her, was the Djinn symbol. Any lingering doubts about this being a fire pledge left her mind. She looked at the door to her left where the bodies had burnt, and she could still see outlines where the girls had basically melted onto the floor boards. Azar wanted to be sick, not from the ephemera of death, which she saw all too often in her job, but the fact that it was her kind that caused such an atrocity. The blood that ran through her veins was the same as this monster, who had planned on killing hundreds of innocent kids.

"I don't think that this place can tell us anything new." Azar choked out the words and Keenan looked at her worriedly. "Let's go down via the fire escape, see if there is anything you guys missed."

They headed to the end of the hall, where a large window opened out onto the fire escape. Azar went out first, hushing Keenan's objections.

"A drop from six stories will hurt but it won't kill me. If the fire escape collapses while you're on it, you'll just be a Jackson Pollock painting on the sidewalk. Now be quiet and let me check!" She bounced around a couple of times and assessed its integrity. It groaned and creaked but it was fine. "Come aboard."

She waved Keenan out the window before slowly

heading down the ladder. One of the rungs had basically melted through and she called Keenan over to look. "Well, I think we definitely know how he got in and out. His hands were still hot enough to melt metal when he left."

They climbed down the rest of the ladder, and the metal warped less and less as they got closer to the ground. If the cops had been searching for evidence from the alleyway, they would have found nothing but a structurally sound fire escape. She highly doubted that if they did find the heat twisted metal they would have put it down to anything but circumstance. It's not like anyone's mind was going to jump straight to 'Fiery Middle-Eastern Genie'.

They walked back around to the front of the building and saw a girl crouching down to place flowers on the memorial. Keenan flashed his badge at her as they walked over.

"Excuse me, Miss. I'm Detective Keenan from the NYPD. I'd just like to ask you a few questions, if that's okay?" The girl nodded and stood up. "What's your name?" Keenan asked in his cop voice.

"Ashley."

"Hi Ashley, this is my associate Azar Nazemi from the FDNY. Do you live up on the top floor?" Another nod from the girl. "Can you tell me anything about Kate and Alana? If they were in any kind of trouble, acting strange, anything like that?" Kate Matthews and Alana Fitzpatrick were the two girls who died in the fire.

"No, nothing like that. It was coming up finals week and everyone had been staying in to prepare. They were really serious; they didn't even have boyfriends. We would have known if they did, you can't keep a secret in a sorority." The girl didn't smile, and neither did anyone else. Ashley looked like a deflated doll, like she'd blow away with a stiff gust of wind.

"What about any of the other girls in the penthouse? Anyone angry or been acting weird? Perhaps someone with a vendetta against the sorority in particular?" Ashley shook her head.

"It isn't like the movies, you know? The whole Greek life in NYU is really small in comparison to most colleges. We are kind of like one big community. Not competitive or anything like that. I told this to the police when they interviewed us. We weren't mean girls or frenemies or whatever. We concentrated on school, and maintained a good GPA average so we could keep the penthouse." Ashley's eyes were starting to get big and watery and Keenan said a quick thank you, gave the girl his card and strode away. She didn't know what it was about female tears, but they seemed to make even the toughest man uncomfortable.

"Let's move onto Coney Island," Azar suggested and they headed back to the subway.

CHAPTER 4

A s soon as they got to Coney Island, Keenan scrambled out of the car again and she laughed. Maybe, subconsciously, she'd taken the corners a little too fast and ran a couple of orange lights, but she hadn't done anything illegal. She definitely hadn't put them in the way of any real harm.

"When I get back to the station, I'm going straight to Traffic and telling them to pull your license," he shouted. This just made her laugh harder.

"I've been driving since the automobile was invented. You just need to relax more and work on your control issues. We both know you were never in any danger."

Keenan just gave her a stony stare and walked off, leaving Azar to trail behind.

She could see the ferris wheel slowly spinning in the distance and hear the continuous buzz of people chattering on the boardwalk. The striped awning of an ice cream cart caught her eye and she made a mental note to pick one up on the way home. It would be a shame to come all the way to Coney Island and then leave without having a cone.

They walked toward the storage shed where the fire had been lit, its doorway still sealed up. Keenan pushed open the door and lifted the police tape for her.

The first thing she saw was the charred remains of carousel horses and brightly colored amusement rides. It depressed her a little; it was like someone had burnt down fun.

Keenan led her to the back towards the bumper cars. She could tell this is where the fire started, because the plastic exteriors of the cars looked like a bad Dali painting. The Djinn sign had been permanently burned into the concrete floor of the warehouse. It was at least six feet wide.

"Here is the six point sun again. This was definitely his first fire. He was a little overzealous, even for an Ifrit."

"I agree." The voice behind her made her whirl around, and she stiffened as a dark shadow emerged from behind a pile of boxes. As the light from the windows caught his face, Azar sucked in a shocked breath.

He was Djinn, of that she was sure. His honey colored eyes burned with a supernatural light and he walked with an unnatural grace. He was definitely a full blood.

Keenan stepped forward, flashing his badge. "My name is Detective Reilly from the Arson Unit of the NYPD. This is a closed crime scene, Sir, so you'll need to leave." The Djinn just laughed at Keenan and Azar elbowed him in the ribs.

"He's Djinn," she whispered to Keenan, involuntarily stepping backwards, trying to hide herself from his sight. It was far too late for that, but old habits die hard.

"Jann to be specific; you may call me Bast. What I want to know is why there is an Ifrit in my warehouse again? Coming to finish the job, perhaps?"

He was practically on top of her in the blink of an eye, his face inches from hers. Time seemed to shudder to a stop as she stared at his face. The man was beautiful but he wasn't perfect. His nose was long and thin, with a slight hook at the end, as was common among the Persian people. His face was all hard angles, and Azar could see tiny scars littering his skin. One above his lip, one on his cheek and one slicing from the underside of his chin, right along his square jaw to end next to his ear. It looked as if someone had tried to slice his throat and failed. It wasn't physical perfection that made him beautiful, but rather the intensity of his eyes.

Reality crashed back in as Keenan whirled towards Bast and drew his gun. The Djinn merely laughed and grabbed Azar by the shoulders, lifting her five inches off the ground. "And telling a mortal our secrets? You have been a very naughty little Ifrit, haven't you?"

Keenan flicked the safety off his gun and aimed it point blank at Bast's head. Bast ignored him as if he didn't exist, just an annoying fly that just wouldn't go away. His grip on her shoulders was firm, bordering painful but she schooled her features into a neutral, almost bored expression. Azar hoped the Jann weren't like wild animals and could smell your fear, because if so, then she was one dead half blood. But if she didn't do something about Keenan's cowboy stance soon, he was going to be nothing but a pile of gore within five seconds.

"Keenan, put down the gun. Bullets can't kill a

Jann; they are creatures of air and smoke." Azar pushed the words past the terror clogging her throat. "I didn't light this fire. I think there's a Rogue carrying out a fire pledge in the city. Not me," she clarified quickly.

He seemed to consider her intently. The Jann was huge; easily over six and a half feet and his shoulders were so broad she wondered if he had to turn on his side to get through the warehouse door. Bast released her shoulders but ran his hands up her neck to cup her cheeks, rubbing his thumbs over her cheekbones.

"I'm glad it's not you, little Ifrit, because I would really hate to hand you over to the Council. I wouldn't want that pretty little head to be separated from that delightful body," he purred at her.

Terrified or not, Azar didn't like being manhandled. She lifted her leg and kneed Bast in the crotch. The Jann fell to the ground and grabbed his package, making a sound somewhere between a groan and a chuckle.

"You can't shoot them, but a kick in the nuts still hurts like hell," Azar told Keenan, who was standing there staring down at Bast with a wince on his face. "Look, Jann, I didn't light those fires. I don't go around endangering innocent lives to get my Djinn rocks off." Azar sounded confident but she fervently hoped that this Bast wasn't a lackey of the Council or else she was in a lot of trouble.

"I have to give it to you, you definitely have spirit. For a half blood, you definitely inherited the Ifrit temper. Come to my office, and you can tell me why you think an Ifrit is trying to attempt a fire pledge when there hasn't been one done since Tokyo in 1923."

Bast stood up slowly, still holding onto his package as he limped towards a side door. The word 'Office' was written in large black letters, still recognizable even though the door had been blackened by soot.

The office was filled to the brim with greenery. Potted plants and hanging baskets of flowers and ferns littered every available surface. Every plant was thriving, running down and tangling with each other until they were a indistinct, green mass. Some type of climbing plant wrapped around the legs of the big oak desk which was almost too large for the pokey little room, and plants littered the edges of the desk until there was nothing but a tiny workspace in the middle. The leaves of the desk plants reached down to their floor compatriots and ended up in a wild tangle of branches and leaves around the middle. Bast motioned them to sit and wandered around to the other side of the desk.

"So tell me why you think this is a fire pledge? When the warehouse burned I obviously knew it was an Ifrit, but I just thought it was sparked by their natural dislike of the Marid." He stroked the leaves of the maidenhair fern on his desk and Azar could have sworn it wrapped around his hand like it was caressing him back. She looked at Keenan and noted he was looking at the same thing, but his face was so calm you'd think he'd seen plants hugging their owners every day of his life. Azar shook her head.

"But you aren't Marid. Why would they attack you?" Though, now she thought about it, a Jann this close to the sea was a little strange. Jann were usually desert dwellers, or they inhabited wide open spaces where you could see undulating countryside for miles and miles. Not crowded inner city amusement parks.

"A Marid put a hotel out here in 1829 and before you knew it, it became its own little oasis. He gave it to me in 1980 when he went back to the homeland to die. I bought up most of the amusements soon after that. So if the Ifrit was a little bit out of touch with Djinn society, he may still think it belonged to

Moselle, the Marid. We don't exactly have a Djinn Weekly to keep us up to date on the gossip," Bast said with a grin.

Azar laughed as well. If they did, it would probably be like a trashy tabloid. But, instead of people getting abducted by aliens, headlines would read: "Ifrit vows to swim across the English Channel" or "Ghul turns vegan and protests outside Djinn Council." Alien abductions and Bigfoot wouldn't be that out of the ordinary for the Djinn.

Azar was a little stunned that there had been two Djinn so close for all these years. She rather arrogantly assumed that there were only a few Djinn who'd crossed the ocean to come to the New World. In hindsight, maybe she had just stuck her head in the sand because she was sick of running. She liked her life here; she had friends and a great job. It was easier to think that there was no real threat than to have to live continually on the move.

Shaking her head, she focused her thoughts. She needed answers about this Ifrit. She could leave the soul searching for another day.

"I," she started, but Keenan cleared his throat. She rolled her eyes. "Er, we, think this is the first in a series of arsons, all with the Djinn emblem as their ignition point. Here, a sorority house at NYU and a dodgy little apartment building over in Brownsville. I was sure that this was the Marid hit, being so close to the ocean, but with you here it could be either Marid or Jann. The Sorority house is obviously the Sila hit; an all-female house at an educational institution is a bit of a no-brainer. I have no idea what the apartment fire could mean. There are just too many variables. There is going to be three more strikes and we have no idea where or when." She met his eyes and held them, imploring him to do something. "We cannot let this be another Great Fire of London. New York is too densely populated and the technology has become too great. It risks exposing us all." She had pushed thoughts of all the possible destruction to the back of her mind, but saying it out loud reinforced it. If the fire pledge was successful, millions would die. She was out of her depth, her knowledge of her own kind far too limited. They needed help. The help of the one Djinn she knew for certain didn't do it. "And we'd like your help."

"Azar!" Keenan jumped to his feet. "Are you crazy? He is a possible suspect, and you want to bring him into a police investigation? For all we know he could be in on it, as some kind of insurance scam." Keenan still had his gun in his hand as if it was some kind of security blanket. The only person he could successfully shoot in this room was her. She wasn't immune to bullets because she was technically half human.

She knew there was far greater threat to her in the room than Keenan's gun. If Bast knew that she hadn't done her servitude, he'd be obligated to tell the Council. To not report such a thing would put him in the firing line. But she had to take the risk. She owed it to the people she worked with, her friends, the hot dog vendor, even the uppity woman and Snookums the dog. She owed it to every person in the city who had made her life here so good for so long.

"Millions will die if we don't, Keenan. So will you help us?" She met Bast's eyes and let her vulnerability show. His golden gaze held hers until she felt as if she might suffocate if she didn't look away. But she held on, her chin raised. She would not back down. His mouth curved into a smile, and it held both respect and bemusement.

"Sure, little Ifrit, I'll do whatever I can to help, but what will I get in return?"

"How about if I promise not to kick you in the family jewels again?" Azar didn't negotiate. Either he cared or he didn't, but either way she didn't want his help if it wasn't given freely.

Bast threw his head back and laughed. "Deal, Ifrit. What is your name anyway?"

Azar hesitated. If she gave him her real name, it would be easier for them to track her down if he turned out to be a rat.

Who was she kidding? If he wanted to turn her in, the Council had ways of tracking her down with or without her name.

"My name is Azar." She involuntarily hunched down into her shoulders as if she could already feel the cold wind of the guillotine that was poised above her head at this moment. Her fate was now in a stranger's hands.

"Azar; I like that. It means 'little fire' in Persian."

She'd already known that; after all, she had the internet at home too. Although Bast sounded as if he could speak ancient Persian fluently. She knew Jann were long lived, far longer than the Ifrit, but not quite as long as the Marid. Considering the Marid lived for a thousand years and the Ifrit for approximately three hundred and fifty, his age would probably remain a mystery.

She looked over at Keenan, who was looking at Bast with barely contained suspicion. Well, at least he wasn't giving her that look any more.

Bast reached into his drawer and pulled out a

tourist map of New York. He spread it across his desk, and the plants lifted their leaves just a little bit higher to make way for it. These plants were seriously starting to give her the jeebies.

"So, show me where the fires have been?" Bast handed a black marker to Keenan, who took it and circled Coney Island, the sorority house near NYU and the apartment block in Brownsville. Bast took the pen back off Keenan and drew a large perfect circle around all three of them. "This is your ground zero. He's going to try and make sure that each hit is roughly in the shape of the Djinn emblem, so that should give us some idea where. It is the potential targets that will be harder to narrow down. If we can't work out what he is going to target, we don't stand a chance because the area is too large." He drew the Djinn symbol on a piece of paper perfectly, naming the points. "So we have the Sila for certain," he crossed off their name, "and maybe the Marid or the Jann." He put a question mark next to both their names.

"What about the apartment block? From what I know, there are no ties to any of the Djinn in that place. It was just a little run down hovel filled with single parents and people with nowhere else to go." Azar tapped her finger on the map. They needed to figure out why he chose that apartment in particular. "Keenan, can you find out everything there is to know about that place; the site, the building and the people who live there? There has to be some connection."

"I'll do it as soon as I get back to the station. Speaking of which, I think we should be going." Keenan stood and gripped her elbow, pulling her up and directing her towards the door in one smooth movement.

Azar swallowed down her irritation. He was out of his element here and for a control freak like Keenan Reilly, this whole situation would be a real bur in the ass. She could put up with him being a bit handsy for a little while longer. She shook her elbow gently out of his grasp and turned back towards Bast. He'd come around to the front of his desk and was leaning against it with deceptive ease.

"Would it be okay if I came and saw you after my shift tomorrow? We still need to work out where he will attack next. There can't be too many Ifrit running around New York." She put out her hand to shake his. Bast placed his hand in hers, then tugged her close to his body.

Before she could register what had happened, Bast's lips were on hers and he kissed her softly. His breath was like the warm summer winds of her homeland. Azar lost herself in that kiss; it was like molten lava being poured over her body. So much electricity jumped between them that they could have powered Coney Island for a week. Keenan cleared his throat loudly. She shook her head and pushed at Bast's chest.

Bast let her go with a wolfish grin. "Oh, it'll be my pleasure, Little Fire. You drop by any time. I'll be waiting right here and we can pick up where we left off." A lopsided grin curled his lips. "With the conversation I mean."

No one in the room believed that's what he meant. Keenan had dragged her out of the room and then out of the warehouse before Azar regained anything resembling coherent thought.

Keenan didn't say a word to her the whole way back to her apartment. Azar didn't know why he had his panties in a bunch. She was the one that just got violated by a sexy, golden eyed Jann. Okay, so violated may be the wrong word. The kiss was electric and made every nerve ending in her body tingle. They were still tingling now.

After parking the Shelby, she walked him back to his squad car.

"It's against procedure to make-out with

suspects." Keenan's voice was gruff as he stared into the distance.

"Well, luckily Bast is not a suspect and I am not an officer of the law." Azar leaned against the side of his car as he climbed in. "Let me know if you find out anything useful about the apartment fire." She pushed off the car and walked towards the security door of the apartment. It was a pretty nice apartment block for the area; the neighbors were reasonably friendly and the security was good.

"I don't want you meeting that guy by yourself," Keenan yelled out through the open car door. Azar shot him a half-hearted smile over her shoulder.

"If Bast decides to cause trouble, there's not a being on this earth that could protect me, even the mighty Keenan Reilly." She turned back around and went into her building, the door shutting with a slam behind her. There was no going back now.

CHAPTER 5

Azar was glad to be back on shift. The team at the firehouse welcomed her back like she'd been gone a month rather than a day and life settled back into its boring routine. But she couldn't get the impending destruction out of her head.

"Hey Az, you with us today?" Joe asked. He had volunteered to spot her while she lifted weights on the chest press. She gritted her teeth and did another rep. Strength training was mandatory and every crew member found the time to head to the weight room at least once a day. She nodded at Joe and he put the bar back on the struts.

"Sorry Joe, I'm just a little distracted." She stood up and her aching muscles protested. She'd tried to work out her emotions with sit-ups last night. So now not only was she sexually frustrated and terrified, but every part of her torso ached liked someone had beaten her with a baseball bat.

She wiped down the bench and dabbed her face with her towel. She took a giant slurp of her protein shake, and momentarily wished she'd laced it with painkillers. However, she should have known better than to over do it, so she was going to endure the repercussions with grim determination. She gingerly walked behind the bench as Joe took her spot.

"Is there something wrong? Old Maconi is a good listener," he grunted between reps. Azar sighed heavily. The firehouse was sometimes like a knitting circle; gossip spread like wildfire. It wouldn't be long before he found out anyway

"I slept with Keenan Reilly the other day."

Joe slammed the bar into the support struts and flew into a sitting position.

"You did what with your archenemy, Reilly? The same man you called a chauvinistic snake charmer? The same man to who you can barely say one civil word?"

Joe's shock was kind of amusing and Azar gave him a sheepish grin. If someone had told her a week ago she would get sweaty with Keenan Reilly on her couch, she'd probably punch the person in the mouth and tell them to get their head read. Irony can be a snarky bitch sometimes.

"I don't know, it must have been the smoke fumes. Or maybe it was the year since I've had sex. But it just kinda happened. One minute we are arguing and the next minute we are doing it on the couch." Azar's cheeks reddened as she remembered exactly what they did on that couch.

A couple of the other guys had heard Joe's exclamation and had come over to see what the gossip was.

"Did I just hear that right? Did Nazemi sleep with Reilly?" McAdams called from where he was running on the treadmill.

McAdams was almost as bad as a little old housewife and this news would soon be known by everyone. The conversation buzzed as the information was whispered from one person to another. She wouldn't be surprised that if by the time the guys out doing the equipment checks heard it, the story had morphed into her and Reilly eloping to Las Vegas and having a threeway with a show girl. She let them go; she was glad that all they had to worry about was her sex life. A call went over the line and everyone stopped to listen.

"Truck 61, Ambulance 34. House fire at 2240 Mayfair Street."

The whole house went into work mode. Striding to the truck, they stepped into their turn out gear and climbed in as the roller doors opened. The sirens went on and they sped down the streets. McAdams leaned across the backseat to Lieutenant Ryan, her superior. Lieutenant Ryan was a nice guy, if a bit on the gruff side. He took his responsibility to his team very seriously, and that was all anyone can ask from someone in charge. He wouldn't send them in to bad situations for possible glory, and they would give him their trust and loyalty.

"Guess what I just found out about Nazemi here? Apparently she and Detective Reilly were doing the two man tango all night after that apartment fire over in Brownsville," McAdams mock whispered

Lieutenant Ryan raised both brows. "I thought you hated Reilly? Or is that only from the neck up?" he asked, a stupid big grin on his face. Apparently being gruff didn't exempt him from teasing her too.

She just rolled her eyes as the rest of the crew ribbed her good naturedly. Joe laughed from the opposite side of the truck and she slapped his leg.

"These guys are going to go on about this for

weeks because you Italians only have one volume level; Sicilian!"

Joe just gave her an innocent look that was ruined by his smug grin. They really were like one big family, equipped with far too many teasing big brothers. But she loved them all, and would never want to see anything happen to any of them. Especially not being burned alive by a massive fire demon.

They pulled up to the call out address and already Azar could see the smoke billowing out of the front windows of the two storey house. There was a woman pacing the footpath, ringing her hands and Azar prepared herself for her orders. She let herself live in the moment. Everything else could wait until the end of her shift.

Hours later, Azar stood out the front of Bast's warehouse and tried to psych herself up to go in. The sun was beginning to set over the Coney Island boardwalk, and the tourists had thinned out. Azar had always loved Coney Island. She loved the sound of the squealing children going around on the old carousel and the smell of corndogs and sea salt that always permeated the air. It made her feel happy. She loved walking down the boardwalk, eating an ice cream and watching the waves lap at the sand.

She had never even contemplated that perhaps Coney Island had been started by Djinn, or that she had been so close to detection all these years. Maybe she walked past this Moselle, or even Bast.

She shook her head, a tiny smile curving her mouth. No, if she had seen Bast before, she definitely would have noticed him. He was not the kind of person you'd miss, even in the bustling crowds of Coney Island. It wasn't just his height, or even the mesmerizing gold of his eyes. Bast had charisma, an energy that pulled at everyone around him. If she had seen him before, she wouldn't have forgotten. He was the kind of man from which late night fantasies were made.

Her phone vibrated in her pocket, shaking her out of her daydream. "Azar."

"It's Keenan. I dug up what I could on the family that lived in the apartment over in Brownsville. They were at their mosque when the fire started. They are a family of refugees; both parents and three kids from Syria, been in the States for about four months. The father is unemployed, but in Syria he was an engineer, the kids haven't started school yet. I can't see any connection apart from the fact they are from the Middle East." His voice was all business, no hint that they had ever been intimate. Azar squashed down the feeling of disappointment; she had far more important things to worry about.

"That doesn't seem like much of a connection. I'm at Bast's office now. I'll run it past him and see if he has any ideas. I'll give you a call later on." Azar ended the call before Keenan could start nagging about her meeting Bast alone and slipped the phone back in her pocket.

She lifted her chin and pulled her shoulders back. She'd procrastinated enough. She ducked under the police tape and walked through the charred warehouse to the office. Taking a deep breath, she knocked.

"Come in." Bast's smooth melodic voice sent tingles down her spine.

She pushed into the room. The foliage seemed more suffocating today. The plants shied away from her as she brushed past them.

"Azar, it's nice to see you. Don't mind them, they don't like your heat. It's an instinctual thing." Bast stood and walked around his desk toward her, his hand outstretched but she waved him off.

"It's nice to see you too, Bast. Excuse me if I don't

shake your hand. The last time had some undesired results."

Bast just laughed and raised an eyebrow. "Undesired? I think not. In fact, I think you desired it very much. There is a pull between us that I had to explore. But if our little kiss made you uncomfortable, then I humbly apologize. Won't you please take a seat? No Detective Reilly today?" Azar shook her head and sat down on one of the antique chairs. She hadn't noticed them yesterday, too shocked from the appearance of another Djinn, but they looked old, maybe Louis XVI. She rubbed her hand up the warm wood. It was spectacularly made and kept in immaculate condition. It sat on a genuine Persian rug that looked ancient.

"Keenan is working on getting us info about the apartment block fire. The family who live there are refugees from Syria. They've only been here four months." She chewed her lower lip as she thought. There had to be a connection there. Why that family? Were they Djinn themselves and if not, why target that family in particular?

Bast tapped his finger against the map that was still spread out on his desk thoughtfully. "They must have been the pledge for my race. The Jann are the Djinn that provide an Oasis for those in need. If you'd lived in a war torn country your entire life, surrounded by genocide and mass bloodshed, constant wars and dictatorships, I imagine a little apartment in a shitty area of town would seem like an oasis of peace for such a family."

Azar nodded, it made sense. What didn't make sense is why they were targeted specifically. How would the Ifrit even know about some family that had just got off the plane from Syria? It would have made more sense for him to hit Central Park or some other leafy area that provided a calm refuge in the normal chaos of New York City. She didn't realize she'd been thinking out loud until Bast answered her question.

"It would be very hard to light anything on fire in Central Park; too many witnesses and good Samaritans willing to extinguish it immediately. Besides, I don't think lighting a trash can on fire would gain much favor with the Balraka, do you?"

Azar shuddered when he said its name.

Balraka.

She hadn't told Keenan the whole truth about the fire pledge. Apparently, when done correctly, the fire pledge raises the embodiment of the very first Ifrit, Balraka. It was apparently so ferocious and deadly that the other Djinn cast him into the pits of hell, chained in manacles of ice, for all of eternity. They created a failsafe so that his prison could only be opened by each race providing a tribute.

A thousand years later, another crazy Ifrit discovered that if he destroyed something that was beloved by each of the races, he could temporarily release Balraka into the world, and Balraka would rain down fire and destruction upon everything he could reach. And his reach was long. Entire cities had burnt to the ground. Fiery destruction was like ambrosia to the Ifrit.

However, the magic that had chained Balraka in the beginning would eventually drag him back down into his icy prison to wait until some other crazy Ifrit would try another fire pledge. Many of the Great Fires of history were due to fire pledges releasing Balraka.

"We should tell the other Djinn. A fire pledge is in no one's best interests and they need to keep their eyes open," Bast continued. "Also, *Azerasr* is only six days away, and if I was doing a fire pledge, that is when I'd want my big finale." Azar had forgotten about *Azerasr*, the Ifrit Day of Celebration.

In the old days, the Ifrit used to burn whole villages to the ground to honor their race. But in modern days, the Ifrit mostly just created big bonfires or torched a few cars. Well at least that's what she had heard. She'd never actually celebrated it or met any other Ifrit. But she'd met an Eastern European werewolf in a bar once, and he'd known a lot about the Djinn. He'd happily told her everything he knew over a few dozen jugs of ale.

She had to tell this to Keenan. She pulled out her phone and dialled Keenan's number.

"Keenan, it's Azar. Do you want the good news or the bad news?" She heard him sigh on the other end of the line.

"Give me the good news first. I need something positive at the moment."

"The apartment fire was the Jann pledge. So that narrows down the spots where we need to look for the next targets. But it was too specific. The other targets have been general targets, their correlation to the Djinn races clear. But the Syrian family must have been known to our Rogue, and on more than just a nod in the hallway kind of way. It was personal. He knew that they were refugees and he knew that the apartment was their oasis." She could hear him scribbling notes down on the other end. "Now, for the bad news; I think he's going to hit the next three places in the next six days to coincide with an Ifrit Fire Celebration."

"Way to hit me with a quick one-two." He sounded more disheartened than he had at the beginning of the call. He was so out of his depth in this case, and there was only so much Azar could say to help him understand. There are some things that are difficult for even the most open minded human. A world full of other beings, of which the Djinn were only a small percentage. Azar honestly believed in that old human saying that ignorance was bliss.

"Sorry about that Keenan. But hey, forewarned is forearmed, right?"

"Right. I'll call around to your place tonight to check on you." He didn't give her time to disagree, hanging up in her ear. It was almost kind of sweet that he wanted to check on her. Then she remembered he was a cop and probably just wanted to grill her for information.

Bast was looking at her like she was an abstract painting he couldn't quite understand. His intense gaze was making her a little warm in her own skin, like she was set to slow burn, and that was really saying something for an Ifrit. She lowered her lashes and cleared her throat. It was almost painful to look into his deep, golden eyes.

Get it together, Azar, she chastised herself, *there is absolutely no point to lusting after one of the Djinn, espe-*

cially if you want to stay out of shackles for the next hundred years.

She needed to break the sexual tension in the air before she decided to screw caution and do him right there on the desk. She didn't think he'd put up much resistance. "Well, we aren't going to warn anyone sitting in your office. Do you know where we can find any other Djinn?" She couldn't believe those words just passed her lips. She had spent years in hiding, and now she was throwing herself in the deep end.

Bast's lips curled into a devious grin that made her heart leap but her stomach sink.

"Yes I do. But we are going to have to stop by your place. You'll need to change."

She had a sneaking suspicion she was going to need that ice cream first.

Azar looked at the black leather mini skirt in between Bast's thumb and forefinger.

"No, no, no, no!" she said, shaking her head vigorously. "There is no way I'm wearing that out of the house. Ever."

She bought the skirt to wear as a biker chick outfit for Halloween one year but she'd chickened out and gone as SpongeBob SquarePants instead. There was a good reason for that. The thing was miniscule. If she even leaned forward too much, it showed things that should never be seen outside the bedroom. She was going to throw it out but had never gotten around to it, a mistake she sorely regretted now. It was bad enough that Bast had already talked her into wearing her ex-housemates spangly gold halter. It had a plunge at the front that almost went to her navel and the back barely covered her slave mark. She'd been very adamant that Bast leave the room when she changed into it. He complied like a gentleman of course, but there was a sad little boy pout on his face as he did. If she wore the skirt as well, she may as well be naked.

"You won't fit in where we are going in jeans, no matter how delectable they make your ass look. This place has a definite 'less is more' policy when it comes to compulsory attire."

She sighed and snatched it out of his hand, then pointed to the door. He waggled his eyebrows as he left, his smirk both annoying and sexy as hell.

She shimmied out of her jeans and slid on some lacy underwear. If she was going to flash everyone, she was going to do it in her good panties. She went to her ensuite and piled her hair on top of her head, added some dramatic eye makeup and a little bit of lip gloss. She looked like a high price hooker. She slid the skirt up over her thighs, sucking in a breath as she zipped up the back. Sitting back on the bed, she slid on her Houboutins. They looked like Louboutins, but with a few decimal places less in the price tag.

Standing, she looked at herself in the full length mirror. She sighed and pulled open the bedroom door, startling when Bast was directly on the other side.

"I was coming to see if you needed help with the zip," he said huskily. His eyes felt like a caress as they took in every inch of her body. "But I can see you have managed just fine." His words slid over her body and wrapped around her mind. Her heart began to thunder in her ears. She was sinking into the quicksand that was Bast and she wasn't even smart enough to struggle. He pressed her up against the door jamb and lightly ran one finger down her collarbone.

His lips followed the path he had just traced, and Azar gasped at the heat of his tongue touched her skin. "Why can't I resist you?" The whisper of his breath on the skin where his tongue had just been made her shudder.

Azar let out a whimper as Bast's mouth climbed up the side of her neck to the point of her chin. His hand roamed around the curve of her hips and his large body made hers feel small. He wrapped his arms around her waist and pulled her close, kissing her like it was the silver screen. Her body slightly dipped back and with such passion that it threatened to overwhelm her completely. Her arms were around his neck, holding on to him because she knew her knees were like water. He lifted her, sliding his hands under her ass, pressing her back against the wall.

"We'll warn the Djinn tomorrow," he murmured between kisses, his hands running over her lower back. She tensed as she remembered her slave brand. Even though she knew that Bast wouldn't be able to feel it, it sent a cold rush of reason into her passion muddled mind.

"Bast, stop. We can't do this. Keenan and I have something going on and it just wouldn't be right." It was a little white lie, but it was a necessary one.

Like a perfect gentleman, Bast stepped back immediately. His eyes were still smoky with desire but he nodded once. Azar felt bad that she hadn't stopped it earlier but she'd been bombarded with sensations that had disconnected her body from all rational thought.

She straightened her clothes and touched her hair. "We should go."

Bast led the way out of the room, pausing to hold the door for her as they left the apartment. It was going to be a long night.

Azar wasn't overly surprised that they stood outside of Blue Smoke, a fetish club opposite St John's Cemetery in Flushing. Ghuls. She could almost smell them from outside the front doors. Bast was whispering something in the bouncer's ear, and the colossus was nodding like a docile servant. Bast looked amazing in a black silk shirt that made his skin glow and his honey colored hair shine like spun gold. He wore tight black jeans that sculpted his thighs and butt. Until this day, Azar would have argued that no man looked good in skinny leg jeans, but just one glance at the way the denim hugged his hips made her mouth water and changed her opinion for life. The fact he looked so amazing just made her even more frustrated with herself. She had enough to deal with, she didn't need to be panting after a Jann like he was water and she had been walking through the desert for a year.

"Let's go." Bast reached out and offered her his hand. She begrudgingly took it and felt a searing warmth run through her body. She made a mental note to touch the next Djinn that crossed her path. Maybe the reaction wasn't Bast specific and happened between all Djinn. And maybe pigs flew the Transatlantic flight path.

They passed through the velvet ropes and the thump-thump of the music became almost unbearable as soon as they stepped through the door. The lights were dim, and Azar strained to see her surroundings. She could make out the dark outlines of the people that were writhing around on the couches and beds that dotted the room. The scent of sex and the steady pounding of the music made heat pool in her belly. People gyrated against each other on the dance floor in an animalistic version of the mating dance.

A huge bar lined one of the mirrored walls and the overhead lights were encased in royal blue shades, casting the bar in an eerie deep blue light. Bast guided her towards the bar, his arm wrapped around her shoulders, buffering her from the people on the dance floor and the men that were eyeing her scantily clad body like she was a feast. Azar would have been more indignant about the sleaze-bags if she wasn't so distracted by the feel of Bast's hands on the bare skin and the curve of his body tucked tightly next to hers.

Once they had reached the bar, Bast caught the barman's attention. He was young, and the mischievous glint in his eye, as well as the tattoo's, marked him as a bad boy.

"Two double vodkas and orange." The guy behind the bar just nodded and turned to make the drinks. Azar opened her mouth to protest, but Bast cut her off. "You need to relax. If you wind up any tighter you are going to go supernova and a Rogue Ifrit will be the least of our problems."

He had a point. She could feel the fire bubbling to the surface, and she wasn't sure if it was her surroundings or the sexual tension that was making it so hard to keep it leashed. Either way, she had to take it down a notch otherwise these humans were going to see more of her than they bargained for. The bartender returned with their drinks, and Bast paid the man.

"Keep the change." The barman nodded and produced a lopsided grin that would have melted the heart and dropped the panties of any girl in the room. Well, if he wasn't standing beside Bast. Everyone paled in comparison. It was like a candle standing next to the sun. "I'm looking for Lila."

The bartender pointed to a hallway that was to the left of the bar. It was roped off as well, and two burly bouncers manned the entrance. Bast sauntered up to them as if he owned the place and Azar shuffled along awkwardly in his wake. He said something to the biggest bouncer in a low voice that she couldn't hear, and the big man opened the velvet rope as quickly as the bouncer at the front.

They treated Bast as if he was some kind of VIP in the club. The idea of Bast attending a Ghul fetish club every night made her stomach turn. Bast waved her forward, and then held her elbow gently as if she was made of crystal.

The hallway they walked down had little cubby holes with sheer curtains, so you got a vague impression of what the occupants were doing. Azar's cheeks had turned red and she'd gotten a very thorough sexual education by the time they made it to the end of the hall. The end room was three times the size of the cubby holes and had heavy curtains to ward off unwanted eyes. Bast slipped between the curtains, pulling Azar along with him.

The sight that greeted her had her stunned. The

room was packed with bodies, some having sex against the wall, or on the floor, others perched on couches. What was really weird was the naked woman licking the foot of a man whose head was thrown back in ecstasy. She wasn't the only one. Two other men were doing the same to one woman in the corner, each held a foot and lapped at the soles as if they were made of ice cream.

"What the fuck?" she whispered.

At least she thought she whispered it, but every eye in the room suddenly swiveled to her. Well, except one couple in the corner who were still going at it like wild monkeys. She doubted anything could have gotten their attention at this point. Bast rolled his eyes at her and led her further into the room, standing slightly in front of her.

It's a little too late for that now buddy, Azar thought, as she grimaced at his broad shoulders.

All three Ghul's had stopped what they were doing, and their conquests looked distraught. Azar wanted to tell them to go home and take an iron supplement, but she resisted. The foot-licking woman sauntered over to them, without putting on any clothes, and stood in front of Bast. Her smile was that of someone who knew a person intimately and Azar wondered if she and Bast had been lovers.

The idea made her stomach curdle. She guessed they'd found the infamous Lila.

"Bast! To what do I owe this unexpected pleasure? Not that pleasure with you is ever unexpected," she purred.

Bast leaned down so that she could kiss each of his cheeks. Lila pressed her body sinuously against his, her hands rubbing his shoulders and simultaneously pulling him closer. The man whose foot she had just been licking shot Bast a look that could kill. Bast untangled himself from her groping hands and her beautiful visage turned into that of a sulky child.

"I'm not here to rekindle anything, Lila. I'm here with a warning for the Ghul."

Lila turned back towards the bodies lying around the room and snapped her fingers once, waving them out the door. They jumped up like good little lap dogs, even the monkey sex couple who had apparently finished the deed.

Bast waited until the last one had left the room before he continued. "There is a Rogue Ifrit trying to create a fire pledge in the city. He's already completed the Marid, Jann and Sila tributes. We believe he'll complete the remaining three before *Azerasr*." Lila's fellow Ghul were now standing on either side of her, eyeing Azar suspiciously.

Lila's eyes flicked to Azar, her upper lip curling with distaste. Azar wasn't sure if her disgust was because she was half human, or if it was her Ifrit side that had her non-existent panties in a twist.. "Is this the little trouble maker? I do hate the Ifrit. Always so bad tempered. They never know how to have a little fun. But maybe this one does? Is she your new pet, Bast? A little on the plain side, and far too tall. Not to mention a half blood."

Azar ground her teeth, her hands flexing at her sides. She'd like to smack the blood-sucking little Barbie doll back into the rotting grave she crawled out of.

Bast rested his hand on her arm as if he could read her thoughts. "Azar just happened to be the first to read the signs. She has nothing to do with the fire pledge. I don't need to tell you how bad the return of Balraka would be for all of the Djinn. I'm fairly sure you had a club similar to this one in San Francisco when the Rogue Elziah successfully completed the pledge. A lot of Djinn were lost during that fire, as well as humans." Lila's companions were nodding in unison, matching frowns marring their otherwise attractive faces. If anything they looked confused. Obviously neither one of them was the brains behind the Ghul. That left Lila as the mouthpiece.

Lila was still staring at Azar with a face that made the pretty Ghul look as if she'd eaten something sour. Annoyed, Azar leaned towards Bast and ran a hand over his broad shoulders and down his arm, pressing herself slightly closer as if they were lovers. Sure, it was a petty thing to do, and she guessed that made her a bit of a tease, but it was totally worth it to see the little blonde jerks face harden. Bast looked down at her, his face not changing but there was an amusement in his eyes and perhaps a hint of promise, which made Azar's pulse race. She was probably going to regret her impulsive move, but it was still worth it. Lila stood ramrod straight, the smirk no longer gracing her too perfect face.

"The Ghul thank you for the warning Bast and I'll pass it on to the Council Sitter. But I don't think we'll have that kind of problem here. We have good security, and Lemar out the front is a Were. We usually have a strict policy of no non-Ghul Djinn in the club and he can smell them a mile away. We like to keep out the riff raff, and I don't like to share. But I have always made an exception for you, as you know. You are welcome here anytime." Her tone implied that Azar was not. The look Lila gave her could have laid waste to an entire city.

Azar just jutted out her bottom lip in a fake pout

and then smirked. Like she would ever come to this place for fun. That being said, she was going to stay out of this side of town for a while, and well away from any darkened car parks.

Bast sighed and shook his head. "I thank you for that Lila but this really is a serious threat. You need to warn the other clans…" Bast's voice faded out, like someone turning down the sound on an old AM radio, as an unfamiliar chill ran up her spine.

It was like something tugging at her, trying to draw her in while simultaneously trying to get her to throw up her lunch onto Lila's crimson carpet. It was like the feel of the fire, if the fire was doused in oil. She turned and headed back down the hallway to the bar. It could only be one thing.

"He's here."

She didn't know if Bast had followed her or not. She could feel where the Rogue was in the room, feel his fire tugging at hers challengingly, and she was helpless to resist. She started to run, her heels wobbling awkwardly on the plush carpet, and a disembodied part of her mind hoped that she didn't break an ankle.

She rushed past the barman and pushed her way through the sweaty bodies that were grinding against each other on the dance floor, limbs and bodies so entangled that moving through them was like wading through molasses. Dread washed over her in waves, as she fought the warring desires to draw closer and flee.

A scream pierced through the music, and Azar knew she'd been too slow. She threw the last few people out of the way, not even trying to mask her inhuman abilities. What she saw on the other side of the crowd stopped her in her tracks.

A few seconds seemed like minutes as her brain processed the human torch in front of her. To the left was a dark haired man with cold eyes and a humorless smile. He pointed to her, and she could feel the chill running through her body.

Finally, her training overrode her shock. She tackled the women who was encased in fire to the ground and smothered the flames with her own body. The woman's pain filled shrieks echoed through the club and the smell of burned flesh and hair was pungent in the air. Bast was soon on her too, helping to bat out the flames with his jacket. Azar yelled to anyone who would listen that she needed a wet bed sheet from one of the private rooms.

The burned woman's blue eyes rolled around her head, standing out against the raw burnt skin of her face. Far too long later, someone handed Azar the sheet she'd asked for and she laid it over the woman's body, making soothing noises that were drowned out by the victim's moans of pain. Suddenly, Lila was there with the paramedics and Azar moved away so they could work. She got to her feet and turned around, looking for Bast. What she found was four of the FDNY's finest firemen with their mouths open and a very angry looking Keenan Reilly.

CHAPTER 6

Fortunately, the firemen recovered first. "Holy shit. Is that you, Nazemi? What are you doing here?" That was Hal, a married lieutenant from the 52nd fire house. The FDNY was a close knit group, so to her horror she knew every man there, and they sure as hell knew her. Female fire fighters weren't that common, even in an equal opportunity society.

God, she was never going to live this down. Men could be as gossipy as woman, arguably more so, and by the time she went to work tomorrow, every fire-house in the city of New York would know that Azar Nazemi had been at a fetish club, wearing basically nothing. Some of the other guys looked at her approvingly, grinning like idiots.

Their smiles made the look on Keenan's face significantly more ominous. Bast came to stand next to her, wrapping his arm around her shoulders. Keenan's face grew darker, and he strode past them towards the victim. He gave out orders to the uniforms doing crowd control as the paramedics wheeled the woman to the ambulance. Hal seemed to have recovered from the shock of seeing her in the club and was directing his crew to evacuate the building and check for spot fires and accelerants. Bast guided her towards the exit.

"Don't leave yet, Nazemi. I need your statement," Keenan yelled from the other side of the room. Azar sighed. She knew he was going to make her wait until he'd interviewed every other person who'd been in the club. It was going to be a long night. She plopped down on a nearby chair and settled in to wait. Bast sat opposite her, his face grim.

He cleared his throat, the way boyfriends do when they are about to give you the 'let's be friends' speech and Azar went on instant high alert. Nothing good ever came from an uncomfortable clearing of the throat, especially when the person doing the clearing was as self-assured Bast.

"When you were putting out that girl, I saw something I probably shouldn't have." Azar blushed, unconsciously tugging on the hem of her skirt. She was pretty sure the whole club saw something that they shouldn't have. Bast was shaking his head. "Not that. Well yes, I saw that too, but I meant something else, something not nearly as delightful and far more problematic. On your back."

Azar eyes widened. He'd seen her slave mark.

Another Djinn, who was duty bound to hand her over to the Council, had seen her slave mark. Her eyes darted towards the door. She could run. She had passports and cash saved up; she could go to Australia or South America. She eyed Bast. She wouldn't be able to overpower him, but she could probably outrun him. She slipped her high heels off under the table. She poised to stand, eyeing the exit, but Bast reached over and put his hand firmly on her arm.

"I'm not going to turn you in Azar. There is no love lost between the Council and I, and I'm fairly sure that Lila and her posse didn't see. My own slavery was less than... pleasant, and I am in no hurry to inflict such a punishment on you. I just wanted you to know that your secret is safe with me." His eyes hardened at his last statement, and she shuddered to think what could make such a calm person tense up until he resembled stone. "Also, if

that mark was stopping you from taking our friendship further, well, everything is out in the open
now." One side of his mouth turned up in a lazy half
grin. Damn, he was sexy.

She knew she should still run, but she wanted to
trust Bast and she really, really, wanted to stay.

A mumbled, "thank you" was all Azar could
manage without tripping over her words and they
sat in silence. She turned the night over and over in
her mind; meeting Lila, briefly seeing the Rogue
Ifrit, the girl's screams, Bast knowing she hadn't
served her compulsory servitude. It was too much
for one girl to take.

She slumped forward, resting her head on her
folded arms. She let the picture reel of the night's
events spin over and over in her mind until she
somehow went to sleep.

Loud voices brought her out of her troubled slum-
ber. She opened one eye and saw that it was Bast and
Keenan arguing over who knew what. Their voices
were hushed yells, which was kind of redundant
because it meant that they were talking to each other
at a normal volume, but with a bit more palpable
tension.

"I don't care what the hell you are, you hurt one hair on Azar's head and I'll find a way to stuff you back into whatever rusty tincan you came out of." Keenan's voice took on even more of an Irish lilt when he was angry. She tried to hold in a smile and failed. It really was quite a sweet thing for Keenan to say, no matter how misguided.

She slid her open eye to Bast. His smile was amused and a little condescending. "I have no intention of doing any harm to Azar. I know about her little predicament and I can promise you that her secret is safe with me. She knows that, and now you do too." He turned and looked at her, a mysterious smile spread across his face that made her heart stutter in her chest. "Good morning Sleeping Beauty."

Oops, busted.

She struggled to get her stiff muscles into a sitting position. She looked at the time on her phone. It was 2 a.m..

"Can we get this show on the road? I have a shift tomorrow and I'd rather not fall asleep on the job."

Keenan glared once more at Bast and then sat down opposite Azar. He pulled out a notepad and pen and sighed. "Start from when you arrived at the club and try to leave out anything that might get me sent to the department psychologist when they read my report."

It was forty five more minutes before Azar finally stumbled up to the door of her apartment. Bast stood behind her. She thought he and Keenan were going to come to blows over who got to drive her home. Keenan eventually gave in. He had to go back to the station to complete a mountain of paperwork and chase up the results from the techs. However, Azar could tell that he hated watching Bast help her into the passenger seat of his fancy European car. The smug look on Bast's face probably didn't help either.

Now she was pressed between the door and Bast's hard chest. The irony wasn't lost on her. How a person ends up in this position twice in one week, with two very different but equally as incredibly delicious guys, was completely beyond her. But she wasn't going to fall in the same trap twice. She quickly slipped her key in the door and unlocked it, keeping the doorway blocked with her body. She turned back towards Bast, looking up into his incredible golden eyes and his white smile and her willpower began to falter.

No girl, you are a mess, her better judgment argued. *Your life is a mess, your sex life has gone from non-existent to complicated in the blink of an eye, so the last thing you need to do is add this two hundred odd pound hunk of trouble into the mix.* She nodded to the sensible voice in her head.

"Thank you for driving me home, Bast. I've got it from here. No need to come in." Bast just continued to smile as if he could read her mind. Hell, he probably could. The thought sent a blush directly to her cheeks. He leaned down and lightly brushed a kiss across her parted lips.

"It was my pleasure. Anytime you want me to take you home, day or night, for whatever reason, you let me know." His grin was pure wickedness. "I'll pick you up tomorrow night. We have a few more people to warn." He gave her another whisper of a kiss on the corner of her mouth, turned and sauntered away. Azar just stood there, gaping at his back, hoping her legs would solidify enough to help carry her inside her apartment.

Her shift the next day was wonderfully mundane. They had the usual traffic accidents and trash can fires coupled with in-house equipment maintenance checklists to fill out. The simple routine helped Azar unwind a bit, keeping her mind occupied enough that she didn't worry herself to death over New York City's impending doom.

She picked up a pizza on the way home and sat down to devour it with a couple of fingers of scotch in front of the TV. She was halfway through her first slice when there was a loud knock at the door. Azar sighed. She knew that her good vibe couldn't last all night, but she was hoping she'd have a couple of more scotches under her belt before reality set in. She threw the other half of her pepperoni pizza slice back in the box and opened the door. Keenan was standing on the other side, his usual stony cop glare gracing his otherwise beautiful features.

"Reilly, to what do I owe the pleasure of this visit?" Like she didn't already know, but old habits died hard and she couldn't resist needling him a little.

He quirked an eyebrow and she let a small smile curl her lips. She turned and walked back into the living room before he had time to give her some smart ass answer. She flopped down on the couch and picked up her half eaten slice of pizza. "Want some?" Keenan eyed the couch like it was covered in fungus but he eventually sighed and sat down beside her, picking up a slice of pizza and demolishing it in half a bite.

"Eating like that is going to give you indigestion," she chastised.

Keenan merely grunted and took another huge bite.

They sat in companionable silence until the pizza was gone, and they'd both knocked back a few more fingers of scotch. Keenan finally turned to look at her.

"I want to go with you and Bast tonight, wherever it is you are going."

It was Azar's turn to sigh. She knew that one was coming. He was getting all macho on her, beating his chest in the direction of another alpha male and doing everything short of peeing on her leg to mark his territory.

"I'm sorry to disappoint you, but you can't. If the other Djinn even get even a whiff that you might know more than you should, well, it won't just be Bast and I with our heads on the chopping block. That's not a metaphor either. They literally cut off your head." She downed the rest of her drink. She couldn't stress the danger of his knowledge enough. She wasn't even one hundred percent certain that the Djinn couldn't read minds.

A lot of the races kept their secrets to themselves. They weren't exactly a trusting bunch, and it was better to have an ace up your sleeve than to be an honest dead man. She said as much to Keenan.

His face turned red and his fist slammed down on the coffee table, making glasses and pizza crusts jump into the air.

"I hate this. This guy is a lunatic and you're going around, putting yourself in harm's way and I can't do a thing about it. Remember that girl from last night? Well she died this morning, in horrible pain that could barely be masked by morphine. They had to put her into a coma to give her some relief." He ran his hand through his already messy hair, and Azar guessed he'd done that very gesture quite a few times today.

She felt a rush of sadness at the girl's death, and an overwhelming sense of guilt followed right behind. Tears blurred her eyes and she blinked rapidly to clear them. Keenan looked over at her, and his face quickly turned from anger to guilt. Reaching over, he pulled her into the crook of his arm, his warmth chasing away the chill that had seeped into her body. A tear leaked from the corner of her eye and fell onto his stretched cotton shirt.

"I'm sorry. I shouldn't have told you like that," he murmured as he kissed the top of her head.

"I should have reacted quicker. I just stood there,

wasting precious seconds staring at her like an idiot, and maybe that could have been the difference between life and death. Now an innocent girl is dead and I may have been able to prevent it." She sniffed. All she could think about was the girl's wild blue eyes and her cries of pain.

Keenan squeezed her tighter to his body and rubbed her back. "You couldn't have known. It isn't your fault; it's the fault of that monster. But I promise you Azar; we will get him and make him pay for what he did to those girls."

She tilted her face up so their lips were only inches apart. She held her breath as he leaned closer, gently touching his lips to hers. But Azar didn't want gentle. She wanted to exorcise all the anger and fear in her body with hot, mindless sex. She deepened their kiss and pressed her body towards his. His hands slid down her back to her butt and he pulled her onto his lap. Her hands were under his shirt and running over the hard muscles of his chest in an instant. Keenan had somehow managed to get her tank top off, brushing the pads of his thumbs across her silk covered nipples. She was reaching for the top button of his jeans when there was a knock at the door.

"You have to be shitting me," Azar swore.

Keenan also let out a few choice words that were usually only heard in a men's locker room. They both knew who it was, and it just added to Keenan's already bad mood. Azar was frustrated and grumpy as well, but deep down inside, a little part of her leapt with joy at the thought of seeing Bast again. Not that she'd ever admit it, even under threat of death.

Azar wiggled her way off Keenan's lap and pulled her shirt back over her head as she shuffled to the door. She looked out through the peep-hole just to be sure and could see Bast standing there, dressed all in black and looking like a golden eyed devil. The corners of his mouth were slightly turned up as if he knew a really good secret and he wasn't going to tell. She pulled open the door, one hand on her hip.

"Good evening, Azar. I hope I'm not interrupting anything?" She would bet her record collection that Bast knew exactly what he was interrupting.

She just raised her eyebrows and stood aside to let him in. Keenan was standing when they got back to the living room.

"Ah, Detective Reilly, nice to see you again." Bast's tone insinuated he would rather have poked bamboo under his fingernails than spend another minute in Keenan's company.

"If you two can restrain yourselves for fifteen minutes, I'm going to have a quick shower and then I'll be ready to go." Keenan merely stared daggers at Bast, but Bast wore the same self-confident expression that seemed to be permanently etched onto his face.

"I'm going anyway," Keenan muttered and walked towards her. He wrapped his arms around her back and kissed her possessively.

He kissed her with such fiery passion, that she wasn't sure it hadn't somehow branded his name across her ass. He broke off the kiss and shot one more ominous glare across at Bast. Then he left, slamming the door on the way out.

She could only shake her head. She would never understand men. Keenan wasn't stupid, he could feel the connection between her and Bast. It was a tension in the air that was thick enough to choke a horse. But the fact was, despite what she said to Bast last night, she and Keenan had indulged in one single, but still pretty amazing, hate-fuck, but that didn't give him rights. She liked him, though. She could tell under that under all that suffocating bravado was a man who cared. He cared about lives, and protecting the innocent, and putting bad guys behind bars. It was like he was designed to test her.

She motioned for Bast to sit. "Make yourself comfortable." She walked into the bathroom and slammed the door shut, frustrated.

Azar emerged thirty minutes later, dressed in her usual outfit of black skinny leg jeans, combat boots, and a black tank. She also threw on a leather jacket in deference to the cold, not that she actually got cold or hot, but it paid to keep up appearances.

"I hope this will do for wherever we are going, because there is no way I'm going to put back on the skank couture. I'm actually going to shove it down the garbage chute as soon as I buy trash bags. Anyway, most of it melted last night when I was putting out the fire," she said nonchalantly, but in truth it hurt too much to think of the girl who was beneath the fire.

Bast looked her over, his golden eyes darkening and his tongue darted out across his bottom lip. It made her feel naked. And hot. Bast cleared his throat. "I think that will do very nicely. We should go."

Bast looked flustered, and she smiled to herself. It was nice, and slightly terrifying, to know that she wasn't the only one who turned into mush. She grabbed her phone and ID and stuffed them in her back pocket and motioned Bast out the door.

She regretted forgoing the stairs in lieu of the elevator almost instantly. The sexual tension in the small metal box could have suffocated a fish. She could practically see the pheromones pouring off Bast's skin. She forced herself to focus; New York was about to burn to the ground and all she could think about was getting laid against the elevator wall. She'd gotten worse than a hormone riddled teenage boy.

They reached the front of her apartment block and she saw Bast's Maserati double parked on the street. She drooled, not even caring if she looked ridiculous. Bast held the passenger door open for her and she slid into the plush leather seat. Even his car oozed sex. It was a sleek charcoal grey and smelled of the indescribable aroma of Bast.

"So, where are we off to tonight? Not another Ghul fetish club, I hope? I don't think I could deal with more naked Ghul's," Azar asked warily. The thought of Lila still left a sour taste in her mouth.

Bast was quickly around the other side of the car and slid into the driver's seat. "No. Lila will get the word out to the rest of the Ghul. We are going to visit a Shaitan."

"What!" Azar's head whipped towards Bast and her hands banged down against the dashboard.

In her shock she forgot to moderate her strength and the airbag sprung out of the dash and pinned her back against the passenger seat. It was lucky that she was tall otherwise it would have pounded her square in the face. As it was, she was fairly sure her collarbone would be sore for a couple of days.

Bast sighed. "And now we are going to have to take your car."

CHAPTER 7

An hour of bad traffic later she parked her Shelby in an underground parking complex in Hoboken, New Jersey. It figured that the Shaitan would end up in New Jersey. They were in the seedier part at the back of Hoboken, near the projects on Jackson and Fourth, and Azar was really worried about her car. If anything happened to it, she was going to toast Bast until he bought her a new one, in mint condition. Bast guided her across the street and around the corner and she could feel the vibrations of the heavy metal music beneath her feet. Bast had filled her in on the details of the Shaitan on the way over.

The club they were going to was called The Onyx; a metalcore club owned by a half-Shaitan/half human Djinn. Azar tried not to be nervous. Hadn't she just given the speech to Keenan about all Djinn having the right to choose to be good or bad?

But the Shaitan were bad news. There was a reason that modern Christian religions had based their Satan on the Shaitan. They were cruel and twisted, demons in their truest form. They fed on the energy created by negative emotions. Fear and terror were the most potent, but they could also feed on anger, envy and malice. Azar didn't exactly know how they fed on negative energy. Deep down, she really didn't want to know. Needless to say, she pitied the poor woman who had sired the half-Shaitan.

Bast was talking to the bouncer at the door, and the man was shaking his head. Bast was making passive hand gestures and the bouncer had his head cocked, listening to someone speaking in his earpiece. Another man appeared in the doorway and said something to Bast. Azar wished she could hear the conversation over the thumping bass notes drifting out the front door. The new guy gave her a hard look before nodding and motioning them in.

Bast grabbed her elbow firmly and followed the man through the entrance doors, into the club. The man was dressed the same way as the bouncer out front; black cargo pants, a tight black t-shirt, heavy lace up combat boots and a state of the art wireless transmitters in his ear. The crowds in the club parted for them as they moved through the main room.

The décor couldn't have been more different from the Blue Smoke Club. The only lighting in the room was above the bar, except for the strobe lights that flickered around the dance floor from the stage. The patrons were mostly dressed in black, heavy eyeliner rimming they eyes of every girl and more than a few of the guys. Every single one of them was throwing their head around so vigorously that Azar was surprised they didn't all go home with whiplash.

The band up the front of the dance area were sweating and jumping around on stage, while the lead singer screamed incoherently into the microphone. The whole atmosphere was barely contained angst in black lace. The Onyx was obviously a popular place, it was wall to wall bodies. Azar was glad that Burt, the Fire Marshall, wasn't here because he'd be having a heart attack. The club was definitely over-capacity.

The bouncer led them out the back of the main room, down a corridor that was painted completely black except for a small red door right at the end. It definitely felt ominous, or that may have been the residual effects of the Shaitan who owned the place. The bouncer knocked on the red door. Getting whatever answer he needed on the other side, he motioned them through and shut the door gently behind them.

They stood in front of a desk occupied by a man dressed completely in black leather. His head was down as he studied a sheet of paper on his desk intently, ignoring the other occupants of the room completely. Whatever, it gave her more time to stare. Although all she could see was messy black hair that stuck out at odd angles from his scalp.

The man, er Shaitan, flexed incredibly broad shoulders and dropped his pen with a sigh. He uncurled his body as he stood and Azar noted that his height easily matched that of Bast's. However it was the fact that every available inch of skin below his chin was covered in tattoos that really shocked her.

Two flaming skulls laughed hauntingly on either side of his neck, intricate patterns ringed his biceps and forearms and a dagger thrust through a heart peaked out from the gap in his laced black leather vest. They were just the ones she could pick out without staring too intently. Tattoos ran into more tattoos until he looked like a rather scary story book. The thin slice of skin that showed between the bottom of his vest and the top of his tight leather pants also had ink adorning it, though she couldn't make out the pattern. Maybe he really did have every inch of skin tattooed. She thought about asking, but then remembered the old saying. Curiosity killed the Ifrit.

When Azar finally drew her eyes away from the man's hip bones, she realized that he was watching her just as intently. He was as dark as Bast was golden. His face held an angular jaw and pale skin, a dark five o'clock shadow, and two black, dead eyes that looked as if they could see her soul. She didn't like the feeling. The Shaitan came around the desk to stand in front of them.

"What do you want, Bast? I'm too busy to play games with you tonight. Who's the Ifrit?" He cut his dark eyes to her and she felt them appraise every inch of her body. She fought to control a shiver. She steeled her spine and raised her chin. She wasn't a princess who needed rescuing. And she definitely didn't need a man to talk for her. She opened her mouth before logical thought had a chance to step in.

"My name is Azar, and you are?" She put out her

hand against her screaming sense of self preserva-
tion. The Shaitan gave her a mirthless smile and
took it, gripping it almost painfully.

"Donovan. I don't usually let other Djinn into my
club, but Bast informed me it was urgent." He
wrenched her away from Bast's side and closer to his
own body until his mouth was next to her ear. "Are
you the reason for this... urgency?" He whispered
the last word, making it sound somewhere between
a threat and an invitation. It sent tingles through her
stomach, and she couldn't tell if it was fear or attraction, or some perverted combination of both. She
went with righteous indignation, and stuffed the rest
of those messed up sensations back in their box.

Azar was getting real sick of everyone using her
good manners as a way to try and get into her pants.
She shook Donovan's hand loose and stepped back.

"No, I'm not. Don't manhandle me again, either.
It has unpleasant consequences. Ask Bast."

Donovan merely smiled creepily.

"She's tougher than she looks Donovan, I
wouldn't get on her bad side." Bast was smiling but it
didn't reach his eyes. "So can we cut the crap
already?" Donovan shrugged and leaned back
against his desk.

"It's come to our attention that there is a rogue

Ifrit trying to complete a fire pledge. We believe he's going to try and complete it on *Azerasr*. He's hit the Jann, Marid, Ghul and Sila pledges already. All that is left is the Shaitan and the Ifrit. We thought you should know so you and the other Shaitan in the city can protect yourselves." Bast's tone was nonchalant, as if Donovan's wellbeing was the least of his concern right now.

Donovan looked thoughtful, and he was studying her in a way that made her feel like a bug between two pieces of glass. His thoughts were basically written on his face.

She rolled her eyes. "No, jackass, it isn't me," she said in a huffy voice. It was like these Djinn didn't even think any other Ifrit existed. The Shaitan's eyes narrowed. People with good life expectancies didn't insult the Shaitan. Obviously Azar hadn't gotten the memo.

Donovan stood up straight and then bowed slightly at the waist, his eyes never leaving hers. "The Shaitan thank you for the warning. Unfortunately, I am the only Shaitan in New York City, so this news is especially disturbing for me." His tone was artificially polite. She didn't know how he made a simple thank you sound like a giant 'fuck you.'

Bast cleared his throat, bringing everyone's attention to him. "He hit Lila's place last night."

Donovan threw his head back and laughed. The sound was at odds with the man in front of her. It was kind of like watching a snake roller skate. It was unbelievably strange but slightly heart-warming at the same time.

"I hope he burned the place to the ground. God, I hate that uppity little bitch. Seriously, the way she acts, you wouldn't think she gets her rocks off by licking sweaty feet and grave robbing." Azar's warmth towards Donovan was rapidly increasing. They could definitely bond over their mutual dislike of Lila.

Bast shook his head. "Unfortunately, no. He set a mortal on fire, and she died this morning."

An emotion briefly flickered across Donovan's face but Azar had no time to analyze it. It could have been sadness, but that seemed unlikely, or maybe glee at someone's suffering, which was more likely to be in the Shaitan's emotional wheelhouse. Her opinion of Donovan was getting more complicated by the second. His face returned back into its hard mask of neutrality, and she wanted to rewind time so she could see that fleeting expression again, to study it and work out what it meant. Donovan didn't fit inside the box she'd placed all Shaitan.

"That is unfortunate. But again, I thank you for the warning. I'll have my security put on high alert. Now, let me walk you out." That was it, they were dismissed.

Donovan ushered them out the door and back towards the dance floor. She trailed a little behind them, appraising the crowd. People danced violently to the music, most with more metal on their bodies than a Transformer. She was slowed down even further by an impromptu mosh pit in her way, and she didn't know if they were having fun or some kind of involuntary seizure.

Someone walked across her path and blocked her view of Bast and Donovan. Manic eyes glared at her and a hand clamped over her mouth before she could yell for Bast, his other hand gripping the back of her neck painfully. She recognized the face immediately. The Rogue. Blackness swam in her eyes as his fingers pressed against hard against her arteries of her neck, cutting off her blood flow. She could feel the waves of menace permeating from him. He made her skin crawl as he tightened his grip even more.

"You're in the way again, half blood. You've

drawn attention to me and now my work is going to be harder to achieve. But I will complete the ritual and you will be my glorious finale." His teeth flashed in the strobe lights, a disturbing grin twisting his face.

Then he was gone, melting back into the crowd so quickly she wondered if he was even there to start with.

Azar stood still in the sea of people, shocked to have been in the presence of such evil. He made Donovan look like a Presidential candidate. She shook herself out of her stupor and pushed her way through the crowd towards Bast and Donovan. She knew the Rogue was going to hit right now. She surged forward and all but tackled Bast.

"He's here!" she yelled above the music. Donovan went on high alert, his finger instantly going to his ear to warn his security team. Someone pulled the fire alarm and the sprinkler system was activated, water pouring down on the people jammed tightly into the club. Azar desperately searched around for any signs of a flame, but she picked up nothing.

People were starting to run for the exits, pushing and shoving each other to get to the door first. Donovan's security were trying to maintain calm and still be on high alert for the Rogue, but there were too many panicked people trying to climb over one another to get the exit doors.

Burt the fire marshal would definitely be having a coronary right about now.

"Bast, do something!" Azar yelled over the terrified screams of the humans. Bast jumped up onto the bar, without using his hands and looked out over the crowd.

Almost instantly the crowd stopped and turned simultaneously, all eyes focused on Bast. Standing with his arms spread wide, his eyes closed against the chaos in front of him, the only sign he was doing anything strenuous was the two little creases marking the smoothness of his forehead. Then, simultaneously again, everyone in the club turned and filed calmly out of the exits in four distinct lines.

Azar gaped at the sheer power. There must have been five hundred people crowded into the club, and Bast had reached into and controlled the minds of every one of them. A shiver ran across her skin. She hadn't realized that the Jann even had such ability. She silently added a few hundred years to his age. He had to be older than she first guessed to have accrued that much raw power.

He looked down at her from his perch on the bar, and saw her look of horror. The strain was gone from his face but his eyes still glowed like shining, golden orbs and his pupils were practically non-existent. He blinked once and his eyes went back to normal. He smiled at her and gave a self-depreci-ating shrug. Like what he had just done wasn't both terrifying and awe-inspiring.

Azar cast her mind around the now empty club, but she couldn't sense the presence of a fire or of the Rogue. She cast out her mind further, taking in the surrounding streets and apartment buildings and still sensed nothing. The Rogue wasn't in the area.

"Dammit!" She kicked the bar. Bast jumped down, landing with perfect grace beside her.

"Is he gone?"

She nodded, too angry to reply. He'd been right there, within her grasp and she'd lost him. She'd frozen up like a deer in the headlights and given that psychotic firebug a chance to escape. She was such an idiot.

Donovan strode over, looking as deadly as she knew he was. His black eyes looked hard and cruel, his mouth was twisted in a mean grimace. To say he looked angry would be an understatement.

"Where is he?" His voice was a low growl.

A security guard strode over before she had a chance to answer, and she breathed a sigh of relief.

She couldn't be sure that she wouldn't wet herself if Donovan turned his wrath on her. The guard was some kind of Were and his body was poised for a fight; from Donovan or the Rogue, Azar was not certain.

"We've searched the club and the surrounding streets. We picked up the scent of Ifrit but we are unsure if it was the Rogue or the girl." He jerked his chin in her direction.

Donovan and the Were turned to stare at her, their thoughts transparent. What if the Rogue really wasn't here at all? What if she was the Rogue and this was all an elaborate ruse to throw the only Shaitan in NYC off her trail?

"Don't be a jerk, Donovan. It isn't me. It's not my fault that your pet can't tell the difference between two different scents. Maybe his nose is impotent?"

The Were snarled and took a step toward her. She narrowed her eyes and stepped up to meet him face to face. She needed to vent some frustration and smashing this asshole's nose would help a lot.

"What'd you say to me? I'm gonna tear you to pieces, bitch!" the Were growled, his eyes flashing yellow and his teeth lengthening.

"Not if I barbecue your fuzzy ass first, fleabag!" The fire rippled under Azar's skin, begging to get out. It seared blissfully where her wings would burst through her back. The flames pushed through her flesh and made her hands glow like white-hot embers. She knew she was reacting more violently than she normally would, but it was the last straw in a day that had just been too much.

The sound of laughter penetrated the red haze that surrounded her. She whipped her head around to see Bast doubled over, laughing. Even Donovan was chuckling. She shot them both daggers and stepped away from the Were. She hoped he knew how lucky he was.

Azar crossed her arms over her chest. "Look, he was here and he was pissed off. He said that I was ruining his plans and that I would be his big finale."

All the humor left Bast's face in an instant. It didn't take a genius to work out what the threat meant. He was going to use her as the Ifrit pledge.

"I can loan you Jerry for protection," Donovan offered, indicating the Were next to him. Jerry's jaw dropped and a look of horror froze on his brutish features, rekindling Donovan's fit of giggles.

"Thanks for the offer but I'd rather take my chances with the Rogue. Besides, I'm not his only target. You are going to need all the help you can get to protect this place and any else you value." Even as

Azar said the last part, she knew it sounded dumb. Shaitan didn't have little cottages in the woods where they went when the world got too rough for them.

To her relief, Donovan didn't laugh at her again. In fact, he looked almost pensive. He nodded and turned, giving orders to Jerry, who immediately strode off into the darkness of the club. Azar got the overwhelming feeling that there was more to Donovan than what showed on the surface. He was a man with secrets, like all Djinn. But somehow, she didn't think his secret was related to a mass grave out in some far flung national park. Maybe, just maybe, the big bad Shaitan wasn't as bad as he seemed.

"Do you have a girlfriend?" Azar asked. Both Donovan and Bast looked at her like she'd lost her mind. "What? It's a legitimate question."

"No, I don't. Are you offering?" Donovan raised his eyebrows. He really was kind of attractive in a bad boy way, but Azar shook her head.

"No, sorry. I have enough problems." Wasn't that the truth. Her eyes slid to Bast, who smirked back. "What about a pet puppy?"

"No"

"Goldfish?"

"No"

"A secret love child?"

Donovan hesitated briefly. Bingo. "No."

But the hesitation had been too long. He obviously wanted to keep it a secret, which was fine with her. She met Donovan's hard eyes and gave him a reassuring look. She'd keep his secrets, but one day, she might need to use it as collateral. She wasn't against racking up debts for the greater good, even if she never intended to act on them.

She elbowed Bast in the stomach and he let out a cough. "Everyone has secrets. It's none of my business what they are. But if it were my secret, I'd ensure that it was extremely well protected for the next four or five days. Better yet, get them the hell out of New York City all together." Bast looked at the gold Rolex that shone on his wrist. "We should get going, Azar. I wouldn't want the good Detective trying to put a bullet in me for having you home late."

Donovan raised his eyebrows at Bast's words.

Azar tried to copy one of those nonchalant shrugs that everyone liked so much.

"Like Bast said, everyone has secrets."

CHAPTER 8

Azar popped one eye open and looked at the clock. Nine A.M. She had a brief moment of panic before she remembered it was Sunday and it was her day off. She rolled out of bed and padded out to the kitchen in an oversized T-shirt with the FDNY logo on the back. When Bast had dropped her home last night, she'd been glad that there was no Keenan waiting at her door. She poured herself a bowl of cereal and got out the ingredients for *Zareshk Polow*.

Every Sunday she went over to Joe's house and had lunch with his family and *Zareshk Polow* was her contribution to the meal. The whole ritual made Sunday her favorite day of the week. She liked cooking the traditional meal because the smell of the spices reminded her of her mother, who'd made the dish every year for Azar's birthday, right up until the year she died.

As nostalgic as cooking the dish was, it was eating at Joe's place with his family that really made the day. Every time she went there, she would walk into the same setting; the kids would be running around screaming, Joe's father would be sitting in Joe's favorite chair watching the football or baseball, depending on the season, and Joe's mother and his wife Linda would be in the kitchen cooking enough food for an army. Then Joe's sisters and their families would arrive to add to the mayhem. Eventually all the kids would be banished outside to run off some energy and a huge football game would ensue until Mama Maconi called them all in for lunch. It was a beautiful family environment, filled with so much love that they generously shared with her.

She had just put the rice on the stovetop to steam when there was a knock at her door. She wandered over and peeped through the hole.

Keenan was there holding a tray with two cups of coffee and a brown bag that she hoped contained some form of pastry. She looked down at her bare legs, shrugged, and opened the door with a smile.

"Well, hey there, Sailor. What's in the bag?" She

stood aside to let Keenan past. He looked at her legs, then through the door, then back at her legs before he entered. She smiled to herself as she shut the door and followed him into the kitchen.

He placed the coffees and the paper bag on the counter. "I bought us some doughnuts. I thought you could tell me how it went last night with Bast." He sniffed the air. "Something smells really great in here." He wandered over to the pot where the rice was steaming on top of sliced potatoes and lifted the lid. Azar picked up the wooden spoon and whacked him on the knuckles.

"Hands off or you'll ruin it. I have lunch at Joe's on Sundays and if you ruin my *Zareshk Polow*, Linda will track you down and set a mob of angry children onto you." She leaned onto the kitchen counter and pulled a doughnut out of the bag. Keenan rubbed his red knuckles, pouting as he came over to join her. He stood behind her, so close that she could feel the warmth of his body on her back and the rough brush of his denim jeans over the back of her thighs.

"I didn't know you could cook," he whispered in her ear. He rested his hands on her hips and pulled her back until she was nestled against his body.

"I, uh, can't really. I'm just good at one or two things." Her thought processes were getting foggier the further up her ribcage his hands ran. "You have forty minutes until this dish burns. So if you're making a move, you better make it quick, Reilly."

Keenan flipped her around and his mouth covered hers in a searing kiss. His hands slid to her ass and he boosted her up onto the kitchen bench. He pulled her shirt over her head and started nibbling and kissing his way down from her neck. He got down to her hip bone and grinned up at her.

"I'm good at one or two things too." He hooked two fingers under the waistband of her panties and slowly slid them down her thighs, trailing lingering kisses in their wake. Once they got to her knees, he let them slip down her dangling legs and she kicked them over her feet. He kissed his way back up her leg and bit the delicate skin of her inner thigh. Azar's skin felt hot and chilled simultaneously, her breathing short and sharp. He pulled her towards him and hooked her knees over his shoulders, gently nudged her backwards until she was lying on the kitchen bench. His hands held her hips up off the bench top.

He leaned forward and Azar could feel his warm breath on her center. She held her breath as he stilled, only inches away so that she could feel the heat of his skin. It seemed like an eternity before she felt the flick of his tongue on her clit, and a moan bubbled up from her throat. He flicked his tongue more vigorously and Azar squirmed on the bench, trying to pull him closer and hold on to sanity. The man had a tongue like a sea serpent!

"Holy fuck," Azar moaned as his tongue swirled and caressed. His hands massaged her ass and stroked up and down her spine. Her back arched upwards, her thighs so tight around his head that he was probably going to have a headache later, but she couldn't bring herself to care about anything but the amazing sensations he was producing with his mouth. The pressure built up in her groin until she knew she was close.

Keenan must have sensed how close to coming she was, as he pulled back and moved her legs to his waist. Azar was surprised to see that at some point he'd already shucked off his jeans and his shirt quickly followed. She sat up and wrapped her arms around his neck, and he moved them straight down onto the kitchen floor. He pulled a condom out of the back pocket of his discarded jeans. He slid it onto his straining cock.

Azar couldn't help but smile. "Do you carry one of those in your back pocket all the time?" He grinned sheepishly and knelt between her legs. He pressed his body to hers, leaning in to kiss her, his tongue delving into her mouth and she could taste a faint trace of herself on his lips. All coherent thought left her mind as he slid into her body. He groaned into her mouth as his pace quickened and Azar shattered around him. She bit his shoulder to muffle her cries. He slowed a little and then rolled them over so she was straddling his hips.

She grinned down at him and moved against him slowly, her body undulating over his until he picked up her rhythm. His hands ran over her breasts and the rough scrape of his thumbs over her sensitive nipples made her body clench around his. As the warmth grew in her body, her pace quickened, and Keenan was thrusting up to meet her, his hands pulling down on her hips so he was buried deep inside her.

Their bodies shone with sweat and their groans of pleasure echoed around the room. The waves of ecstasy battered at Azar until she once again tipped over the edge and Keenan was right behind her. Her body arched backwards and Keenan sat up and wrapped his arms around her waist, dragging her back down until she was gasping for breath against his chest. Their bodies shone with sweat and her hair stuck to her face.

"You weren't kidding about being good at that," she said between gasps for breath. Keenan ran his fingertips over her shoulder blade gently.

"I'm a man of the law. I never lie." Azar scoffed and Keenan grinned. "Well, at least not about the important things." He pressed a kiss to her neck. "Like how hot I think you are, and how badly I want to be inside you again." He pressed another kiss to the curve of her shoulder. Azar glanced at the Hello Kitty clock on her wall, a gift from the guys at the station house for her last birthday.

She raised her eyebrows. "You know, we still have another fifteen minutes. If you work fast we can make all your wishes come true," she purred.

"All my wishes? I don't think there would be enough time in a month to do all the things I wish to do to you. But we could probably knock one or two off the list." He slapped her ass cheek. "But not on the kitchen tiles. My fantasies don't involve my ass cheeks turning into popsicles."

Azar climbed to her feet, and Keenan stood up after her. He ran a finger down between her breasts and she was struck again how sexy this man was. Suddenly, he bent over and deadlifted Azar over his shoulder.

"Keenan, put me down," she half squealed, half

giggled. Keenan just ignored her and deposited her on the couch laughingly.

"Now about those wishes," he murmured in her ear, "do I get three?" He nibbled on her earlobe.

"I'm not that kind of genie," Azar whispered back breathlessly.

"Are you sure? Because I think I wished for you every night that I was alone in my bed. Now hush, I'm working on a time limit here. Lucky for you, I do my best work under pressure."

He wasn't wrong.

Twenty-five minutes and two more spectacular orgasms later they were lying on the couch naked and sweating. Azar eased herself up and wandered over to the kitchen. Standing back at the stove top, she sautéed off the barberries, and layered up the *Zareshk Polow* in a big casserole dish. Keenan was pulling his clothes back on and tossed Azar her shirt. She stretched out her shoulders languorously before pulling it over her head

"I have to shower before I go to Joe's," she told him. Keenan immediately started to undress again and Azar laughed. "Alone. If you help me shower, I will never get there and Mama Maconi will assume I'm dead and call the police." Keenan sighed and buttoned up his shirt again. He came over to the kitchen and swiped some of the rice out of the casserole dish. Then he moaned long and low, his face disturbingly similar to his 'I'm about to come' expression.

"Holy crap, this is great. You weren't kidding about doing this good." He took another spoonful of rice.

"You weren't either." She gave him a saucy wink as she wandered up the hall. "And stop eating my food. The threat about Linda wasn't an empty one, you know."

Twenty short minutes later, Azar was dressed in a knee length sundress and sandals, as was appropriate for a traditional Italian Sunday feast. She'd put on some lip gloss and pulled her dark hair into a ponytail.

When she got to the kitchen, it was empty but there was a note on the bench written on the back of an envelope that contained her power bill.

"Got called into work. Warehouse fire in Canarsie. We still have to talk. K xo"

Azar smiled at the xo, gathered up her casserole dish and locked up her apartment.

Joe lived around the corner from her, in a street

lined with row houses just off Linden Boulevard. It was a nice street. Neighbors sat on their front porches, minding everyone's business, and kids played on the sidewalk. Joe's place was a pretty standard row house; three levels including the basement, a postage stamp sized front yard big enough for the trash cans and a few flowers. A small backyard had just enough room for a grill, a patch of grass and a kid's swing set.

Azar pulled into a spot on the front of the house, looked at herself in the mirror to make sure she didn't outwardly look like she'd just had wild sex and walked up the steps to the front door. She could hear the noise of the kids running around the house and it made her smile. No wonder Joe talked so loud, he was probably partially deaf from the years of competing with his sisters to be heard and now the constant high level of noise inside his own home.

She hammered on the door to be heard above the thundering of little feet inside. The door was opened by a little boy dressed in an Ironman outfit, complete with mask and glowing round arc reactor in his chest. Azar guessed it was Joe's four year old son, Tommy. She schooled her features into her best straight face and gazed down seriously at Tommy.

"Sorry Mr. Stark, I was looking for the Maconi

residence. I must have taken the wrong turn off Linden." She gave the boy a look of mock confusion. The little boy removed his mask and smiled.

"No Az, it's just me!" he giggled and grabbed her hand, pulling her into the hustle and bustle of the sitting room. "Az's here," he yelled to anyone who cared before running off to join his cousins, who were doing laps around the sitting room in a boisterous game of chase. Linda stuck her head out of the kitchen and took in the chaos around her.

"That's it, everyone go play outside. That includes you Joe!" Azar looked over to where Joe was holding a little boy upside down by one leg with a huge grin on his face. Linda sighed. "It's like I have four kids sometimes, you know?" But she was smiling as she said it and Azar knew the love the two shared.

Joe lowered the kid to the ground and shooed him outside. He came over and kissed his wife, then wrapped Azar in a warm brotherly hug.

"You look awfully happy today. What put that big goofy smile on your face? Or should I say who?" Azar swung a punch at him in the shoulder but Joe danced out of the way, laughing. "Coming outside for a game of football?" He asked as he backed towards the door, in case she took another shot at him while his back was turned. He knew her too well; she wasn't above the cheap shots.

"Of course, I need the opportunity to pound you one for having such a big mouth! I'll just put this in the kitchen and let the chaos die down a bit first." She hefted the casserole dish.

Mama Maconi stuck her head through the kitchen door and took the casserole dish from her hands. Azar bent so she could get the ceremonial kiss on both of her cheeks.

Mama Maconi was a tiny woman, and if Azar was any closer than four feet away, all she could see was Mama's tight grey bun that perched perfectly on the top of her head.

"Azar, my beautiful girl, you look wonderful. Too skinny though. You need to eat more. How have you been? A pretty girl like you needs to find a man and get married. My bridge partner's son is back in Brooklyn and he is quite the catch. I could get him to call you, if you'd like?" Linda made tiny but vigorous head shakes behind Mama Marconi's back. Then, just in case Azar didn't quite catch the hint, she stuck a finger down her throat and made up-chuck motions.

"That's okay, Mama. I have to work with all those men at the fire station. That's enough testosterone for me right now." Joe's mother wouldn't reply to anything but Mama from the adults or Nonna from the kids.

Mama Maconi just shook her head, muttering how you weren't young forever and something about bambinos before waving them away and waddling back into the kitchen. Linda grinned and rubbed her pregnant belly. Joe and Linda took the procreation of bambinos very seriously. They had three boys already, and Linda had secretly confided they were going to keep going until she finally got a girl. Joe was adamant that he had too much testosterone for them to have anything but boys. They were even running a pool at the firehouse about the sex of the baby. Odds were twenty to one that it was another boy. Azar had put a cool Benjamin on the fact it was a girl. She hoped so for Linda's sake.

Azar wasn't sure how she ended up adopted into this family, but she was thankful. They were a wonderful piece of normalcy in her otherwise hectic life. Linda poured Azar a glass of wine and herself some grape juice and told Mama Maconi that she was going to watch the game out back. Mama was the captain of the kitchen, and heaven help anyone who interfered.

Out on the small back deck, Joe's sisters Tina and

Louise were already sipping wine. They both got up and gave her the classic Italian two cheek kiss before they settled back down on the wide comfy chairs that took up most of the space on the deck.

"So, we heard from a little birdy that you and Keenan Reilly did the nasty." Louise grinned at her and waggled her eyebrows.

"If by a little birdy you mean that six foot four turkey over there, then you heard correctly." Azar waved her hand in the direction of Joe. She should have known he wouldn't have let the news stay at the station. The three women hooted and demanded details. She shook her head; she didn't kiss and tell, despite their persistence.

"But it was only the once, right?" Linda asked, looking at Azar suspiciously. Azar felt her face get red, and the blush slowly spread down her neck until she felt like she was red all over. All three women looked at her with their mouths wide open. "More than once? When?" Linda exclaimed. They all leaned forward in their chairs.

Azar downed the rest of her glass of wine and then poured another one from the bottle in the middle of the table.

"This morning," she mumbled.

Azar just wanted to lie down and die with

embarrassment. Every week she would come over here and grumble about her dislike of Keenan whenever his name was mentioned, which was usually in connection to him sleeping with some poor girl. She'd go on and on about how she wouldn't sleep with Keenan Goddamn Reilly if he were the last man on earth. She still kind of disliked him until he took his clothes off. Then she liked him very much. The man had a body made for sin and a talent in the sack she had rarely seen in her hundred odd years. But when he had his clothes on, he was possessive and demanding, not to mention a chauvinist to the core.

When you added Bast to the mix, her love life was just a confusing mess. She knew Bast wanted her. She saw it in his eyes every time he looked at her, felt the very real evidence of it last night and now he knew her secret, there was really nothing stopping her. Except Keenan Goddamn Reilly. Until she worked out what they had together, she couldn't really give in to her hunger for Bast. Not that she and Keenan could ever be together; he was human, she was Djinn. It was just too dangerous for both of them.

"Earth to Azar, a penny for your thoughts?" Linda nudged her with her arm.

"From the look on her face, I'd give her far more

than a penny for her thoughts," Tina chimed in. "Keenan Reilly is such a hottie, and I heard from the girl who works in the clinic on East 22nd street that he is a monster in the sack. I love Paul, but I have to admit, I'm kind of envious!" Paul was Tina's husband. He sold electrical goods and was a little spongy around the middle, but he had a quick smile and he loved his wife.

"I don't know," Azar sighed. "Keenan is great until he opens his mouth. When we are, uh, in bed, he's perfect. Plus, he knows some tricks that would not only blow your socks off but would shoot them straight out of the tri-state area. But when he's not busy doing those things, he's arrogant and opinionated. And then there's this other guy who's just like me and he's smoking hot too but as equally unavailable, emotionally I mean."

"What do you mean just like you? Another firefighter?"

Azar grimaced. Whoops. She reminded herself to slow down on the wine before she spilled everything.

"No, he's Iranian. Sometimes it's just nice to have a shared history," Azar lied. It was partially true, after all.

"I didn't think that kind of thing mattered to you.

This isn't about the guy you got caught with by the guys from the 285 the other night? The one at the Blue Smoke club? Hal's wife called me at nine the next morning to tell me that little tidbit. I don't even think I was the first on her call list. I think she'd called the entire school emergency phone tree by the time she got to me," Linda said and winked.

Azar panicked. "I'm kinda seeing this guy, and his uh, cousin owns the club. It was just a wrong place at the wrong time kind of thing." It was all partially true, but it sounded lame, even to her own ears. She didn't even care that the entire FDNY was talking about her; if not about the whole Keenan and Azar affair, then probably about her little foray into a pervert bar practically naked. For a brief moment, she was kind of glad that she had bigger things to worry about or else she would be truly horrified.

The two bottles of wine on the table were now empty and Louise and Tina had that cheery glow of the newly tipsy.

"Is he as good looking as Keenan Reilly? I'd really like to have your problem. Good looking men throwing themselves at me left and right until I had to beat them back from my door with a stick just to get to work every morning," Tina sighed wistfully.

"I'm sure Johnny wouldn't mind if you beat him

with a stick every now and then," Louise teased her sister.

Tina's husband Johnny was a tough as nails construction worker from the Bronx. Tina and he had met at a friend's wedding and hit it off straight away. They'd married a year later and had their first child a year after that. Azar knew the only reason Joe had approved of the match back then was because he was pretty sure he couldn't take Johnny in a fight. Years later, everyone could see how much Johnny and Tina adored each other and their little girl. He was rough around the edges and he wasn't Italian, but he fit in with the family just fine.

"I promise you, I get out my door just fine every morning. Until last week I didn't have any romantic prospects. But you know what it's like, it's either feast or famine in this city." They all gave sympathetic murmurs and the topic changed to the fact Tommy refused to wear anything but his Ironman suit.

Azar joined in the conversation, giving advice where she felt she could, but generally just feeling amused. Tommy was going to provide Joe and Linda with some serious problems when he hit his teenage years. Mama Maconi said Tommy was just like Joe when he was a boy, and from what Azar had heard, that meant wild and rebellious. Mama said Joe was the cause of every one of her grey hairs.

She finished her wine and joined in the game of football. It was wild game with no rules, and the kids were covered in dirt and grass stains. Azar couldn't get into it as much as Joe because she was wearing a dress, but she kicked off her shoes and ran around after the kids. She held down Joe so the kids could all pile on top of him in a ferocious game of stacks on, and Johnny ran out to hold down his legs as the kids tickled him until he cried for mercy.

Soon, Mama Maconi was calling everyone in for dinner and clucking at the grass stains on everyone's clothes and knees. The huge dining table, set with lots of mismatched chairs and china, was soon crowded with adults. The kids had their own table in the corner, where they didn't have to worry about manners and the conversation centered on the newest video games rather than taxes. Food was passed around and plates were piled high. Papa Maconi said Grace and soon enough everyone dug in like they'd been starved for a month. The laughter and conversation was loud and raucous as always. She'd been seated between Linda and Johnny, which meant if she turned to her left she could talk about something other than her love life.

"So, how's business Johnny?" Azar asked between mouthfuls of baked Ziti.

"Yeah, not bad. Working for a new outfit here in Brooklyn so I can come home to Tina and Stellah earlier every night, you know? But they are a bit shady this new crew; I think they might be owned by the family if you catch my drift. But I don't mind, they pay better than the Bronx and I keep my head down and just get on with my work." That was a lot of words for Johnny, who usually gave her monosyllabic answers.

Obviously, Brooklyn had some pretty famous gangsters in its time, mostly in the forties and fifties, but that had quieted down now. But they were still there and although they didn't have the power that they had sixty or seventy years ago, it was assumed that they still had some form of operation in Brooklyn. However, no one really blinked an eyelid at such things anymore; they'd become part of the landscape of Brooklyn.

"Be careful," Azar cautioned. "They aren't the type to think twice about putting you in a bad situation that you can't get out of." Azar had met some gangsters in her time. In the old days they had a strict moral code, but that had slowly eroded over the years into the free for all that was around now. There was no honor amongst thieves these days.

By the time the food was finished and the coffee and the cake savored, it was time to go home. Azar could barely stand. She was glad she had to wear dresses to these dinners because if she was in her jeans, the top button might have flown off and poked out someone's eye. She offered to wash up, as she did every week, and was shooed out of the kitchen by Mama Maconi and Linda.

Azar wandered into the living room and sat on the couch arm next to Joe, as all the seats were taken by the men. They were a very traditional family; guests and men weren't allowed in the kitchen and the women weren't allowed to mow the lawn or barbeque. Not exactly a division of labor, especially when Linda and Joe's sisters worked a full day as well, but hey, old habits die hard.

When Azar was convinced that she could actually fit behind the wheel of her car again, she took her leave. She kissed everyone on both cheeks, including Johnny who wasn't actually Italian but accepted this intimacy with good grace and Papa Maconi who kissed Azar's cheeks hard enough to leave a bruise every week. Mama Maconi hustled her out the door with leftovers to "fatten her up" and Joe saw her to her car. He whistled at the beautiful Shelby and ran a hand over the roof. Joe suffered from serious car envy; he only had a beat up Honda and Linda had a minivan to transport the boys around every day.

"Do you want me to leave you and my car alone for a minute?" Azar asked laughingly.

"Yes, please. Leave the keys too," Joe said, holding his hand out eagerly.

She smacked it away, laughing. There was no way on earth that she would let Joe drive her car. He was a hot blooded Italian who believed, like almost every man, that he was really meant to be a Formula One driver. That meant going too fast, and taking the corners like Michael Schumacher. Azar popped him in the arm hard and slid into her car.

"Thanks for lunch!" she yelled out the window as she put her foot on the gas and roared away.

CHAPTER 9

Azar was brought out of her food coma by someone standing over her bed. Her scream was quickly covered by a hand.

"It's only me! Don't panic the neighbors or they'll call the cops. And then Detective Overprotective will come over and we'll have to do that whole Shakespearean drama again." Bast's golden eyes glittered down at her in the moonlight as he sat on the edge of her bed, looking like the star of a dirty dream.

"Jesus H. Christ Bast, are you trying to scare the life out of me? What part of 'threatened by crazed Ifrit' don't you understand? You just don't walk into a woman's bedroom like that!"

Azar's heart rate was racing so fast it that it felt

like it was going to burst from her chest like a face-hugger from the movie Aliens. Like having Bast in her bedroom late at night wasn't bad enough, but she was also naked. She'd come home from Joe's place, stripped off all her clothes and fell into bed to sleep off all the food she'd eaten. She pulled the sheet tighter around her body, but Bast had already noticed her bare shoulders and was appreciating the outline of her body under the sheet. She tried desperately to think of something to distract him.

"Uh, what time is it anyway? And how the hell did you get into my apartment?" She could see Bast's teeth gleam in the moonlight. Obviously not her most subtle change of topic.

"It's 12:15 a.m. I tried knocking but no one answered so I closed my eyes and wished myself into your apartment, of course. That's the Jann specialty; transporting desperate souls to places that contain great beauty. And I am desperate," he purred. "And you are very beautiful." He leaned closer and put a hand on the either side of her body so that her breasts were pressed close to his chest and his mouth was inches away. Every nerve in her body went on high alert.

"Don't worry, Little Fire. I'm not going to jump your bones tonight. Fortunately for you, you've been saved by the bell. Or in this case by Donovan." He leaned closer so that his cheek brushed hers and his lips were near her ear. "When we do make love, and it will happen, you will beg me to join you under that sheet." He kissed the pulse point just below her ear and moved off the bed, a hand running down over the curve of her hip. "I'll wait for you in the kitchen." And then he was gone.

Her body was on fire. Her heartbeat had gone from Kentucky Derby to the running of the bulls in Pamplona. She threw the sheet off to cool herself down and took a few deep breaths. She wondered if it was possible for the Djinn to have a heart attack. She was tempted to have a cold shower but decided she should see what Bast thought was so important that he got her out of bed at midnight. Pulling on her jeans and a cable knit jumper, she shuffled out to the kitchen barefoot. Bast had brewed some coffee and set the mugs on the counter.

"What could Donovan want so badly that he had to send you around at midnight?" Azar yawned deeply. Her body might be wide awake but her mind was still wistfully looking for some good REM sleep. She took an appreciative sip of her coffee.

"The Onyx burned to the ground tonight," Bast said conversationally. Azar almost dropped her cup.

She sloshed hot coffee onto her hand as she righted it. Bast reached over with the dish cloth, blotting the coffee off her hand before refilling her cup.

"Why the hell didn't you lead with that? Was the club full?" She knew that nightclub fires usually had a high number of fatalities; not just from smoke inhalation and burns, but from hysteria and the trampling that came with it. They'd caught a little bit of that behavior the other night before Bast stepped in.

"No, Donovan had closed it down for a few days under the guise of necessary maintenance. He had guards there twenty four hours a day but the Rogue managed to sneak past. One of the Were security guards got pretty badly burnt trying to combat the fire and the other security guards had to pull the guy out."

Azar shook her head. Weres had greater healing abilities than humans, but it was still completely possible for them to burn to a crisp or pass out from smoke inhalation.

Azar went to the couch and started pulling on her boots. "We need to go to The Onyx and see if we can help Donovan. Maybe we can find something before the police arrive."

Bast was leaning back against the kitchen

counter, his head tilted as if listening. Then there was a loud knock on the door. Lucky Mr. Grimond next door was deaf, with all the knocking going on at her door at such an ungodly hour, otherwise he'd definitely complain to her landlord.

"No need. They came here." Bast strode over to the door and pulled it open. Six Were's and Donovan piled into her tiny living room. Azar shot Bast a dirty look, and he just grinned. She was sure he invited them here so they wouldn't all have to pile into his office and crush his precious plants.

Azar vacated the couch so two of the big Weres could sit down. They were all pretty big actually; five were muscle bound giants, with shoulders like barn doors and no obvious signs of a neck. Jerry from the other night was amongst them. The sixth Were was still very tall, but his body was a lean, tanned muscle, and his abs rippled beneath his tight white tee as he walked. His hair was strawberry blonde and his eyes were the strangest shade of khaki green. It was a jaw dropping combination. He reached a level of physical perfection that surpassed even Keenan and Bast. Definitely some kind of jungle cat, Azar thought appreciatively.

The sixth Were caught her studying him and winked. "Jaguar, because I know you are wondering," he said in a Texan accent. Azar gave him a sheepish look. It fit perfectly though; the lean muscle, the loose limbed swagger and his ability to be solitary in a room full of people. She would probably peg the other five as wolves, the more prolific of the Weres.

Donovan took the remaining chair. He looked terrible. His clothes and face were stained grey with soot, and his hair stuck up at all angles; well, more so than usual. His jaw was tense and his mouth was drawn into a tight slash. His eyes glittered with an anger that she was glad wasn't aimed at her. She patted him a couple of times on the back, the way one would pat a Rottweiler that you thought was friendly but didn't really know. She probably would have given him a hug if she wasn't a little worried about him snapping her in half in a fit of rage. He looked at her and his eyes softened a little, but the rest of his face remained a hard mask.

She walked tentatively over to the single couch chair and sat on the armrest.

"I'm assuming you and your little posse here want in on the search for the Rogue?" Donovan's eyes went hard again and he nodded curtly. "I'm really sorry about the club. Is the security guy okay?" Donovan nodded again, but it was Jerry who answered.

"Simon only got some superficial burns. A couple of days rest within the pack and he'll be fine." Azar only knew a little about Were culture, but she knew that their normally speedy healing abilities were even more accelerated when they were within their family groups. It said something about the depth of his injuries that he would have to be within the pack for a couple of days to heal. Though, Azar was pretty certain that anything short of decapitation would be "superficial" to this bunch.

"So, he snuck past you guys again? I'd really like to know how he keeps doing that."

A chorus of growls resounded throughout the room.

"Geez, I'm not disparaging your sniffer skills, calm the hell down. All I am saying is that you guys can smell me from the ground floor, yet he can sneak right into an empty room and wander around undetected? As far as I am aware, there is no ability that allows us to mask our scent."

Everyone was silently contemplating this little fact when there was another knock at the door. All six Were jumped to their feet in a second and stealthily walked towards her front door. No matter how hard she strained, she couldn't hear a single footfall. Damn, they were good.

"Relax guys. I highly doubt the Rogue is just going to knock at the door." At least, she didn't think so. She walked over to the door with more confidence than she felt. The last thing she needed was for it to be Mr. Grimond next door, coming over to see what all the noise is about, and instead get torn apart by angry werewolves.

Azar peaked out the viewer. It was Keenan. She almost wished it was Mr. Grimond. She sighed and opened the door. Keenan leaned in and kissed her cheek.

"I saw your light on so I thought I'd come and keep..." He stuttered to a stop when he saw her apartment filled to the brim with men. Big, bulky and mostly hunky men. "Uh, keep you company. But I can see you're about at capacity for company." He eyed every man in the room warily and they eyed him back with equal hostility. Azar thought she might gag on the testosterone.

"Okay everyone, let's just ratchet down the macho factor for a second. This is Keenan Reilly. He is an arson investigator for the NYPD. He is investigating the fires. Keenan this is Donovan, he owns a club in Hoboken." She indicated Donovan, who looked like a serial killer she'd dragged in off the street. Probably not the most reassuring first impression.

"The detective and I have already met tonight. He took my statement; he wanted to know if I burnt down my own club for some reason." Donovan's voice was gravelly with anger. Not at Keenan, she hoped, because that would not bode well for Keenan's life expectancy.

"Standard procedure," Azar assured him, "and this is Jerry and... uh I have no idea who the rest of them are." Jerry gave a little finger wave and the other werewolves remained silent. The Werejaguar grinned at Keenan and came over to shake his hand.

"I'm Oliver, nice to meet you. I also happen to enjoy investigating the apartments of pretty girls in the middle of the night." He winked at Azar. She really didn't need another outrageous flirt in her life, but she still blushed an unattractive shade of red. He was just so damn hot. Like melt-your-panties-into-a-puddle-on-the-floor hot. And funny. Funny was her kryptonite. He was going to be trouble, but she couldn't help herself, she grinned back. He had managed to lower the room's tension level a little.

Keenan turned and looked at Bast. "Of course you're here." There was a note of resignation in his voice, as if she and Bast were a package deal. Azar wasn't sure when that had happened, but she knew it meant trouble.

Bast gave him a megawatt grin. "I was here before the others arrived."

Azar shot him a dirty look but it just bounced off Bast's shield of self-assurance. She pulled a bottle of scotch out of the top cupboard and poured herself a shot. She looked at the group of men still covertly staring at each other and she pulled out her shot glass collection, dusted it off and then poured everyone a round. Oliver came over to lean on the breakfast bar next to Bast. One of the other Weres came over and picked up six shot glasses in one hand, passing them around to Donovan, Jerry and the other Weres.

"To The Onyx," Azar toasted. A murmur went around the room and everyone downed their shot. Keenan stood on the other side of the breakfast bar with her.

"So I didn't realize you all knew each other. Are you all part of the same social group?" Keenan asked warily and Azar could have slapped her forehead.

"Bast and I are old friends," Donovan responded, but he'd noted the not so subtle insinuation. He eyed Azar with curiosity.

"Well, as fun as this is, can we get on with it so I

can go back to bed?" Azar crossed her arms over her chest. She was too tired to walk on eggshells.

"I agree," Oliver said seriously. "Let's get on with it so I can go back to her bed."

Ugh, there was that blush again, but she gave Oliver a mock glare which only made him smirk more. Trouble. With a capital T.

She turned to Keenan, who was trying to casually scan the room for potential threats. "Donovan and his friends are helping us track down the arsonist. They have a skill set that will make it far more likely that we will find this monster before the cops do. So if you're going to share info, do it now before this psycho barbecues me as well."

Keenan's head whipped around so fast that Azar wondered if he'd given himself whiplash.

"What do you mean, barbecues you as well?" Whoops, Azar had forgotten that she hadn't told Keenan about the Rogue's threats when he had been here earlier. They'd been too preoccupied with other things. Everyone conveniently found somewhere else to look, except Oliver and Bast, who were watching on as if they were about to see a train-wreck. She shot Bast an appealing look and he just shrugged. Asshole.

"The Rogue cornered me the other night at

Donovan's club. He said I was going to be his big finale. I think he means for me to be the final tribute." Azar braced herself for impact, but Keenan turned on Bast. He stepped around the counter and got up in Bast's face.

"How could you let this happen? You were meant to be protecting her, staying close to her!" He poked Bast in the chest and all the Weres took a collective breath in. "And now a crazed genie wants to make her into a bonfire?"

The forbidden secret.

Donovan looked a little shocked that Keenan had just blurted it out liked that. Azar's knees went weak and Oliver wrapped an arm around her waist quickly. Now they were all in a world of trouble. This is what happened when you told humans things they weren't supposed to know. Bast's eyes narrowed and he looked as angry as Azar had ever seen him, which was to say he look mildly peeved.

"I'd like to get a lot closer to her, and I will very soon. However, Azar can protect herself. She's not a weak little damsel that you humans seem to enjoy so much. It's you who needs to be careful. You are the only person putting Azar in any danger right now!" His eyes glittered like sharp pieces of amber.

Keenan seemed to snap out of his caveman rage

as the realization of what he said dawned on him. He looked at her, and at the room full of people, and then back at Azar.

"Fuck."

Grinding her teeth, she strode around to the other side of the bench, getting up his face. She wanted to scream at him. Instead, she pulled back her fist and punched him in the nose. She heard the crack. The Weres all sucked in a gasp. "What the hell do you think you are doing? What part of deadly secret did you not get? You have no idea what you've done to all of us!"

Keenan was doubled over holding his nose, blood gushing from it steadily. Oliver looked practically gleeful as he grabbed a dish towel and held it to Keenan's bloody face. After he'd wiped some of the blood away, he tipped Keenan's head back and examined his nose, which seemed to be sitting at an odd angle on his face.

"I think she only dislocated it. If you hold still I can pop it back into place."

Keenan nodded through watery eyes and held still. There was another audible pop and more groans of sympathy from the couch.

Azar wasn't even looking at Keenan; she knew he'd be fine. She was looking between Bast and

Donovan, trying to predict what might happen. When she'd let it slip to Bast that Keenan knew about the Djinn in the warehouse, she'd been in shock from finally meeting another Djinn. Plus, he'd caught her in a tough position; either let Keenan shoot him and fail, or warn Keenan and save them all a lot of bloodshed. That had been an easy decision at the time. Bast gave off that kind of reassuring vibe anyway.

Besides, in reality, the worst case scenario for Bast was the proverbial slap on the wrist. However, Donovan was a whole different kettle of fish. The Shaitan were the most heavily monitored of all the races. Their predisposition towards violence had the potential to bring a lot of negative attention to the Djinn. Any small infraction could result in them getting their head irrevocably removed. Keenan Goddamn Reilly had really put him in a bad position and all three Djinn in the room knew it. He'd have to turn her in. Probably Bast too, though those two had some kind of strange alliance going on that Azar didn't really understand. But Donovan and Azar barely knew each other; he had nothing to gain by keeping her secret and everything to lose.

The Weres were looking in any direction but at the three of them. The Djinn Council had no authority over the Were races. She could tell the whole pack that she was an unslaved Djinn who had told a mortal the forbidden secret and they would probably just pat her head then send her on her way. She rubbed her temples and tried to think what she could offer Donovan to stay quiet. She didn't possess anything of any real value; she was going to have to run, again.

"At least give me until after *Azerasr*," she implored. Donovan nodded and looked at Bast, some kind of unspoken communication passing between them. She turned back to look at Keenan. Someone had found her first aid kit and strapped up his nose. It looked pretty professional and Azar raised her eyebrows at Oliver.

"It pays to have a doctor in every group. It's just one of my many talents." He winked at her again.

Keenan looked at her pitifully, like a puppy she'd just kicked for peeing on the carpet. Blood had stained the front of his shirt, and both his eyes were black. "Azar…" She held up a hand to cut him off.

"Just tell us what you know and nothing else. I don't really want to talk to you right now, but unfortunately I don't have the luxury of kicking you out and giving you the silent treatment because a crazy person is about to burn up the city of New

York!" She huffed and crossed the room to the couch.

The two huge werewolves shifted over uneasily, and Azar jammed herself down in the middle of them, just to annoy Reilly and Bast. Keenan shot her another apologetic look, and then a couple of warning looks to the two werewolves either side of her. That made one of them chuckle.

"In regards to evidence at The Onyx, there is no accelerant yet again, just a violent fire that seems to have sprung up out of nowhere." Keenan's voice was nasally and he kept wincing as if his nose hurt when he talked. Good. It'd teach him to keep his trap shut. "Obviously, everyone here knows why that is. Other than that, we found some clothes in a dumpster about three blocks down. We are fairly sure the perp changed out of them and tossed them. They were covered in some kind of hair, smelled a little like dog."

Everyone had a light bulb moment. That's how he could sneak in without anyone noticing. They were sniffing so hard for the scent of Ifrit, the smell of another werewolf would hardly have registered to them.

This brought up another worrying possibility. The Rogue had himself a pet werewolf. Or he was keeping one captive. Apparently everyone else had reached the same conclusion because there was a collective growl around the room. This had just gotten real personal.

"Did they just growl?" Keenan asked no one in particular.

Oliver patted him on the back. "Yeah, they're dogs." Keenan opened his mouth as if to ask something, then closed it and just shook his head.

"We'll check with the pack leader to see if anyone has gone missing or has been suspiciously absent," Jerry said.

Donovan sighed. "I guess that is one mystery solved. Doesn't really help us track him down though." Azar sighed right along with him. There was a clue to the mystery in there somewhere but Azar couldn't find it. Her gut told her that the answer would be found at the Brownsville apartment.

"What else do we have on the Brownsville apartment fire?" Azar asked Keenan.

"Not much more since we did the preliminary investigation there a couple of days ago. I can look into it more if you'd like?" Azar nodded. Something there didn't make sense. It could have been a lucky guess that a refugee family lived there, it was low income housing after all, but it seemed just a little too targeted, a little too premeditated. There was a link there that they were missing.

"I think that would be a good idea. I just have a feeling we are missing something. Now everyone get the hell out of my apartment so I can go to bed." Azar wiggled her way out from between the two werewolves. Every eye turned to follow her as she walked to the door and opened it. Several of the Weres stood, but no one took a step toward the door.

"Azar, I think you need some form of protection," Keenan said, his arms crossed, giving her a no nonsense look even though his nose had swollen to twice its size. Bast and Donovan were nodding in agreement.

"It's the best chance we have at catching this guy in the act. We all know he is coming for Azar, and personally I'd like to be waiting for him." Donovan's face looked downright vicious. Retribution and revenge were right in the Shaitan's comfort zone.

Keenan was looking at Donovan like he was looking at the Devil himself, and in a way he probably was. Azar knew that there was more to Donovan than his Shaitan exterior, but he could probably still rip a person to shreds without a second thought. It was in his nature, just as it was in hers to embrace fire and in Bast's to try to create peace for the worthy, or whatever the hell the Jann did. The skill sets of the benevolent races were a little more ambiguous than the more destructive races.

"I wasn't suggesting we set her up as bait," Keenan growled. It was a little anticlimactic after the werewolf growls, and seemed like a dumb, or brave, thing to do in an apartment filled with things that responded to body language.

Bast rolled his eyes as if coming to Keenan's rescue was getting to be a bore. Azar would be eternally grateful to him if he managed to prevent Keenan from being eviscerated into nothing more than a blood splatter painting on her living room wall.

"The human is right; if something went wrong because we dangled her in front of him and the pledge was completed, well, more of New York will burn than just your bar. I will stay with Azar until the Rogue is caught." He winked at Azar and his eyes said that he was going to protect her body intimately.

"Like hell you will. If anyone is staying with Azar, it's me," Keenan replied. Both the Djinn looked at

Keenan as if he'd suggested killing a T-Rex with a BB gun.

Azar reached the end of her patience. "Excuse me? If it's okay with the big strong men in the room, maybe I could have a say in my own life? I don't need anyone's protection thank you. I am Ifrit, what is he going to do? Burn me? It is impossible to kill me by setting me on fire, so if anyone is safe from this guy, it's me." She lit a small fireball to make a point. "So you can all go home."

Bast was shaking his head. "You are not impossible to kill in more mundane ways, Azar. You are vulnerable, especially from sneak attacks. You must have someone to watch your back. I believe I would be the best option."

Donovan smiled, "Jerry is still available. Actually all the Were are available now that my club was incinerated." As much as Azar was glad to see Donovan in a lighter mood, she'd rather take her chances with the Rogue than sleep in an apartment full of werewolves. But Donovan had a point; a Were would be able to smell the Ifrit before it reached her, especially now that they had worked out his trick.

"Thanks for the offer Donovan. Actually, if it is alright with you and Oliver, perhaps he could sleep on my couch for the next couple of days?" Both Bast and Keenan's heads whipped to the Werejaguar, whose gleaming smile was predatory to say the least.

He strode over to Azar and grabbed her hand, bending at the waist to kiss it gently. His lips were hot, and his tongue flicked out, tasting her skin. Maybe this was a bad idea. "I've never been able to say no to a damsel in distress. Of course I will stay with you." His eyes sparkled with mischief, and he was definitely fucking with all the other Alpha males in the room. That was all.

"Great, then it's settled. Now everyone but Oliver needs to leave!" She shooed out the Were's one by one, then Donovan.

Bast and Keenan were still standing there, side by side, eyeing Oliver suspiciously. She got behind them and gave them both a good shove towards the door. "Out, out, out!"

They finally left with assurances that they would return; both giving warning looks to Oliver as she slammed the door.

Oliver poured himself another shot of scotch. "Girl, you really know how to party. I don't think I could possibly keep up," he teased, knocking back two fingers of scotch. Azar got him a blanket and pillow, and spread them out on the couch.

"Oliver, you have no idea." She shuffled on tired feet toward her room.

"Want me to tuck you in?" he called.

"No, thank you!" she said adamantly, even though her lady bits were yelling back a resounding *YES!*

His chuckles echoed through her closed door. She had a sneaking suspicion the only one she was fooling was herself.

CHAPTER 10

It's not every day that she stumbled into her kitchen, desperate for a cup of coffee and instead finds a very nice naked butt peeking out of her fridge. The ass in question belonged to a very lean and well-tanned Oliver. The man didn't have a tan line in sight, which led Azar to believe that perhaps he did this naked thing often.

She cleared her throat to get his attention. Oliver turned from the fridge, a carton of milk still in his hand. He didn't even bother to cover anything, obviously completely at ease with his nudity.

"Good morning," he yawned as he took a swig out of the bottle.

Azar's jaw dropped to the floor. Now she understood why Oliver spent a lot of time naked. Hell, if she was a man as blessed as he was in that department, she too would spend all her time naked and have absolutely no shame whatsoever. He placed the milk on the counter and set the coffee to percolate.

"Don't take this as a complaint, because you are very pretty, but why are you wandering around my kitchen naked?" Azar had to ask, as she desperately tried to keep her gaze focused on his face and not anywhere else. Like his well-defined abs, or that impressive V where his hips ran into other things.

Oliver grinned. "Like what you see? I slept in my other form last night, and I can't do that in jeans." He sauntered over to the couch and picked up the aforementioned pants, which made the muscles in his thighs ripple as he bent over. "You know you wanna touch these buns," he teased over his shoulder.

Azar grinned to herself. She clenched her fist and let the fire heat up in her hand. A girl deserved a bit of fun when she had several death threats hanging over her head.

"You know, you're so right. I do want to touch," she purred, sashaying over to him. She ran a hand over the hard muscles of his ass, and then pulled back her hand and slapped it. She seared a perfectly shaped hand print onto his ass. Not with enough heat to do any serious injury, just enough to be like a bad sunburn.

All the same, it made Oliver jump about three feet into the air and actually yowl like a scalded cat He turned around rubbing his ass cheek and Azar ran over to the other side of the kitchen, putting the breakfast bar between them. She could barely breathe she was laughing so hard.

"I'm going to get you back for that." He was trying to look at the red mark over his shoulder. She watched him walk in circles, chasing his own tail to try and get a good look. Tears of laughter ran down her face at the sight. "I need aloe vera, it burns," he whined.

"Now you'll know better than to walk around naked and make open ended offers to an Ifrit. If you play with fire, you are going to get burnt," Azar laughed. She'd always wanted to use that line! She took pity on him and tossed him a tub of yoghurt. "Try this, it'll help."

Once she could breathe again, she made them both a cup of coffee. Oliver had gingerly shimmied into his jeans, commando of course. He was really going to feel the denim on that burn today. She offered him his coffee as a peace offering but there was a wild look in Oliver's eye to match the grin on his face and they both promised trouble.

"You won't be grinning when I get my revenge," he said, taking a gentle sip of his coffee.

Azar knew better than to have another poke at him. She didn't know what kind of revenge he meant, but from the glint in his eye, she was either going to love it or hate it. He had that look that mischievous kids get when they'd found a way to pull a prank on the teacher.

"I'm sorry, really, but you were right; I just had to touch." She stifled another laughing fit. "What are we up to today? I don't have to work, and you are on babysitting duty. Is there anything you want to do?" Oliver's grin widened and he waggled his eyebrows. "Besides that; I have enough man troubles without adding a horny Werejaguar to the list. A grumpy Irish cop and a mysterious Jann are enough for any girl." She smiled and elbowed him in the ribs to hide the fact that for a fraction of a second, she'd seriously contemplated the offer. He looked down at her, and his eyes practically smoldered. He knew. She didn't know how he could possibly know she was thinking dirty, dirty things about him, but she'd bet her entire collection of Die Hard films that he did. She blinked at him slowly, keeping her face impassive.

Eventually, Oliver gave a theatrical sigh. "Why are the good ones always taken?" He wrapped an arm around her shoulders and gave her a hug. "How about I make pancakes and we watch Netflix?"

"You really know how to show a girl a good time," she said with mock seriousness, glad the tense moment was over, and sat down to watch Oliver cook without a shirt on. Just because she had man troubles, didn't mean she couldn't appreciate a nice view when she saw one.

They were just finishing up the end of a Yeti movie double feature and the last of the dozen pancakes when Oliver's phone rang.

"Oliver. Yup. Yes. Okay. We'll be right over." Oliver hung up and sighed. "Playtime is over. That was Jerry. The Pack has called an emergency meeting and would like our presence." He uncurled his body from the couch and stretched, looking exactly like the cat he was.

"Why do they want my presence?" She hadn't had anything to do with the Weres in the area for as long as she'd been in NYC. Oliver shrugged as he put a shirt on, much to her regret, and he gave a little wince as he sat back down on the couch to pull on his socks.

She sighed and got ready to go back to reality, which she thought would make a much better fantasy movie than anything about a Yeti.

Azar turned the Shelby onto a dirt trail that looked like nothing more than a fire break. If Oliver hadn't pointed it out she would have driven straight past it. They'd driven north for hours to Sterling Forest National Park in upstate New York.

The national park itself was beautiful. There were deer leaping through the forest undergrowth, and the leaves that littered the ground sent a beautiful woodsy scent wafting through her open window. They were so deep in the forest now that the branches of the tall trees parted only enough to let through dappled light. Rabbits hopped along the forest floor and it all looked very idyllic.

Azar looked over at Oliver, and wondered if he had the urge to get out and chase down all those bunnies. He seemed pretty relaxed, but she would hit the locks in a heartbeat if he even looked at those rabbits longingly.

They were thirty feet down the dirt track when,

out of nowhere, a man jumped in front of her car. Azar slammed on her brakes, stopping short by inches. The guy was huge, bigger than Jerry and the Onyx werewolves by about a foot, both vertically and horizontally. If she'd hit him, she was pretty sure it would have totaled the Shelby and he would have walked away with barely a scratch. Her heart was pounding and the adrenaline had manifested itself as anger. She breathed deep, calming breaths. Oliver shot her a worried look and then wound down the window as the giant man walked around to the passenger side.

"That was close Tao. If she didn't have preternatural speed you would have been a goner. As it is, if she doesn't calm the hell down, you may still be a goner." He shot Azar another worried look. "Then I'll have to explain to your wife why you ended up toasted by an Ifrit because you pulled a stupid stunt like jumping out in front of a car." He sounded totally calm.

The huge werewolf, Tao, just shrugged. "I knew she'd stop. We've been expecting you. Sweet ride," he said appreciatively. The man's voice was gruff and deep; like gravel rolling around the bottom of a forty-four gallon drum. "They are meeting in the common room, you know the way. But stay to the tracks; we've increased security and any outsiders straying from the path will be met with quick punishment." He pinned Azar with a hard glare and she held his eyes for longer than necessary, before lowering hers with a nod. She knew this was bad etiquette in the Were world, challenging a male on his own ground, but they needed to know that she wouldn't be intimidated by a few muscles. Azar rolled the Shelby forward down the bumpy track. This would be hell on her suspension.

Ten more rough miles down the road and they came across a gathering of small hunting cabins, backed onto the face of a fifty foot cliff. Fifteen or so people milled about, their ages between five and seventy. Everyone stopped and looked when the car pulled up, staying poised and alert, until Oliver got out of the passenger seat. Then most people just waved and went on with whatever they were doing before, except one old woman, who hobbled over to Oliver and wrapped him in a hug.

"It is good to see you Cable."

Azar raised both eyebrows and mouthed "Cable?" at Oliver as he hugged the old lady back.

"Oliver is my surname," he mumbled, "and this beauty is Dotty. She is the matriarch of the Sterling Pack and the love of my life." The old woman thumped him in the shoulder and knocked Oliver back with an oof.

"Don't try your sly cat moves on me, Cable Oliver! Better men have tried and I'm too well seasoned to fall for sweet words and a pretty face." She shook a gnarled old finger at his face, but she was wearing a big smile and had a sparkle in her eye that said they'd done this routine many times before.

"You are the second woman to tell me I'm pretty today. If this keeps up, I might get a big head." He grinned at them both and Dotty took another swipe at him but this time he managed to jump away. Dotty turned to Azar, shaking her head at the mischievous little boy that seemed to be alive and well inside of Cable Oliver.

"You must be the Ifrit Azar that Jerry has been telling us about. Please be welcome. We are meeting in the Common Room, which I'm sure that ruffian Tao told you about."

Dotty ushered them both to what looked like a crack in the cliff face from a distance but as they got closer, she could see the edges had been worn smooth from years of shoulders brushing past. They walked through a maze of connected tunnels that gently sloped downwards. Dotty gave Azar the tour as if she were a real estate agent.

"Down the tunnel on your left, we have the communal kitchen and dining areas. Most of the families eat together but the dens do have their own private kitchenettes if a member doesn't feel like eating with the rest of the pack. Everyone likes to just sit alone sometimes, especially the teenagers. They'd lie around all day watching those god awful Werewolf TV shows in their pajamas if their parents let them. Okay, down to the tunnel on your right are the Dens. Non pack members are never allowed near the Dens; a safety precaution, you know."

Azar nodded. The safety of the pack came before good manners.

They walked on and the tunnels wound further down below ground. Just in front of them a little girl ran out of an adjoining tunnel, her face wet with tears. She turned and saw Dotty and the tears doubled in size as they rolled down her little cheeks. She ran over to ageing matriarch and threw herself into her arms. She had something clutched protectively close to her body.

"Kayla, my little pup, what's wrong?" Dotty asked in soothing tones usually reserved for children and men with the flu.

"Caleb broke my truck. He said that girls aren't

allowed to have trucks. He said that it was a stupid truck and he threw it on the floor and broke it."

She sobbed louder as she showed them all the broken truck. It was an old tin toy and it looked like one of the axels had snapped clean in half when it had hit the stone floor. The wheel hung down at an odd angle and it made the truck look as sad as the little girl. The girl was crying so hard that her little body was shaking with every sob and Azar felt sorry for her.

Oliver squatted down in front of her. "Don't you listen to Caleb. Girls are allowed to have trucks. Girls are allowed to have anything they want and when Caleb gets older, I bet he'd give you his whole truck collection just so a pretty girl like you will talk to him."

Little Kayla's tears subsided into violent hiccups and sniffing. "Really, Mr. Oliver? His whole collection?" she asked as her eyes lit up with hope. Oliver smiled and nodded.

Azar squatted down next to him and put out her hand to the little girl. "My name is Azar. Maybe I can fix your truck, if that is okay with you?" She glanced at Dotty for approval.

Dotty gave a quick nod, but Kayla eyed her suspiciously.It would have been drummed into her from her earliest memory not to trust strangers. But eventually she looked at Dotty and Oliver, who would protect her, and at her broken truck that she obviously really wanted fixed, and handed it over.

"I was a blacksmith for a few years, so I should be able to fix this. I'm just going to use a bit of my power?" I directed the last part toward Dotty, who nodded once again.

Azar focused her heat on the tip of her index finger and tipped the truck over to see its broken axel. The steel had snapped off near the front left wheel, and it was easy enough to use her finger to weld it back together again. She also heated the whole axel rod to make it stronger, so the next time mean little boys threw it, it could withstand the impact better.

"Oliver, if you could just grab that bottle of water out of my bag?" Oliver rummaged through her handbag and passed over the bottle.

Azar tipped it over the axle and it hissed as steam rose from the hot metal until it cooled. She spun the wheels and was happy to see them turn smoothly.

She handed it back to Kayla. "Try not to play with it for another hour to let the metal cool completely, but after that it will be stronger than ever. A wild elephant could stomp on it and that axle won't break. But I'd keep it away from elephants anyway, if I was you." She winked at Kayla as the little girl tipped the truck upside down and looked at the fixed axle and then back at Azar, like she'd just seen a magic show.

"What do you say Kayla?" Dotty prompted.

"Thank you for fixing my truck," the girl said genuinely. She looked like she'd found a brand new hero.

"You're very welcome, Kayla. Mr. Oliver is right about those boys though, so don't you worry about what they say." Kayla smiled brightly before Dotty shooed her back toward the Dens.

"Caleb and Kayla are a future mated pair if I've ever seen one. Just can't keep them apart now, even though they are always fighting. Mark my words, in fifteen or twenty years, we'll be attending their wedding," Dotty chuckled, hobbling back down the tunnel. Azar hoped Dotty was still alive in fifteen or twenty years.

Eventually, the tunnel opened out onto a big rounded cavern with large rugs covering the stone floor. Light sconces were fixed to the walls and cast a warm light over the people sitting around a beautifully carved long table. Dotty motioned for them to sit at the two empty seats in the middle.

The group around the table was eclectic to say the least. They varied in age and gender, size and ethnicity. But Azar knew the Alpha straight away. It was like all the electricity in the room radiated from him. He was a middle aged man, maybe in his mid-forties, and he wasn't big like Tao from the trail. He was tall and handsome in a lean, rough way. He had a large scar above his brow and big brown eyes that shined with a shrewd intelligence. This time Azar lowered her eyes and bowed her head immediately. Oliver seemed relieved. The Alpha stood to shake her hand.

"It's a pleasure to meet you Azar of the Ifrit. My name is Anton, the Alpha of this pack. Jerry speaks highly of you."

She winced. She hoped Jerry hadn't told him that she had threatened to make him extra crispy. Anton's eyes gave a brief flash of humor, although the rest of his face remained neutral. Obviously Jerry had indeed related that story.

"That's very kind of Jerry. He caught me on a bad night," Azar apologized sheepishly.

Anton just nodded and motioned her to sit. Oliver sat next to her, Jerry was directly across the table. Anton sat at the end in a especially ornate chair and Dotty sat at the end opposite end in a similar chair. Obviously the Matriarch was a respected position and was probably the Alpha female of Anton's predecessor.

"Let's get down to business. When Jerry brought us the news that the Rogue Djinn was using wolf scent to cover his attack on Onyx, we were very perturbed. We did a quick check of the pack, and have found that one of our young males has not been to any of his college classes in several days." He handed Azar a picture of a handsome boy, in his late teens or early twenties. The kid looked harmless; he was wearing a great big smile that ended with two little dimples in his cheeks. There was nothing remarkable about him, he just looked like the average teenage boy.

"Many of our juveniles live out of the pack, for schooling and to taste a bit of the freedom they've longed for during their youth. Inevitably, they find that living out of the pack is uncomfortable for wolves. Not so much for the cats, of course." He smiled at Oliver. "We questioned his friends and his roommate at his dorm, and no one has seen him or heard from him in almost five days. They said he didn't seem anxious or worried, nor was he seeing anyone. It was as if he just vanished into thin air. They said that some of the other kids in the dorm went on a trip to Las Vegas, and they assumed he went also. We don't believe that Aaron would do so without informing someone in the Pack first and definitely not so close to the full moon."

A woman sobbed down the end of the table, and one look at her distraught face told Azar that this was the boy's mother. The Alpha sent the woman a consoling look as the man beside the woman held her close and rubbed her back, probably Aaron's father. The Alpha continued.

"We don't believe that Aaron is the type of person who would voluntarily plot to hurt people, so we are going to operate under the assumption that he is being held against his will. However, if this assumption should prove false, he will be delivered swift justice in the way of the wolves." Anton looked at Aaron's father, and the man nodded his head in acquiescence.

Azar didn't know what kind of justice was meted out by the wolves, but she had a feeling that it was final in nature.

"We intend to offer you and your compatriots' assistance in tracking down your Rogue and recovering Aaron, one way or another," Anton continued and she nodded her agreement. They could use the wolves' assistance. They were more plentiful in numbers, and could help with the groundwork.

"I can't speak on behalf of my companions, or on behalf of the Djinn Council, but I would welcome any help the Pack could offer. What I do know is that he will make his move in two days' time to coincide with an Ifrit holiday. I'm not sure if Jerry told you much about what he hopes to achieve?"

Jerry nodded, along with the rest of the table, but Anton motioned for her to explain.

"I'm not sure exactly what you know about Djinn history, but Balraka was the first Ifrit. He was so deadly and evil in nature that the other Djinn decided to imprison him in manacles of ice in the very bowels of hell. A particularly crazy Ifrit later discovered he could release Balraka for a short time by completing a ritual called a Fire Pledge. Then Balraka would rise up from the earth and reduce anything he could reach to ash. In a population as dense as New York City, that could mean millions of deaths. We believe that he will try and use my death as the final step of the ritual. I have the human police and also some other Djinn looking for the Rogue, but so far we've come up with nothing."

A man down the end of the table leaned forward to address Azar. "What of the Djinn Council? Why aren't they searching for this Rogue also?" Azar cleared her throat uncomfortably; there was no way to answer this question without sounding completely selfish.

"Members of the Djinn have been informed of the threat and have promised to report it to their Council Sitter. However, due to certain circumstances personally, I can't go to the Council for assistance unless it's absolutely necessary. To approach the Council would result in my head being cut off, so trust me when I say that while it's a possibility, it is definitely a last resort." There was an awkward silence around the table as people weighed up her predicament; one life to potentially save millions. Unfortunately, it was an easy decision when it was someone else's sacrifice. Empathy was fast becoming a dead emotion in a world where social media made it easy to point fingers at other people's failings, while hiding behind a thin veneer of anonymity.

Anton nodded, a small crease between his brows. "We respect that this is your decision to make. None here will inform the Council. However, as a precaution, we may call back any Pack members currently residing in New York City. I shall give you five pack enforcers, and also any others who may wish to help with your search and disablement of this Rogue. I would give you more but I cannot compromise the packs protection, especially in such uncertain times."

Azar nodded her agreeance. She would never expect the wolves to help the Djinn at the expense of the pack. Even the idea was a complete contradiction to their way of life. Jerry indicated that he, Oliver and the other four Were employed by Donovan wished to assist the group and Anton gave his consent.

"We thank you for any help you can offer. If I can find him, I promise I will do everything in my power to bring Aaron back safely." She looked down at the distraught mother and her heart broke for her.

Anton sighed. "That is all we can ask of anyone."

They went through some specifics with the rest of the table's members, discussing which enforcers should go and which were needed within the pack. They also discussed the most efficient way to get every pack member out of New York in two days, and it was agreed that the enforcers sent with Azar would track down any members not reachable by phone, when they were not needed by her.

Azar was struck about how nurturing the pack environment was. Anton cared about every single one of his pack members, and she could see the worry in his eyes over Aaron's disappearance. It was nice to be in a room full of people from whom she didn't have to hide any secrets. The wolves didn't care that she hadn't served her slavery, nor did they care that she had told Keenan such a big secret. They didn't even seem overly bothered that she was an Ifrit, a being so powerful that she could kill maybe a hundred of this pack before they could bring her down. They welcomed and accepted her with a trust that was given freely; but she had no doubt that even the slightest betrayal of that trust would have very deadly results.

"Okay, that's all we can do today. Let's go and grab something to eat and be within the Pack at this hard time." Anton stood first, and then Dotty and then the rest of the table rose to their feet. Anton motioned for Azar and Oliver to join him. "Would you like to stay for dinner?" When Azar shook her head regretfully, he just smiled. "That's okay. I'll walk you to your car."

Anton took them back out through the maze of tunnels and she was glad for the guide. It was a complicated route to say the least. When they finally reached the open air, Azar took a deep breath in. It wasn't that underground home was particularly claustrophobic, but being out in the sun and the air was just more comfortable for an Ifrit.

She saw a small knot of children outside, all crowded around Kayla as she showed off her truck. One little boy stood off in the periphery, kicking the dirt and Azar guessed it was the infamous Caleb. Kayla said something to the group and waved, and then fifteen tiny pairs of eyes turned to stare at her. Azar waved back heartily. Anton gave her a questioning look.

"I fixed her truck and Oliver restored her faith in boys." Anton shook his head, his lips curled in a bemused smile.

They all said their goodbyes, and as they drove away, Azar felt a little sad that she was leaving all that warmth behind.

CHAPTER 11

An hour and a half later, Azar and Oliver were back at her apartment. The enforcers had followed her home and then dispersed out to find pack members who lived in the city but couldn't be reached by phone. They gave her five different cell numbers to reach them on if she needed them and left.

Azar sat on the couch with Oliver. "Does this mean I should call you Cable from now on?"

He screwed his nose up. "Yeah, but only if you want me to spank you silly."

Azar laughed and waggled her eyebrows suggestively. He was joking again. But joke or not, the idea of him spanking her sent little waves of happy down to nether-nether land. She needed to think about

Keenan. Or Bast. She had enough on her plate. She didn't need to add a sexy ass werejaguar to the list. Right?

Maybe she was just hungry. That was the sensation that was making her stomach flip-flop. Not sexual attraction. She was just hungry-horny. Horngry. The sun was beginning to set and she was starved. She ordered Chinese takeout for the both of them, and they settled down to watch the baseball.

At the bottom of the third, there was a knock at the door and when Azar opened it, Bast, Keenan and the Chinese takeout kid all stood in her entrance way.

"So, who do I tip?" Azar grinned as she took the food from a very uncomfortable looking delivery boy and gave him a ten dollar tip.

Bast slipped another twenty in the kids pocket too, muttering something about 'emotional pain and suffering.' Azar thought that meant that perhaps the poor kid almost choked on the tension that was flying around the hallway between the other two.

Azar moved to the side to let the guys in. Keenan kissed her forehead tenderly and Bast kissed both her cheeks, just a little too close to her lips. Azar shook her head. Lucky she got a lot of Chinese food.

She headed to the kitchen to get some plates and forks.

When she finally got into the living room, Oliver was standing up, his jeans unzipped and pulled down to show off the red hand mark on his ass to Keenan and Bast.

"Now I know why you two are having such a fight over her. She's just wild when she gets her hands on you. When she really gets going, she just gets so smoking hot!" His grin was smug and his eyes glittered with mirth. She should have guessed this was how he would get his revenge. Keenan's eyes said he'd like to get his police issued gun out and shoot both Oliver and Bast, and Bast's eyes were just the same mysterious golden orbs she couldn't read.

"Put it away before I give you a matching one on the other side," Azar said as she put out paper plates and cups. She was never a fan of washing up after a party, so she kept some supplies just in case. She went back into the kitchen and got the Chinese food. She sat cross-legged on the floor while Bast sat next to Oliver and Keenan sat on the single armchair. The four of them ate and watched baseball in silence until everyone was stuffed.

"Okay, so what have we got?" Azar finally asked,

resisting the urge to pop the button on her jeans. Oliver didn't resist the urge at all, popping the button and unzipping his jeans until a tiny patch of curls glinted above the zip.

Bast switched off the TV. "I got nothing. None of the other Djinn are unaccounted for. Closest known rogue Ifrit, other than you of course, is in California."

Keenan didn't even seem fazed by the existence of multiple fire toting mythical creatures anymore. It was amazing what humanity could handle with an open mind. He rubbed his temples gently.

"I went and visited the Brownsville apartment tenant today. The only connection I could find was the guy who owned the building; Ellis Fareet. He's a local philanthropist/slumlord who works out of Brownsville and all the other poor areas in Brooklyn. He's known for building not for profit community centers on the cheap and then burning them down to get inflated insurance claims. Insurance companies, and even the Arson Unit have tried to pin something on this guy, but nothing ever sticks. They blame gangs, activist groups or homeless people and Fareet gets his inflated insurance money every time. It's not an unusual practice for the more crooked citizens of New York. We didn't click because he usually makes more money out of his slums by keeping them up rather than burning them down, so we ruled him out when we did our preliminary investigation. But now that I know what I do about your kind," he shot Azar an unreadable look, "I think he could be a real possibility."

Azar pulled her tablet out from between the couch cushions and googled Ellis Fareet. A news article came up from a month ago about the ground breaking at the site of a future Refugee Center that Fareet had funded near the Brownsville Recreation Center. She clicked on the photo of Fareet holding a shovel shaking the hand of another man. They were both in beautifully tailored suits and looked out of place amongst the crowds of refugees who had obviously been invited along to the celebration.

There he was; the Rogue. It made her angry that he was posing like he was a savior when he intended to cause the death of everyone within reach. When he wasn't threatening her in darkened clubs, he looked kind of normal. Probably about as tall as her, thick eyebrows, dark brown hair and a round face. There was nothing unusual about the man at all, until you looked into his eyes. Then there was only darkness and hatred staring back at you. A cold shiver ran down her spine. She nodded confirmation and passed the tablet over to Keenan.

"See the Middle Eastern looking man in the background? That is Zaid Ali, the tenant from the slum building. The man with the shovel is Fareet." He passed the tablet to Bast, who shook his head.

"I've never seen this Ellis Fareet before. I've been in New York a long time, and if he is as high profile as you say, I would have recognized him as Djinn." He passed it over to Oliver, who looked at it, shrugged and passed it back to Azar.

"Maybe we should get one of the wolves to go over and have a sniff, see if they can smell Aaron," Oliver suggested.

Keenan made a call to the station and got an address for Ellis Fareet. He relayed the address to Oliver who text it to the werewolves, along with a very stern message not to engage if they should happen to come face to face with the man himself.

Azar brought Bast and Keenan up to speed about the meeting with the Sterling Pack elders and the missing boy. It was nice to finally have a name for the Rogue. Ellis Fareet; slumlord and all around bad guy. It was satisfying that they had finally made some progress.

Fifteen minutes later, Azar stood up and paced

around, waiting for the wolves to call. She wasn't exactly sure what she would do if they found Fareet at his home. Probably call Donovan and let him tear out Fareet's heart. She hadn't really thought about handing him over to the Council; it would present too many problems for her personally. They would just cut off his head anyway; better to let Donovan do it and get some sort of closure. She cringed at the thought of harming anyone, even the Rogue who wanted to kill millions of people.

The guys were attempting bond over their mutual love of Azar's car. She hated to interrupt but she needed to know if they had a plan.

"What do we do if he is there? Are there any independent Marid still in NYC?"

The Marid were the natural opposites of the Ifrit, and the only ones with the ability to defeat them in a one on one battle. They controlled water in all its forms; from being able to freeze it, to turning it to vapor and sending it back into the atmosphere. The Ifrit were also the natural opposite of the Marid. Nature had a twisted sense of humor at times. When pitted against an Ifrit, their strengths canceled each other out so that it was a test of wills. In Ifrit versus Marid fights, either the Ifrit got turned into an ice cube or the Marid got boiled alive. But every contest could go either way.

Bast shook his head. "Not since Moselle left in 1980. The Marid are few and far between these days."

That would pose all sorts of problems for the Djinn Council. If the Marid were to die out to just a few, there would be no forces to oppose the Ifrit on the Council or to end the Rogues such as Fareet. The Ifrit would be able to rise up and overrun the Djinn Council, and there would be nothing left of the world but smoky rubble. Maybe the Shaitan could possibly step into the breach, in large numbers, but they were also few and far between after years of culling them down one by one. The balance and checks that had been part of the Djinn way of life for so long were failing, and Azar hoped the Council was trying to find a way to bolster it back to the natural order. She and Bast both knew that if not for her unfortunate problem, they could have just called the Council up and they would send out The Adel to deal with him.

The Adel loosely translated to Justice in English, and they were the enforcers of punishments and deliverers of justice within the Djinn world. If a Djinn was seen to be particularly powerful, he or she could be ordered by the Council to spend his or her servitude in service of The Adel. Azar had heard a rumor that some chose to stay on after the slavery period was up, spending the rest of their preternaturally long lives hunting people down like rabid dogs. She could imagine the Shaitan and Ghul doing so, but probably not the benevolent races.

Azar could see that Bast looked troubled. Everyone hoped that one full Djinn, two half Djinns, a pack of Werewolves and one mortal would be enough to beat Fareet, but the odds weren't in their favor.

She would be useless against another Ifrit. Bast was a creature of air and was therefore vulnerable to a fire attack. Donovan would probably have a thirty percent chance of doing some kind of real damage before he was brought down himself. The wolves could probably take Fareet down if there were enough of them, by severing his head from his body, but a lot of the pack would die in the process. Keenan was just a liability.

She slumped down onto the floor and felt the walls closing in on her. It felt like an elephant was sitting on her chest. Great, not only did she faint like a silver screen damsel, but she had panic attacks like a scared little mouse. Her breathing grew choppier so she stuck her head between her knees and took deep breaths.

Two hands grabbed her upper arms and pulled her to her feet, wrapping her into a broad shouldered hug. As she breathed in the scent of Bast, her heart rate slowed and her breathing eased. He whispered soothing words into her hair and rubbed her back with his large hand. His chest felt warm and solid against her cheek, like a beacon of safety in a world that was rapidly spinning out of control. He pulled her back so he could look at her face.

"It will be okay. We will figure out a plan and use what we have to win. There is power in numbers." She nodded and tried to convince herself that he was right. She peeked around Bast's shoulder and saw both Keenan and Oliver were standing. Keenan didn't even look jealous that she was in Bast's arms; his brows were drawn together in concern. A similar look was on Oliver's face. Azar took a deep breath, pulled her shoulders back and stepped out of Bast's arms regretfully.

"I'm sorry. Mini meltdown. I'm fine now." Ironically, Oliver's phone chose that moment to ring and he quickly slid it out of his pocket and answered.

"Yeah. No, meet us at Azar's place. Yeah I'll call them now." He hung up the phone. She wished she could keep her calls that short and to the point. "They went around to Fareet's address but said the place was empty and had been for a couple of days. They could smell traces of Aaron there, but there was no blood. I told them to come over so we can decide what to do next."

She breathed a sigh of relief. There was still hope that they would find the boy alive. They just had to keep him, and New York, that way.

Oliver opened his phone again, and talked briefly to someone; Azar guessed either Jerry or Donovan. It looked as if her apartment was going to be packed to the brim yet again. God only knew what Mr. Grimond next door thought of all the men traipsing through her door at any hour of the day or night. He probably thought she was a woman of ill repute running a one woman bordello out of the building.

Within twenty minutes, her little one room apartment was filled with eleven Weres, two other Djinn and Keenan Reilly. A person sat on every available stable surface she had and some not so stable surfaces. Her coffee table was bent ominously under Tao, the Were from the Sterling Pack. Someone had bought a couple of cases of beer, twelve bags of chips and some nuts. Her house looked like a frat party filled with steroid pumping gym junkies, although she doubted any of them had ever set foot inside a gym in their life. Except maybe Keenan, who chatted to one of the Weres about the Mets chances of winning a World Series anytime this century.

Someone had put on a Guns 'n' Roses album and turned the volume up loud. Apart from Bast and Donovan, who were huddled up in the corner of the room to have a serious conversation, everyone else chatted and drank like old friends. Azar leaned on her kitchen bench and took in the hubbub of her apartment. Oliver drifted over to her side and wrapped a companionable arm around her shoulder.

"They're preparing for the worst," Oliver explained. "They have a party like this before any big battle, to talk about the good times and the people they love, so they remember why they are doing it."

Azar agreed with the concept. If the worst thing happened, you wouldn't want your last days to be filled with worry and stress. There was time to plan and plot later. It wasn't as if Fareet was just going to waltz into her apartment when it was filled to the brim with supernaturals or turn up in Times Square naked proclaiming he was a Fire Genie.

"I can understand that." They stood together in silence for a moment, but Azar had already had her moment of melancholy. What she wanted was a bit of carefree, harmless fun. The look on her face made Oliver raise his eyebrows. He wasn't one to walk away from an opportunity to be mischievous.

"Okay, I'll give you five bucks if you can bounce a quarter off the bench and into Tao's cup without him noticing," she whispered conspiratorially.

There was probably about ten feet between the bench and Tao's cup, which was sitting behind him on the coffee table. Oliver grinned and nodded as he fished a couple of quarters out of his pocket. He lined the first one up and it fell short of the coffee table. Azar raised her eyebrows.

"I've been duped. I was led to believe that you Werejaguar's had above average precision." She gave him a look of mock disapproval.

Oliver just waved her away and lined up his next shot. "Babe, I am above average in everything. Now watch."

He bounced the quarter off the bench with more force, and it went high into the air, sailing down to plop into Tao's cup. Scotch and coke splashed up onto the huge Were's back until Oliver and Azar quickly faced the other way, pretending to be really interested in her oven. Out of the corner of her eye she saw Tao glare around the room and Azar tried not to laugh. She turned and gave him an innocent smile. He glared back at her. She didn't think he bought her innocent act for a second.

Tao fished the quarter out of his cup and wiped it on his pants. Faster than her eyes could follow, he bounced the quarter off the coffee table. The projectile made a perfect arch in the air and landed in the small strip of cleavage that showed above Azar's tank top. Her mouth dropped open and Oliver applauded, and so did everyone else who was watching. Tao bowed and sat back down on her groaning coffee table, resuming his conversation with Jerry.

That one incident seemed to set the mood for the rest of the night. After two more bottles of her scotch and a case of beer, one of the Were's started a rousing game of quarters. The game became so heated that Mr. Grimond came over to see if Azar was being murdered by a serial killer. The Weres laughed it off, took the old man's baseball bat and gave him a beer. Someone ordered pizza, and a heavily loaded pizza boy knocked on the door about one a.m. The Werewolves invited him to stay as well.

Eventually even Bast and Donovan got into the spirit of the gathering, although Donovan led a not so great game of Five Finger Fillet, stabbing one of her steak knives between his fingers and into her chopping board at a speed almost too fast for her eyes to follow. This led to all the werewolves wanting a turn and eventually, to one of the younger wolves nicking his little finger and bleeding on her carpet. By that stage she was too drunk to care about a little bit of blood on her carpet and she just let go and partied like there might not be a tomorrow.

For her, it might be the truth.

CHAPTER 12

Azar felt like she was being strangled. Her eyes felt like they were glued shut and her mouth was like the Sahara desert. She forced one eye open but the light searing her eyeball was so excruciating she quickly closed it again. She'd had it open for long enough to see she was lying across from Keenan, who was on his back snoring. She tugged at her singlet top, which had twisted around her body until one of the straps had almost stretched right across her chest. She seemed to still have her jeans on, and the button was jabbing painfully into her abdomen. She was lying on her side, her body encased in warmth even though she was on top of the blankets. Something warm was pressed against her back. Wait. What?

Azar bolted upright in bed and almost laid straight back down as she was struck with a nasty case of the whirlies. Trying again, she struggled to stay upright until it passed and then looked over. There was a huge jaguar lying on her bed, purring as it slept. She was wedged between a sleeping Keenan and a morphed Oliver. She was so glad she was still wearing pants, otherwise she didn't know if she could look herself in the mirror when she finally dragged herself to the bathroom.

Telling herself that it was Oliver, not a wild jaguar and he wasn't going to bite her hand off, she nudged Oliver's fur covered rump. His spotted fur was so soft, it was unbelievable. She twisted her fingers in his pelt and ran it down his back, making the jaguar purr louder. She pulled her hand away, realizing it wasn't a giant pet cat but rather a man.

"Move it," she croaked, her face flaming red.

The cat slunk off the bed and stretched, and as it stretched its body elongated and shifted into something more recognizable to her as Oliver. Naked, yet again.

"If only I could get you to stroke me like that in this form," he purred at her.

Azar stared daggers at him, no matter how much she'd very much like to follow through with his suggestion right about now. Instead of following through with her poor impulse control, she pushed past him into the bathroom. She splashed water onto her face and brushed her teeth until they squeaked and her breath no longer tasted like the dregs at the bottom of a whisky barrel. She quickly ran a comb through her hair and went in search of coffee.

As she staggered past her bedroom, she threw a quick look at the clock. It was one in the afternoon. She needed coffee, really bad. Her lounge room looked like a boarding kennel/frat house. Beer bottles and pizza boxes littered every surface, and there were sleeping wolves and passed out guys everywhere. There were even two guys asleep under her tiny dining table. She could smell the coffee brewing, and followed the aroma into the kitchen. Bast was standing there, holding a coffee cup towards her like a heaven sent deity.

"I think I love you," she said as she took the coffee from Bast.

"But we barely know each other," Bast replied jokingly.

"I was talking to this hot, dark deliciousness," Azar grumbled as she slowly sipped the liquid gold.

"But we hardly know each other," Donovan quipped. His eyes didn't look so dead today. They looked hot, like how she imagined Satan's to look before he tempted you right into sinning. And you'd love every minute of it. Obviously, she'd killed more than a few brain cells last night. Probably the ones governing her common sense. She ignored them both and focused on inhaling her coffee. Once she was in a caffeinated state of mind, she noticed Oliver was in the kitchen too. "Did the wolves eat the pizza boy?" She was only half joking.

"Bast and I took both him and Harry home." She guessed that Mr. Grimond's first name was Harry. She didn't actually know. He'd introduced himself as Mr. Grimond and she just ran with it. She liked to pretend he was like Madonna or Mr. Ed and only had the one name. She nodded very, very slowly. She had a fifteen hour shift tonight that she wasn't looking forward to. She needed to get everything squared away before that happened.

"Okay, so what do we do?"

Donovan, who looked positively gleeful. "We kill him," he said pleasantly as if he'd just suggested that take Fareet out to a fancy restaurant rather than murder him in cold blood. Azar was glad that Keenan was still asleep, so he had plausible deniability about the murder of a high profile businessman.

There was a murmur of agreement in the kitchen.

"I was hoping for something a little more constructive. Maybe something like a plan on how we are going to find him to kill him?" She was trying to be patient, but a hangover usually made her grumpy, and this hangover was the Godzilla of hangovers. Her head actually felt like Godzilla was stomping on it, repeatedly.

"I was thinking we could run down some addresses and see if the werewolves can't pick up his scent and track him." Keenan's voice came from behind her. "I'm just assuming that they're were-wolves. I was drunk but I'm pretty sure I'd remember someone bringing a pack of wolves to the party." Keenan poured himself a cup of coffee and sighed when he took his first sip.

His hair stuck up haphazardly, big dark circles puffed up under his bloodshot eyes and his permanent squint implied he had a raging headache.

Keenan glared at them all. "How do you people look so good this morning? I swear Oliver was drinking two to my every one and you two went through a bottle of tequila each." He nodded towards Bast and Donovan.

Azar's scotch collection had taken a serious hit

last night. She refused to even look in her liquor cabinet. But hey, if New York was going to go up in flames, she was going liquored up enough to go out in a blaze of glory. Literally.

"Fast metabolism," Oliver answered.

"Djinn can't get drunk." Donovan even looked a little sympathetic as he said it.

Keenan's eyes narrowed. "Azar is Djinn and she was definitely drunk. She was up on the kitchen counter singing 'I Love Rock'n'Roll' by Joan Jett at one point. That's pretty classic drunken behavior." Azar felt herself blush bright red; she didn't remember doing that. She didn't want to know what else she did.

Oliver was laughing too now. "That's because she's half human. After you passed out she reenacted the kiss scene from 'The Notebook' with Bast. Complete with dialogue. It was totally hot."

Holy crap, she didn't remember that either. Her eyes shot to Bast, and he shrugged one shoulder, with that smug grin plastered on his face again. Oliver continued to laugh, so she elbowed him in the ribs hard and he let out a satisfying grunt.

"I don't remember," she said as she stared at her feet, blushing right down to her toes.

She was horrified. Keenan was right there and

she could feel his eyes burning into her skull. However, no matter how horrified she was, she was also secretly disappointed. If there was one kiss she'd want to remember forever, it would be a kiss like that with Bast. She continued to stare at her feet, just in case one of the guys could read the look of disappointment on her face. Once her face had stopped flaming, she looked up but she still avoided looking Keenan and Bast in the eye. She focused solely on Donovan and Oliver.

"We've gotten off topic. Do you think the Weres will agree to Keenan's plan?" She directed at Oliver, who still had that look of mischievous glee on his face. He nodded. "Good. Maybe Keenan can take Tao to work with him and they can figure it out from there. Does anyone have a plan for what we can do once we've found Fareet? Don't say kill him Donovan, it's really not that simple." Both Bast and Keenan spoke at once.

"We sever his head from his body."

"We take him into custody."

Azar shook her head. This is where the plan got sketchy, to say the least. "Keenan, you can't put Djinn in jail. We don't stay there for very long. Bast, if we can get close enough that might be a possibility, but he is going to be on high alert and sneaking up on him is going to be almost impossible."

"Misdirection," Donovan said quietly. Somehow, Azar knew she wasn't going to like where he was going with this. "We make sure his attention is focused on something else, and then we can get close enough to him to take him out." He turned to her, his onyx eyes somber. Even the laughing skull tattoos on the sides of his neck looked deadly serious today. "Azar presents herself to him as an opportunity he can't pass up. While he's focused on her, Bast and I get into position behind him and send him down to hell to meet Balraka personally."

She hated to admit it, but the plan made sense. Of course, she knew that there was always going to be considerable risk taking down the Rogue, but deep down she was still hoping he would accidentally get trapped in a deep freezer somewhere, or the Council would cotton on to the problem of their own accord and deal with it. They had told Lila days earlier of the threat, but Azar wouldn't put it past her to let the Rogue have its way so the Ghul could have a smorgasbord of corpses when Balraka was finished. They were a self-centered bunch like that. Not to mention Lila was a gigantic bitch.

She snuck a quick peek at Keenan. His face

looked like a storm cloud and she wasn't sure if he was still furious from the Bast kissing thing or Donovan's suggestion that she be bait, yet again.

"The Weres could back her up?" Oliver suggested but Azar shook her head immediately.

"The risk is too great. I'd rather not have your deaths on my conscience because I was too chicken to go on my own. You should back up Bast and Donovan. If things go badly, we are going to need everything we have to make sure the Fire Pledge isn't completed." There was another round of nodding. "Okay, it's settled. You guys track him down today, and tomorrow I'll confront him and we'll take this asshole out once and for all." Everyone agreed except Keenan, who still looked like he wanted to murder every person in the room, his face a mixture of anger, frustration and concern.

Azar leaned over and grabbed his hand, looking directly into his eyes. "It's the only way. I'll be fine, I promise. I'm not actually that easy to kill."

Keenan nodded imperceptibly, but she could see the torment in his eyes as he did so. She knew this next part was going to make it even worse. "And I don't want you anywhere near Fareet when this goes down. You can't help and it would make you an accessory to first degree murder. I can't let that happen. If everything goes bad, you need to do what you can to get as many people to safety as possible, as quickly as possible."

Keenan looked as if he was going to crack in two from the warring emotions that played like a slow motion reel across his face. Keenan had a hero complex, she knew that for certain, and right now, he didn't know who he should save. Her, or the entire city of New York.

Finally, he nodded again. He tipped the rest of his coffee down the sink and walked out.

No matter how badly she wanted to go after him, she stilled her feet. He needed time to process and come to terms with his role in the whole scenario, but she just wished that his exit didn't have such an air of finality about it.

Azar walked out of the kitchen and started nudging wolves awake, the human ones at least. She'd let the others wake up the sleeping wolves; she liked all her appendages where they belonged. She got out a trash bag and started cleaning up pizza boxes and beer bottles. Slowly, the other Were-wolves' woke and stretched. Then they morphed back. Naked.

"Uh, I might go shower. Help yourself to break-fast," she mumbled as she ducked into her bedroom. She was pretty sure the walls of her apartment had never seen so many different penises.

Once she was certain they'd all be up and at least partially dressed, she went back out. Her house gleamed as if there hadn't been a wild party the night before.

"Geez, you guys clean fast. Want to come and do it once a week for me?" They'd gotten rid of all the trash and wiped down every surface until it shone. Furniture had been put back to the way it was, and the dishes were all done. Someone was humming the tune to 'I Love Rock'n'Roll' and the whole lot of them were smirking.

"I'm going shopping," she scowled as she pulled on her boots and slammed out the door, Oliver close behind her.

"Where are we going?" he asked, as he shuffled into his own boots mid stride.

"Victoria's Secret. If I'm going to die tomorrow, I'm going to do it in nice lingerie."

To say that Oliver was enjoying their shopping expedition would be an understatement. Azar had spent forty minutes trying on different bras and Oliver had spent the whole time picking out lingerie for her.

The saleswoman had forgotten that she even existed after about two minutes in Oliver's presence, and she could hardly blame the woman. Oliver was smoking hot, like a tanned surfer but with a Texan drawl. It was a strangely alluring combination. Azar had decided on a red lace bra and Brazilian cut briefs. The red looked sensational against her skin. She had her eye on an emerald green one too, but hadn't picked it up. She stuck her head out of the change room.

"Excuse me?" Azar tried to get the attention of the saleswoman but she was too busy flirting with Oliver. Azar tried again. And a third time. Finally she huffed and walked out of the change room wearing nothing but the red lace bra and her own black boy cut underwear. Oliver's mouth fell open as he looked over the shoulder of the salesgirl.

Azar knew she looked good. She was six feet and she had to be fit and strong to be a firefighter. As a result there was only a little padding on her rounded hips, her toned legs went on forever and thanks to the marvels of Victoria Secret, her boobs were so perky they defied gravity. The salesgirl turned around to see what Oliver was gaping at and she gaped too, before snapping her mouth shut and sashaying over to her.

"Is there something I can help you with?" The woman's voice was snippy, obviously upset that her eye sex with Oliver had been interrupted.

"Yes, can I please have the emerald demi over there? Thanks." Oliver sauntered over as the salesgirl strode off. He let out a low whistle.

"Azar babe, you look smoking in that. Screw misdirection, just take your top off tomorrow and you'll make the bad guy spontaneously combust." Azar laughed. That probably wasn't a bad idea, except the rest of her team was a pack of horny werewolves and Bast. She'd misdirect them all into an early grave.

"Very funny, asshole."

But he didn't look like he was joking as he prowled toward her, his eyes hot and predatory. She stepped back into the change room and swallowed down the lump in her throat. Her ass hit the wall and Oliver leaned in close, his eyes eating her up, or maybe watching her for any sign that she didn't want what was about to happen. But she wanted it. Her traitorous body wanted to burn them both up.

The salesgirl came back with the emerald bra, clearing her throat loudly. "Saved by the human," he purred, turning to leave. Both she and the sales-woman watched him go.

Azar quickly tried it on. It looked great, but she knew it would. She threw her own clothes back on and took her selections to the counter.

She maxed out what was left on her credit card, bought four pretzel dogs, three for Oliver and one for her, and then they went home.

The house was blissfully empty when they walked in. The place was so clean that there wasn't even a stray dog hair stuck to the rug. The blood-stain was miraculously gone from her carpet as well. She imagined that the Werewolves would have quite a bit of experience with bloodstain removal.

She only had an hour until work, so she left Oliver sitting on the couch and went and stood under the shower spray for twenty minutes, soaking the warmth right into her bones. She didn't get out until her fingers had started to prune and the water was getting cold. When she was ready, she found Oliver eating cereal on her couch and watching some japanese game show where the objective seemed to be getting hit in the nuts.

When he saw her, he tipped up the bowl, drank the contents down in one mouthful and was on his feet. He beat her to the door and stood to the side, allowing her to pass.

"Ladies first."

"Funny how gentlemanly you are now you've seen me in my underwear, Cable. I'm still mad at you for letting out the whole Bast kiss thing. I don't even remember it and I'm still in deep shit over it. Just doesn't seem fair," Azar huffed as she strode over to the stairwell. She looked over her shoulder and grinned. "First one to the car gets to drive," she yelled and took off down the stairs two at a time, Oliver pounding down after her.

Twenty minutes later, Azar got out of the passenger seat of the Shelby with a pout. She should have known better than to challenge a jungle cat. He'd jumped from one landing to the next without even flinching and beaten her to the car easily. Cheater!

Azar had gotten so used to Oliver following her around that she didn't even realize it would seem odd to the guys at work. Well, until they all stopped what they were doing and stared at her and Oliver as they walked into the room. They hadn't even come up with a plausible excuse why Oliver was with her. She wasn't sure she could pass him off as her cousin looking like the All-American poster boy.

Of course, Joe was the first to come and investigate. "Hey Az, who's your friend?" He stuck out a hand towards Oliver, who shook it. "Nice to meet you; I'm Joe Maconi."

"Cable Oliver, I'm from Playboy. Miss Nazemi is kindly allowing me to follow her around during her day to day activities for our 'Women in Uniform' article, coming out next month." Azar turned beet red as the boys all laughed and wolf whistled. Boy, she was going to murder Oliver for this later.

"Wow, ain't that something," Joe said, his face almost cracking with a grin. "Who else is going to be in the article?" Joe led Oliver over to the table and chairs that sat outside near the trucks, and a dozen guys came over to hear his response.

"Well I've done an article on a police officer, a flight attendant and a NFL cheerleader so far. We were thinking..." Azar missed the rest as she walked towards the lockers. Joe caught up with her as she entered the locker rooms.

"You okay Azar? I mean first Keenan Reilly, then the Blue Smoke club and now posing for Playboy. Are you spiraling? Do I need to get Linda to organize an intervention?" He said it jokingly but Azar knew beneath the humor he probably was actually worried.

"I'm fine Joe. My love life is a mess and I've got a lot on my mind, but I'm getting there. I promise you by Monday, I'll be back to my old self."

Or dead. Hell, they all could be. Azar shook off her melancholy and set out to doing the mundane tasks that kept her mind occupied and her hands busy.

Fifteen minutes after she started, Oliver came to stand next to her as she tested the oxygen tanks, rerolled hose lines and did paperwork. Sensing her mood, he even refrained from making hose jokes. She appreciated his restraint.

She'd been working on menial stuff for about three hours when a call went out over the PA system.

"Truck sixty one, truck eighty five, ambulance thirty one; warehouse fire 52nd street and 2nd avenue." She strode towards the truck, and told Oliver to follow her in the Shelby. She lost herself in the routine of a call out. After almost a hundred years of firefighting, these procedures had become second nature to her; she was pretty sure that she'd be able to do them in her sleep. Although the tools and technology had gotten far more sophisticated in recent years, the procedures were still similar. Fire always behaved the same way, and since the beginning of time it hadn't evolved or digressed. It was predictable in its unpredictability.

With the efficiency of a well-oiled machine, everyone was in the truck and on the way to 52nd street within minutes. Azar took a deep calming breath and waited for the ribbing to begin. She didn't have to wait long. It was McAdams who went first.

"So, in this Playboy article, will there be a photo shoot?" He said it seriously but Azar could see that he was holding back a laugh, along with the rest of the guys.

"I don't know McAdams. Maybe there will be, Playboy isn't really known for its articles. Of course you'd know that. The last time we had a party at your place, there were copies of Playboy everywhere that had all the pages stuck together." Everyone laughed, including McAdams.

"I'm getting my local newsstand to order me in ten copies of that." And so it went.

Azar was glad that the Captain was in the first response vehicle and not the truck, otherwise they'd all be forced to sit through one of those sexual harassment seminars. Again. By the time they got to the corner of 52nd and 2nd, the only person who wasn't buying enough copies of Playboy to wallpaper a room was Joe. He said he was just going to buy one to show Linda, of course.

She just sat back and took the good natured joking. She knew that every single one of them would jump to her defense if someone outside of the station house ever made even a remotely derogatory comment towards her or any woman. They were a nice set of guys, even if some of them were still teenage boys deep down. Lieutenant Ryan had actually been Mr. August in last year's FDNY calendar. They'd all teased the hell out of him about it for a month, including her. She even had a fully signed copy of the calendar at home.

As they turned down 2nd Avenue, Azar could see the huge cloud of black smoke curling into the air above the building. It looked bad, but then most warehouse fires were. Ninety percent of the time they were a melting pot of old wooden frames, bad wiring, boxes and flammable liquids.

Azar went into work mode as soon as the truck stopped in front of the building, taking orders from Lieutenant Ryan and Captain Fuentes, who'd beaten them to the scene in the first response vehicle. What faced them was a huge wall of flames that encompassed an entire strip of factories. The flames were licking at the walls of the warehouses next to the burning buildings.

"We have a chemical fire, possible combustible materials inside. Keep to the outer perimeter in case of reflash. Maconi and Nazemi, I want you in the alleyways around the site, clearing out anyone who might be living between the buildings." Azar nodded and was right behind Joe as they took off towards the nearest alleyway.

At night, the close proximity of the warehouse buildings provided breaks from the icy winds that came off the bay. Refrigerator boxes crammed into the alleys ended up makeshift shelters for homeless people, street kids and addicts.

The alleyways closest to the buildings were clear; obviously people were smart enough to move away from the burning building. A few alleys along, they came across a couple of addicts on the nod against the wall of a building.

"Guys, you have to move it. We need you to leave the immediate area." Joe used his authoritative fireman voice, but the two guys were obviously right out of it. Their heads were just lolling around on rubbery necks. Azar leaned down and hefted one of the guys to his feet.

"Hey, you need to go right now!"

Joe picked up the guy's friend and they frog marched them to the end of the alleyway. The guy she was holding had greasy blond hair and the damp smell of heroin addicts. She half pulled/half dragged the guy to the EMT's.

"Check these guys out. They are pretty non-responsive and we just want to be sure." One of the EMT's took the guys arm and was talking quietly to him in a soothing voice.

Azar shook her head. She saw drug addicts a lot in her job, but the waste of human life never ceased to amaze her. However, she didn't have time to ponder the detrimental effects of heroin for long as she and Joe quickly returned to the alleyways in search for more potential victims. The smoke in the air was so thick that they could barely see five feet in front of their boots. The wind off the bay fanned the fire, making the smoke swirl between the buildings.

Azar looked over at the flames that licked the air, and a bad feeling settled in her stomach. The fire was raging out of control, almost too wild for the kinds of accelerants that would be inside. The fire wasn't telling her anything unusual. There was no one alive in the building. But still, her gut told her something was wrong.

"On your left, Nazemi," Joe said from the other side of the alley.

Azar could see a shadow curled up on the pavement. She crept closer. The figure was scrunched into a ball in the depths of a shadow being cast by a dumpster. She bent down close to the shadow and saw it was a young guy, maybe in his early twenties. He turned his head towards her, and she saw his face was swollen and bloodied.

"Run," he whispered. She heard a thud, and whirled to see Joe go down in a heap, his helmet next to him on the ground.

"Joe!" she screamed before something crashed into the back of her head and the lights went out.

The first thing Azar saw when she opened her eyes was someone's dead face below her. She bolted upwards away from the corpse but her head hit something solid above her. She forced herself to breathe and lowered herself back down to take stock of her situation. She blocked out her surroundings until she remembered how she had gotten to this point; the boy in the alleyway, Joe going down and the blow to the back of her head. She reached around to where the blow had connected and felt her scalp. There was a huge egg and some congealed blood, but it didn't seem too bad.

Once she was calm, she recognized the face of the body below her immediately. It was Aaron. She checked his pulse and breathed a sigh of relief that he was still alive, if only just. She'd been piled on top of him into what appeared to be the trunk of a car.

Azar's wrists were cuffed in front of her and she looked down at the bronze colored metal that gleamed even though there was barely any light filtering into the trunk. Panic set back in.

The son of a bitch had put her into slave cuffs.

Slave cuffs were two thick bracelets that wrapped around your wrists and partially up your forearm. They were chained together and she couldn't melt them down to get them off. They were immune to her Djinn magic. When imbued with the Councils Blessing, the slave cuffs transferred ownership of the Djinn. Once the slavery period was up, the cuffs fell off. Also, the cuffs could only be used on someone with their slave brand still on their body; it was a fail safe to prevent a Djinn being kept against their will at the end of their compulsory servitude.

Things started to click into place. Fareet must have seen her slave brand at the Blue Smoke club when she was putting out that girl and started planning her capture.

She lit up her hand just to be sure she could still reach her fire. She wiggled her fingers like a happy little supernova and she let out another sigh of relief. She couldn't melt the cuffs off, but at least she hadn't been completely immobilized.

Azar felt the blood seeping from one of Aaron's wounds near his stomach. She let the fire die down in her hand, so that it was hot but no longer flaming. She was going to try and stop him from bleeding out by cauterizing his wounds. A large gaping hole in his stomach didn't seem too deep, just long, and she pushed the edges of the wound together as best as she could with one hand and then seared it closed with the other. Aaron's eyes shot open and he screamed. The burn left a perfect handprint on his torso. She hoped it would fade so he wouldn't have to have a reminder of this pain every day for the rest of his life.

"I'm so sorry," she murmured as she held him down. "I promised Anton I'd get you home alive, and I can't do that if you bleed out in the back of this crappy ass car." Tears streamed down her cheeks for the kid. No one should have to go through this much pain. She was saving his life, but death would probably feel like a better option to him at this moment.

Other than the big tear in his stomach, there were a couple of scabbed wounds and newer cuts that had healed up on their own. His face was smashed up, his left eye socket looked like it had been cracked and his breathing was labored.

Aaron had passed out again from the pain and she rechecked him for anything serious. Nothing else was life threatening, probably just incredibly painful. Unfortunately, there was nothing she could do about that.

She looked around the trunk for some kind of weapon but found nothing. There wasn't a tire iron or even a spare in the trunk with her and Aaron, everything had been removed to accommodate them both. The carpet lining was sticky in places, probably from Aaron's congealed blood. The trunk was fairly big, and made of solid metal, so the car was probably something old and American made. Fareet had removed all her turnout gear. Fear curdled her stomach at the thought of Joe lying in the alley way, and she prayed that he was okay.

Azar wondered where Fareet had gotten the slave cuffs. They weren't exactly given out by the Djinn Council as party favors. She focused her power on the chain, which wasn't made of the same thing as the cuffs. This just made the whole thing even stranger. Normal slave cuffs came with a chain made of the same energy absorbing material as the cuffs themselves. This was to prevent the Ifrit from melting the chain, the Marid from freezing it, the Sila from hitting it with a bolt of lightning, the Shaitan from scaring the chain into submission and so on. Azar didn't know what this metal was. It wasn't immune to her powers, but its reaction to it was slow. Where she could have melted the entire car in minutes, the chain had barely warmed. But it had warmed a little, and that was a reassuring sign.

Azar could have just melted her way out of the car, but to do so would cause even more injury to Aaron. Obviously Fareet had guessed she wouldn't put the kid's life in danger and that was why he'd brought him along instead of just leaving him in the alley. This way, he had her cooperation far more easily than if he had to take her kicking and screaming.

She was still working on the chain when the car slowed and stopped. She heard the crunch of gravel as the driver walked around to the trunk. The lid flew open and Fareet's face stared down at her menacingly. He no longer looked average to her. His expression was that of a monster.

"I see you're awake. Probably testing the chain, right? It's a special heat resistant metal that I got from a Russian chemist several years ago. Then I killed him, of course. We can't have heat resistant items popping up in the market, it would be bad for business. But it did come in handy just this once." His voice had that crazy conversational tone that lunatics use. "I wouldn't even bother. It will take weeks to burn through it and you won't even be alive in twenty-four hours. So conserve your strength for the big finale. I promise you it will be worth the wait." He began fiddling around in his pockets, searching for something.

"Why don't you let the boy go, Fareet? You have no use left for him. The Were know that you have him and they are tracking his scent as we speak. If you leave him here they won't be able to find you later on," Azar said nonchalantly, as if Aaron's life didn't matter to her at all.

She looked around Fareet's silhouette and could see that they were still in civilization. She couldn't see a street sign, just a Starbucks through trees but it looked like every other Starbucks on the planet. She desperately looked for weapons, other cars, anything that could help. They'd parked off to the side of the road in a rest area for broken down vehicles. Azar could still see the lines of traffic going past, but she doubted they could see her. But at least Aaron could get medical attention if they left him here.

"Oh half blood, do I look like a fool? The boy stays because he is like a dead weight around your soft human heart, anchoring you in my grasp. Whilst he is under my control, you will stay to protect him. You really are a disgrace to the Ifrit, but right now that works in my favor. Soon you will be my final tribute to the Great Lord Balraka and he will come back to earth and burn this city to ash!" He sounded like a crazed zealot, his voice hitting that slightly higher octave that seemed to be universal to maniacs everywhere and his hands raised in the air like Balraka was in heaven rather than the very pits of hell.

"Seriously, weren't you hugged enough as a child or something? You must know how crazy this all sounds. You are talking about killing hundreds of your own kind." She didn't add that he would be killing millions of humans as well. She doubted he even saw them as anything other than food for Balraka. Fareet just gave her a blank look, and Azar realized that life, be it Djinn, Supe or human, meant nothing to him. It made her so angry. "I am going to kill you. You chose the wrong half blood to pick on asshole," Azar promised softly from the trunk of the car. Her hands lit up again, fire curling from her fingers and she desperately wanted to reach out and fry this mofo. Rationally, she knew that it would probably tickle him, but it was an outlet for her futile rage.

Fareet just laughed in her face. He reached into his pocket and pulled out a syringe. In one quick move, his hand swept down and stabbed her in the ass, then slammed the trunk shut and she and Aaron were in darkness once more. The darkness brought the realization that their chances of surviving this were starting to fade, and fast.

"What the hell?" Her vision suddenly went blurry and her arms got heavy, her fiery hands going out almost immediately. She'd been sedated. She tried to reignite but she couldn't get more than a flicker.

"I'm sorry," she mumbled groggily to Aaron. She failed him.

His response was a bare whisper. "You tried."

The rest of the night passed in a haze. Whatever Fareet had shot into her wore off quickly, so periodically he would stop the car, open the trunk and stab her with another needle. He didn't talk to her again. From the intel she could gather during her periods of lucidity, they were still driving, probably staying on the move so the pack couldn't trace them. She tried to kick out the rear tail light so she could signal to the cars behind them, but whatever was in that drug cocktail had made her weaker than a kitten. She kept working on the chain between her wrists, but she could barely call up enough flame to toast a piece of bread, let alone burn through some kind of super heat resistant metal.

Each time she woke, she checked on Aaron, and he seemed to be better. His breathing had evened out, which was quite a feat considering a good portion of her body weight was on top of his. She could hear his heartbeat and it was nice and strong. That was about as much conscious thought she could muster.

Every time she drifted back into oblivion, she prayed that her supernatural A-Team would be there the next time she woke. Just this once, she wouldn't mind being rescued by a knight in shining armor.

CHAPTER 13

Azar struggled to open her eyes. She could see the light through her eyelids, so she knew it must be morning. She finally forced her eyes open and realized the whole world had been turned upside down. Or maybe it was just her. She looked up, or down, and realized she was hanging by her feet from a chain, suspended about six feet from the ground. The chain was wrapped around her middle, binding her slave cuffed arms to her body and then ran up to loop around her ankles. She turned her head but all she could see was the cool blue water of the ocean and the New York City skyline juxtaposed proudly along the horizon.

She tried to make the synapses in her brain fire, so she could work out what the hell was going on.

She shook her head to chase away the cobwebs that clouded her mind. She must be on a boat; she could see the prow and the odd bit of surf splashed up and hit her in the face as they moved through the choppy surf.

Azar heard a groan below her and looked down. She let out a yell but it was muffled by duct tape that she hadn't noticed was there. Directly below her, Aaron lay on the steel deck, a knife thrust through his chest to the hilt. She frantically wiggled around, trying to loosen the chains that bound her so she could help him. She called the flame to her and arched backwards to touch the chain.

"I would stop and think before you melt through those chains." A shudder ran through her body at the sound of Fareet's cold voice. She whipped her head around looking for the source and found him standing to her left. He was smiling. "I think this is kind of dastardly, even for me. You see, I needed to be sure you would stay exactly where I put you whilst I dealt with other matters, so I devised a carefully laid out plan." He pulled out a knife that had been sheathed on his hip. "People don't know this about me, but during my slavery, I was used as a metalsmith. I had quite an affinity with metals; gold, silver, iron, steel, it didn't matter. I could shape it and mold it until it was something spectacular. My human *master*," he spat the word out like it was poison, "worked me until the skin of my fingers bled. He made a fortune off my labor. People from all over Europe came to his crappy little kingdom to get the finest crafted metals on the continent. That was until he was killed in an unfortunate avalanche on the road to Constantinople from what is now Russia. He was killed instantly, and I was also assumed dead.

"But I digress. This knife is of my own design. It's the sister blade of the one currently pinning our Were friend to the deck over there, like a butterfly to a board. See these hinged secondary blades?" He pointed to what looked like thin flat spikes that molded to the shape of the blade. Two were attached to the tip and another two were positioned midway up the blade. "When they are stabbed into your victim, they sit flush to the blade, making it easy for the blade to slide into the flesh. But were you to try and pull it out," he pressed a finger to the tip of one of the secondary blades and it fanned out, creating an angry spike that sat out at a forty five degrees from the blade, "it would gut you instantly, like a spear gun no? In the case of our friend over here, it would catch on his heart and tear it from his body.

You see, I've precisely placed the blade in his chest so that if you were to do anything crazy, like fall on top of him from a great height, the blades would knick something vital and he would bleed out before you could get your hands in front of you to stop it. If you tried to remove it, well, a lot of important organs would come with it." He took a little bow, as if someone was applauding him for being sadistically cruel.

However, he was right; she was stuck until she could think of another way to get herself free without killing Aaron. He looked terrible, his face had lost all color and a spreading pool of blood haloed his torso. Thankfully, he appeared to be unconscious. The stiller he was, the more likely he would survive.

Fareet stood there with a smile on his face. He knew he had her. For now at least. But there was something she wanted to know while he was feeling so chatty. She started to speak, but the duct tape over her mouth muffled her words. Fareet rolled his eyes and reached over to rip it off. Azar swore a blue streak as the duct tape took a layer of skin with it.

"That hurt!" Her eyes watered from the sting. "What I want to know is how you plan to kill me? From what I hear, a fire pledge means you have to use your Djinn abilities to burn the sacrifice. If you plan to set me on fire, you may as well just drop me back in Brooklyn so I can go get a shiatsu massage at Mama Lynn's Nails and Beauty." *Easy*, she said to herself, *you just need to needle him enough to get him to spill his plans, not enough to kill you on the spot.*

"Oh, that's easy half blood. As you are my final tribute, I have saved the best for last." He reached over his shoulder and only then did Azar see the hilt of the sword strapped to his back. As he removed it from its scabbard, it glowed faintly with a white blue light. Oh, crap. She knew what that was alright.

"Drakhul." Its name choked up from her throat. Drakhul was like Ifrit kryptonite. It could be wielded by anyone to kill an Ifrit, from a human child to another Djinn race. A single knick was deadly to an Ifrit, and the death would be as painful and horrible as any imaginable. It was one of the Great Weapons forged by the first Djinn, when the Council held a lot less sway and every Djinn was as big and powerful as Balraka.

The Great Weapons were an urban legend among the Djinn, and the story of their strength was whispered about by all types of supernatural creatures. All six weapons were said to be lost to time, and quite frankly, no one was too upset by the fact. The last thing the Council needed was for some back-water Djinn to stumble across one of the most powerful weapons ever created and then get it in their head to overthrow the only system of gover-nance the Djinn had ever known.

"Where did you find it?" She whispered.

"It was buried in the ice above the avalanche that killed my human master. I was lying on my back in the snow, amongst the mud and ice that had poured down on top of our caravan. I was so sure that I was dead, that a shard of ice must have buried itself in my body because the cold was that excruciating. I was staring at the ice wall that had been exposed when the cliff face had given way. Drakhul was buried so deep that all I saw at first was a faint glimmer in the ice. It was no more than a flash, but somehow I knew it was important, that it was calling to me. I dug for months at the ice to chisel my way towards it, and when I finally knew what it was, well, I knew it was a higher power that had gifted me my reprieve from slavery and granted me this powerful weapon. I knew that Balraka wanted me to save him from his icy prison." He walked along the deck, waving Drakhul like a pendulum. If she had any doubts about his sanity before, she knew he was completely nuts now.

"So I escaped from Europe in case the Djinn Council discovered that I had not perished with my master, came to this barbaric new world. I gained power until I was sure that after I had released Balraka, I would be able to rule in his stead amidst the chaos. I cannot free him this time, but I shall never stop searching for a way to unlock the bars of his cell. Until then, I can create a world for him to rule."

Fareet had Drakhul thrust in the air like a conquering hero of old, and the whites around his eyes showed, making him look as crazy as he obviously was.

Azar knew that the likelihood of her surviving the day just dropped dramatically. Drakhul could be the tool of her freedom or her doom but only time would tell which way it would go. However, she would fight hard to make sure she was victorious, because quite frankly, the excruciating agony that would follow a cut by Drakhul was not the way she wanted to die. Now all she needed to do was figure out a way to take it from him without letting the blade slice her in any way. *Should be easy enough*, she lied to herself.

"I can see the cogs turning in your head half blood, but it is useless. You will be my final sacrifice and the city of New York will burn. Now if you could just stay right there, I have some cattle to herd into a suitable holding pen. We want Balraka to have a nice feast when he finally arrives!" Fareet all but skipped off towards the metal stairs that led to the lower decks.

As soon as he was out of sight, Azar looked around for a way out of this mess. They were obviously on a ferry; she could see the NYC Department of Transport logo spray painted to the side of the boat. Given the direction they were heading in relation to Skyline, she'd say it was the Staten Island ferry. At this hour of the morning, it would be filled with hundreds of commuters, tourists and children on school excursions to the Statue of Liberty. Hundreds of people who were about to become breakfast for Balraka. She had to stop hanging around and do something.

Aaron was still prone on the deck beneath her, and she couldn't risk jostling that knife, just in case Fareet was as precise as he claimed. Her hands were cuffed behind her back, so she couldn't climb back up the chain towards the crow's nest to free herself from the chains without falling. She could try to swing and melt the chain simultaneously, but she would have to time it perfectly so that she didn't land on Aaron. It would be worth a shot, but the margin of error was large, and then Aaron would bleed out in seconds. She only had one more plan, and she just prayed that Aaron was conscious enough to help.

"Aaron! Can you hear me? I need you to wake up." To her surprise, his eyes popped straight open.

"I'm alright. Well, not alright, but I'm conscious," he said, his voice stronger than she'd expected. "I thought it would be better if I didn't let him know I was awake. He likes to do things when I'm awake." The faint tremor in the boy's voice let her know what he meant. Fareet tortured Aaron when he was awake. It was just another nail in Fareet's coffin.

"You did good, Aaron. It was best to let him think that you were unconscious. It's what he gets for underestimating a Were. You are much tougher than anyone thinks. I know this first hand. I've met your Pack. You guys are strong, tough and resilient." She was psyching him up, because the next part of her plan wasn't going to be pleasant. "I think Fareet is going to try and burn down New York, and right now we are the only two people on the planet that can stop him. So I need to get down, and to do that, you're going to have to do something really brave."

"That means painful, right?" There was a thin

note of teenage sarcasm mixed in with the fear in his voice, and that gave Azar a little bit of hope.

"Yeah it does. Sorry kid, I really tried to think of another way but they all end up with unsatisfactory endings." *Or you dead*, Azar thought. Aaron was a smart kid though; he knew what she meant even if she didn't say it aloud. "I don't think Fareet was bluffing about the knife in your chest. I think what he underestimated was my experience with trauma cases and your cast iron will."

Azar analyzed his chest wound with the critical eye that had been drummed into her from years of training. If you worked in the emergency services on the streets of Brooklyn, chances were you had attended your share of stabbings. Fareet had stabbed him on the left side of the chest, just below his pectoral muscle. The blade was on a twenty degree angle in his chest, probably so he could insert it between Aarons ribs. Azar gave thanks for small favors. It was going to hurt, but with a bit of luck, he might survive until she could get help.

"Okay Aaron, here is the plan. It's going to hurt like Hades, but I'll be able to get down there and help really quickly. What I need you to do, on my word, is jerk up and to your right just a half an inch. Your rib bone should stop you from going too far off course. Your lung might collapse, and it's going to get a lot harder to breathe, but the knife will be away from your heart and I might be able to move you to safety. Okay?" Aaron's face was twisted in pain already, but he had a stubborn look on his face that kind of reminded her of Tao, so she knew he understood.

"Alright, get ready! Remember only half an inch." She twisted her body so she started to swing out on the end of the chain. She called her flame again and arched backwards so she could touch the chain with a fingertip. She felt the metal soften and melt almost immediately. She swung out to the furthest point and blasted the chain with everything she had.

"NOW!"

Aaron's scream of pain drowned out the sound of the chain snapping and she thudded to the ground right across his legs. She rolled off him as gently and quickly as she could, folding her body through the loops of her bound arms like a circus contortionist, so that her hands were finally in front of her. She crawled up to Aaron's torso. He was white and sweating with pain, his breathing labored. Blood bubbled from the small hole in his chest.

Azar tore off her shirt and pants to use as pressure bandages. Aaron's eyes widened a little at the sight of her taking off her clothes and she smiled at him reassuringly.

"Don't go getting any ideas, Kid. I'm going to try and use them as pressure bandages to slow down the bleeding a little. I'm hoping that the combination of pressure and your accelerated healing will keep you stable enough until I can get you help." She tore her shirt in half, and pressed a wadded up piece to the wound on his front, wrapping it as tightly around the knife as she could. "Okay, now I'm going to roll you to the side a little so I can get my hand under your back. I'm going to melt the metal around the knife so it slides out." She gently curled his free side up and pressed her palm to the metal deck around the knife. When it was hot enough, she gently lifted Aaron into a sitting position by his shoulders, the knife sliding out of the melted metal flooring as if it were butter. She could smell the burning of his flesh as the heated metal pressed against his skin. She sat him up and pressed the other half of her shirt against his back wound before wrapping her pants around his torso as hard as she could.

Aaron had begun to pant in pain, and she grabbed him around the waist and deadlifted him to his feet. "I'm going to put you somewhere a little less exposed. Now that you aren't a bargaining chip, I don't think Fareet would hesitate to make your injuries a little more permanent." She searched around the deck, desperate to find somewhere that wasn't out in the open. The Staten Island Ferry had four decks, only three open to passengers. From her position on the top deck, she could already see that the Fareet had cleared out the third deck. On a normal day, it would be packed full of people taking pictures and kids hanging over the railings. She gently eased him down the ladder to the deck.

Azar peeked through the windows of the top deck cabin, and it was dark and empty. She tried the door, but it was locked. She put her hand around the door handle and melted it open. She had to hurry, Fareet would be able to sense her using her power. She helped Aaron into the cabin and lowered him to the floor between the seats right at the back. It wasn't ideal, but it was darkened and it might keep Aaron off of Fareet's radar.

"Whatever happens, don't move. Anton wouldn't forgive me if you survived this long and then you died through misguided heroism." Aaron nodded reluctantly. He didn't look like he would be going anywhere fast.

She left him there and ran down along the side of the ship towards the stern, where the stairs to the lower levels were located. The wind whipped her hair into her face and water splashed up from the side of the boat to leave droplets on her skin. Only she would have to save a city wearing nothing but her underwear, and not even the pretty Victoria's Secret stuff she'd bought with Oliver.

She still had her hands chained in front of her, and she would be useless until she could find a way to get them free of the chain. She slid around the corner of the deck and came face to face with Fareet.

"I should have known you wouldn't stay where you are supposed to. You've been ruining everything from the beginning, why would you stop now?" he shouted, his face reddening with anger. Azar back peddled away from him and the stairs. Fareet strode towards her, unsheathing Drakhul, so Azar did the only thing she could think of. She freed her inner Ifrit.

She hadn't turned completely Ifrit in almost a century. The need to keep hidden far outweighed the need to give into the other half of her nature. The remaining clothing she was wearing, her singlet and underwear, turned to ash in microseconds as flames engulfed her torso and spread to her limbs. Two huge fiery wings burst from her back, unfurling like flaming petals. Even the individual strands of her hair caught fire and stood up from head like a raging candle flame. Because she was only half Ifrit, she maintained her human anatomy, rather than morphing like a full blood.

Fareet just sneered. "Impressive for a half blood, but we both know that there is no way you can defeat me."

But he didn't change form. Azar realized that he couldn't be full Ifrit and wield Drakhul without significantly raising the odds of killing himself in the process. Just a single errant flame lick against the blade would be a mortal blow, as equally deadly as a blade through the heart. The same rule applied to her, but it evened out the odds a little in her favor. Although her fire wouldn't harm him, the Djinn were faster and more agile in their natural form. They could fight longer, harder and with more resilience than if they were in their far more clumsy human forms. It also gave her an aerial advantage. She had wings, and Fareet was earthbound.

"It's time for you to meet the Balraka in hell, Fareet!" Azar shouted, spreading her wings out around her and taking to the air. She'd apologize to Donovan for stealing his line after this was all over.

Fareet charged at her, brandishing Drakhul with skill that was long forgotten in this modern age. He was quick on his feet, and Azar was unused to using her wings, so the first swing of the sword almost ran her through the chest before she could dodge backwards. It was then, in that split second, Azar took the greatest gamble of her life.

She thrust her slave cuffed hands out in front of her. Drakhul hit the chain connecting her slave cuffs together, and slid through it like butter. She sent a small prayer of thanks to whatever deity looked out for half blood Djinn that got themselves into ridiculously dangerous situations.

The consummate swordsman, Fareet didn't even hesitate over her freed hands, and attacked again while Azar was on the back foot. He continued to attack high, so Azar couldn't take to the air again. She pulled her flames in tight, so that she looked as if she had rippling orange skin. She dodged Fareet's swings until she was almost backed up against the cabin of the ferry. This was not going very well. Her eyes darted around the deck for a weapon as she barely missed a swipe to her neck.

Azar saw an emergency ax six feet behind Fareet's back, and she knew that it was her only chance of gaining the upper hand. As Fareet leaned into his next swing, Azar waited until gravity pulled the long blade down to its lowest point and then flew backwards and up, flying high over his head with one big push of her wings. Then dived down towards the deck. She hit the boards at a run, and smashed through the safety glass with her fist. The glass gouged cuts into her hand as she pulled the ax free. She heard Fareet's footsteps closing the distance fast and she cast out her preternatural senses, waiting for the perfect moment.

When Fareet was in swinging distance, Azar spun, turning to the left with the ax extended in her hands, and she narrowly missed a blow that the Rogue had aimed at her rib cage. She let the momentum of the turn continue to spin her until the ax met its target, sliding into Fareet's body, severing his arm. A disassociated part of her mind watched the arm drop to the deck with morbid curiosity.

Fareet howled in pain and he dropped Drakhul to grab at the bleeding stump of his arm. It wasn't a mortal blow, not by a long shot. If he went full Ifrit, he could pick up his arm and reattach it no problem. Azar desperately hoped he wouldn't do that, but even if he did, at least he would no longer be wielding a sword that promised certain death. Azar was sure that she wouldn't have been able to dodge its kiss forever.

She swung the ax again while Fareet was

unarmed. Like a true soldier of old, he sensed the attack and dodged the swing as he jumped to his feet, his severed arm still held in his left hand, and turned full Ifrit in the blink of an eye. Azar didn't realize that a full blooded Ifrit could change forms that fast. Fareet's visage as he stood before her was so awful that it chilled the blood in her veins.

In his Ifrit form, Fareet grew a full two feet, and sprouted wings twice the size of hers. His wings easily spanned ten feet either side of his body. His torso broadened and changed and his human feet turned to goat hooves. His face elongated, and although his features could almost be recognizable as human, they were twisted and cruel. He looked truly demonic.

Fareet placed his severed arm against the stump of his bicep and fire engulfed the limb, fusing them back together in a spray of white hot flame. And that was that. Her tactical advantage was gone. She was now out matched and out Ifrited. She was a dead Djinn walking.

"I am going to crush you!" Fareet bellowed in an unearthly tone. His voice sent shivers down her spine and she was glad she had wings, because his bellow made her knees turn to water. He reached down to grab Drakhul, but it was gone.

She whipped her head around, desperately searching for the sword, but her eyes fell on Aaron. He had the sword clutched weakly in one of his hands, the other arm pressed to the wound in his chest. He must have snuck around behind them during the fighting. Azar gave a little internal cheer, but as Fareet's dead eyes fell on the boy holding the sword, her cheer turned to horror.

Azar rushed towards Aaron, but she was too slow and Fareet reached the boy first. His swung a huge flaming hand and backhanded Aaron across the face. The force of the blow flung Aaron's body backwards into the guardrail at the stern of the ferry and she heard his bones crack as they met the unforgiving metal. His feet left the ground and his body teetered on top of the railing, the sword still in his hand, before he toppled backwards into the water below.

"No!" Azar and Fareet yelled in unison. They both stood there in shock, staring at the empty stern. And then Fareet went batshit crazy.

"You have destroyed everything!" he screamed hysterically, his flames so hot and high that he was melting all the metal around them, including the deck.

He charged at her and Azar stumbled backwards in the face of such molten anger. She turned and ran, hoping she was more agile in her smaller form than Fareet. She could hear the flapping of his huge wings behind her, and realized he'd taken to the air. She could never out manoeuvre him this way and she was damned if she was going to die running away. She stopped and turned, facing Fareet with her chin raised and belligerence in her eye. She would die with honor and fight until her last breath

"How does it feel to be beaten by a half blood?" she taunted.

"Who said I was beaten?" Fareet sneered at her. He raised his arm and she saw a blade glint in his hand. It was the sister knife of the one that had pinned Aaron to the deck.

As it always happened in life-altering moments, time slowed as she watched the knife leave Fareet's hand and fly through the air. Her body was lodged in the quicksand of time, too helpless to move, and then she felt a burning pain as the knife's blade lodged itself in her chest. Direct hit. She clutched her chest as she fell to her knees, a painful gasp wracked her body as her lifeblood poured into her lungs.

Fareet was in front of her in an instant, his eyes taunting her. "You thought one such as you could beat me? You were mistaken. Now your death will release hell on earth, and you'll know in your final moments that the deaths of all those you hold dear happened because you were too weak to stop it." He reached down to grab the hilt of his knife, ready to twist and remove it, taking along her heart and her lungs and finishing the job. "Now I have a date with a God that I must keep."

But Azar had stopped looking at his deranged face. Behind him, a water vortex rose up from the sea and a woman in light blue leather was standing atop its foaming crest, like it was an elevator or something as equally mundane. The water swirled and bent, depositing the woman on the deck. Azar's jaw dropped in shock. In her hand was Drakhul.

Fareet noticed too late that Azar's attention was no longer on him, and he turned just in time to see the blade swing that would remove his head from his body.

She let her body collapse to the side, landing face to face with Fareet's decapitated head.

"No, you were mistaken," she whispered, and then let death take her.

CHAPTER 14

Apparently there was no rest for her, even in death. She didn't know if she believed in heaven or hell, or even an afterlife, but she imagined it wouldn't be this loud. She could hear voices shouting, and hands pawing at her body.

No, she sighed to herself, *there was only one conclusion. She wasn't dead at all.*

She couldn't open her eyes but she could feel warm hands on her face. She needed to know if the boy was okay.

"Aaron," she managed to whisper, but she wasn't sure that anyone could hear her over the noise.

"The boy is fine. He's with Tao now. Don't try and talk, I'm here. Everything will be okay." She knew Bast's voice. She knew the feeling of its silken notes as they slid over her mind. He was close to her face because his breath whispered across her skin. His thumbs stroked her cheeks, brushing away tears she hadn't realized she'd cried. Bast didn't have to worry about her talking, because even breathing was becoming impossible as the blood filled her lungs.

"Mira, do something! She's going to bleed out here on the deck. There has to be another way." Bast's voice was rough and angry, and she could hear his raw desperation.

"I can only slow her heart rate right down until we can get her to the Council doctors. But she's Ifrit, Bast. Cooling her body until her heart barely beats is going to be excruciatingly painful for her. She cannot die; this I agree. If Fareet's blow kills her, the Balraka may still rise."

"He didn't kill her with Ifrit fire," someone else argued.

"That's not a risk I'm willing to take."

Azar shuddered internally at the thought. If her death meant that Fareet still won, then she would fight death with everything she had.

"Do it," she whispered again, sure that only Bast could hear. She could feel the warm blood gurgling up her throat and spilling over her lips. Bast's hands tighten around her face. He leaned forward and kissed her lips gently.

"If it is the only way. Donovan, hold her feet. Oliver, make sure she can't arch her torso. Mira, she better live, or so help me, I will find a way to make the Council's life hell. The Balraka will be the least of their problems." He continued to stroke her face with the pad of his thumb.

Azar felt two hands on her chest, either side of the knife protruding from the middle. "I understand Bast. I will make this as gentle as I can, but it will still feel like torture." And with that, Azar felt waves of cold seep into her chest.

She screamed as the ice cold froze the fire in her body, the pain spreading through her veins until every inch of her flesh burned with it. Her body convulsed as the ice crawled its way over her skin, until the very air she breathed felt like ice shards stabbing at her lungs. And suddenly the pain was gone.

Azar was no longer bleeding out on the deck of the ferry. She was standing in the warm wind of her homeland. The winds shifted the sand in undulating waves and the hot summer sun beat down on her face. In front of her was a crystal blue pool, so clear that she could see the small fish swimming around on the bottom. Palm trees swayed gently in the breeze, the rustle of the wind through its fronds the only sound in the place.

"Fuck! I'm dead," she yelled into the nothingness and flopped down onto the sand. Fareet had won, and by now Balraka was probably razing her city to the ground.

"You're not dead Azar," a familiar voice murmured behind her. She knew that voice. She whipped around to see Bast's smiling face. She threw herself into his arms.

"Are you sure? This seems like heaven to me." She wasn't lying, the place had a beautiful tranquility that filled her body with peace.

"No, Little Fire, this is an Oasis of the mind. I didn't want you to suffer. But you are still very much alive. I will have it no other way." His brow creased with determination, and his arms tightened around her body. Azar reached up and stroked away the frown. It looked so wrong on his face.

"You know, if this was my Oasis, neither of us would be wearing clothes." She raised her eyebrows at him, and he finally smiled. In the next instant she could feel that warm wind over every inch of her body. She looked down and saw she was naked. There was no wound in her chest, or bump on her head. In fact, her entire body was flawless. The little scar she had from where she fell through the floor of a burning house during a call out two years ago was gone. Her boobs seemed perkier, her hair shinier and her legs longer. She was definitely dreaming this one up.

She looked over to Bast and realized he was naked too. He was even more beautiful naked. A large scar ran down his chest, framed by golden curls of chest hair. There were many more. She'd never thought to ask where he'd gotten all the scars. But it was his imperfections that made him irresistible.

"Is this more to your liking?" He asked, his voice like a caress.

"Is this all a figment of my imagination?" Her voice was a hoarse whisper.

"With a little help, but essentially this is all you. This is your oasis, and my consciousness is here with you, because you wish it to be so. But whatever happens here is just a dream." He ran the back of his fingers down her arm and goosebumps popping up in their wake.

"Then I want you to make love to me." In this tranquil place, her worries about doing the right thing were gone. It was like someone had set her free. Life. Death. Duty. It all blew away on the warm desert wind. She didn't have to worry about Keenan, or the Council, about Fareet or Balraka. All she needed to do was be happy. She was pretty sure it wasn't slutty if it happened on another plane of existence anyway.

Bast gave her a whisper of a kiss as a response, not closing the distance between them. His hand ran across her stomach and up between her breasts to cup her face. Only then did he pull her closer, so she could feel the solid warmth of his body against the soft curves of her own. She could feel his hard shaft pressed against her stomach.

"I think you've bewitched me, Azar of the Ifrit. I don't know how you did it, but you've buried yourself inside my soul." He kissed her deeply, his tongue slowly stroking hers. His hands never stopped exploring her body, like he was mapping out every inch and committing it to memory. He broke off the kiss to scoop her up and lay her down delicately in the sand. The little voice inside her mind that seemed to only exist to think absurd things at inopportune times, delighted in the fact that this was her imagination, and therefore she wouldn't get sand in places that sand should not go. But even that annoying little voice died away when Bast took one of her nipples in his mouth and his roaming hands came to rest on the soft curls at the tops of her thighs. She gasped as his fingertip found the sensitive nub of her clit and massaged it ever so gently.

But she didn't want to wait, didn't want to waste precious minutes on foreplay.

"I want you now Bast." She tugged at his golden hair, so soft between her fingers. Bast gave her nipple one last little nip and moved so he was poised on his elbows above her. She looked up into his golden eyes that promised everything and smiled.

Bast smiled back, and then his smile turned to a frown. An angry frown.

"I have to go. They've knocked you out, and you are getting medical care, but I must leave. I cannot maintain the connection." Even as he said it, the oasis was drifting away. But Azar was certain that the tune to the Rolling Stones song '(I Can't Get No) Satisfaction' was playing in the air when the world finally went dark again.

Azar's eyes opened slowly on the stark white room around her. What she wouldn't give to wake up in her bedroom for once. This room looked like a maximum security psych ward. The door was thick solid metal, the walls were smooth and the furnishings were minimal. Just a single bed, and a toilet and sink combo in the corner. Azar was under no illusion to where she was. She was in a Council prison cell.

You save a city and you get thrown in jail. That's gratitude Djinn style. She tried not to feel bitter about the fact, but was failing miserably.

Attempting to sit up, she set off some kind of alarm because she was attached to several monitors, and was hooked up to an IV through a needle in her hand. She gazed down at a big square dressing decorating the space in-between her breasts.

She was wearing white pajama pants and a wrap top that was tied up to the side. Slave garb. She felt her panic rise in her chest and the heart rate monitor started to protest loudly. She tore at the cables attached to her chest. She needed to get out of here. She couldn't serve her slavedom now, she would be dead before it ended.

As she ripped at the cables and tubes attached to her body, the door opened and a woman rushed in. It was the same woman from the ferry and Azar searched her fuzzy brain for her name.

"Calm down, you're going to tear out your IV," she said in a melodic, soothing voice. "I'm Mira. Do you remember me?" She gently pushed her back down onto the bed, and Azar felt herself sliding back from hysteria.

Where the hell did she think she was going anyway? Did she really think they were just going to let her waltz out of the Council prison, through all the Adel and be on her merry way? Azar let out a defeated sigh, and stopped resisting Mira's hands.

Mira was still talking to her in soft tones. "That's good. Now, let's just get these reattached. Bast would kill me if I let anything happen to you."

Mira had a beautiful face. She reminded Azar of a siren, all golden, Nordic beauty. She had white blond hair that flowed down her back in soft waves, and gentle light blue eyes the color of the Adriatic Sea. Her skin was a creamy shade that you only ever saw in Renaissance portraits. She was still in the light blue leather outfit she wore on the ferry, and up close Azar could tell that it was well worn and buttery soft, moving with her body like a second skin. She was tiny and Azar would be surprised if Mira pushed 5'3 in heels.

"How do you know Bast?" Azar asked, eying the beautiful woman and telling herself not to be jealous. Apparently, she didn't control the urge that well because Mira took one look at her face and laughed.

"We don't know each other like that. I'm Moselle's daughter. Bast and I have known each other a very long time." Her response seemed legit.

Moselle had gifted his part of Coney Island to Bast before he died, which seemed a little odd considering he had a daughter to inherit it. Azar briefly remembered what Bast had said about Moselle going back to the motherland to die, and murmured her sympathies.

Mira smiled sadly and waved her hand. "It was a long time ago now. The pain of his loss still hurts, but I understand that it was his time to go. He led a gentle life and he didn't approve of my choices, so we did not speak much in his last centuries. I was glad that Bast was there for him. My father lived a full and happy life and died at peace with the world. That is all anyone can ask." Mira pretended to concentrate on the monitor attached to her chest, but Azar could see her blinking rapidly. She changed the subject to something less painful for the woman.

"Are you Adel?" Azar whispered quietly. It was like asking the woman if she was the boogeyman. The Adel were the hell hounds of the Djinn world. They were shrouded in myth and stories, each one scarier and more brutal than the last.

Mira nodded as she finished reattaching the

wires that Azar had torn off, and sat down on the end of the bed. "I am. I have been Adel for over three hundred years."

Azar let out a gasp of surprise. Three hundred years of slavery? Azar looked at her wrist and noticed she did not wear slave cuffs. She was obviously one of the few who chose to stay on after their servitude was finished. She didn't look like a homicidal maniac or someone who enjoyed killing. In fact she looked almost beatific.

Mira laughed at her again. "I get that look a lot. The Adel are like any other kind of enforcement group. You have those that have to be here through conscription and those who are only here because they like the feeling of power. Then there are a few who start out for the right reasons, but have trouble taking orders from the Council, especially when it involves seemingly senseless killing. And then you get the few who get conscripted but stay because what we do makes a difference to lives, both Djinn and human. We make the world safer for everyone. That's why I have stayed for so long. But being in the Adel is not for everyone." Mira's beautiful face looked sad for a minute and she turned her face away. Azar got the feeling she was thinking about something in particular.

But the look was fleeting and her face was pleasantly happy again when she turned back to Azar. "Now I have to get your account of what happened. There will be a trial for Fareet, just as a matter of course. I can promise you that he is very, very dead. Also, there will be another trial for you, in regard to your unserved slavedom and unsanctioned disclosure to a human. Normally, that would mean instant death for any Djinn, however, given your circumstances and the powerful connections you have, the Council has decided to give you a trial instead. Your fate will be decided by vote."

Azar was confused. What connections? Did she mean Bast and Donovan? Maybe Anton from the Were's? She didn't think any of their opinions would hold much weight within the Council. She felt like Alice down the rabbit hole, except instead of getting to Wonderland, the rabbit hole was filling up with water and she was drowning. She felt helpless.

"Just start at the beginning," Mira said soothingly.

As Azar recounted her version of events, she went with the honesty is the best policy plan. Lying about everything would get her nowhere now. The tiny Marid recorded Azar's statement in a small notebook, her hands flowing so fast you could barely see the pen. She told her about her mother, growing up on the run, her job as a firefighter, discovering the Djinn mark at the site of the apartment fire. She hesitated over the parts about Keenan, but she knew that Donovan would have already told the Council about Keenan's involvement. She was a little angry, but she couldn't blame him. If the Council had found out he'd omitted that fact, and she was sure that they would have, he would have been imprisoned or even faced death right alongside her. The Djinn were a hard bunch like that.

So instead, she explained about Keenan, about her feelings for him. She explained how he had helped her find Ellis Fareet, had investigated the fire and kept their secret at the expense of his own career and even his life. She explained about meeting Bast at Coney Island, and Lila, who didn't inform the Council about the Fire Pledge.

Mira frowned at that and her eyes turned hard as she scribbled something angrily into the margin of the notebook. Azar thought maybe the uppity little Ghul might get a visit from a very grumpy group of Adel soon. She told Mira about meeting Donovan and her meeting with Anton, the Alpha of the Sterling Forest Pack.

"Yes, we have already spoken to the Alpha, and the boy Aaron," Mira told her.

"Is he okay?" Azar asked. She dreaded the answer, but at least he was alive and coherent if he was giving statements.

"He's damaged, mentally and physically. But he has a strong spirit and the love of his pack, so I am sure he will make a full recovery. He was most anxious about your welfare. It appears you have made a lifelong friend out of this ordeal," she said with a gentle smile that made her face glow.

"However long that may be," Azar said quietly. They both knew that there was a possible death sentence at the end of her trial. Mira nodded sadly, but urged her to continue the story.

Azar sighed heavily. She told Mira of the plan, and how it went wrong. She shivered as she remembered being stuffed into the trunk with what she thought was the dead body of Aaron, and about the wounds that riddled his poor young body. She explained about the drug, the heat resistant metal that Fareet had forged, his explanation about how he faked his own death and found Drakhul. She explained everything that happened on the ferry, right up until the time that Mira arrived.

"And that's it," Azar said, closing her eyes. She felt as if she had just signed her death warrant, as well as Keenan's and maybe even one for Bast.

Mira stood up and came to the head of the bed. "I'll inform Bast that you are awake. He has been quite the burr in the Adel backside while you have been resting these last two days." She leaned over to cup Azar's cheek. "Do not despair Azar; you are a hero. That makes you someone worth saving. I will make sure they know this." Azar was shocked by the intimacy of the action, and just mutely watched as Mira turned and left, the door to her cell closing with a gentle whoosh of air.

It was another two days before Bast was allowed in to see her. The Adel treated her kindly, taking her off the monitors after Mira's visit. A nice doctor came to visit her several times to change her dressings and ensure she was healing properly. The IV was taken out of her hand, and she was encouraged to drink and eat soups, which she did with the ferocity of a person who hadn't eaten in a week. Mira came to visit her several more times, but Azar was itching to see a familiar face.

When Bast walked through the door, Azar did something so out of character that it shocked them both. She burst into tears. Bast had her in his arms before the first tear could slide down the length of her face and he murmured reassuring things into her hair. She just sobbed.

Everything that she'd been storing up, the fear during the fight with Fareet and the injustice of being locked away in a Council cell, it all just bubbled over to form a monsoon of tears that she couldn't control. Bast manoeuvred her over to the bed and sat down, pulling Azar onto his lap. He let her cry until her sobs turned into whimpers, and her whimpers turned into hiccups.

When the tears had stopped falling she raised her head and looked shyly up at Bast's face. "Sorry."

He kissed her lips gently. "Don't be. It's been overwhelming for me too. But everything will be okay. You have my word."

Azar nodded and sat up, pulling herself together. Bast stroked her hair away from her face and looked at her with so much compassion that she almost burst into a fresh round of tears.

"Thanks for coming to save me. I didn't think you would track me down on the ferry until it was too late." She rested her head against his chest, not ready to give up the warmth of his body yet. Bast had one arm tightly around her, and he didn't look ready to let her go either.

"The Weres tracked you to the ferry terminal.

Keenan flashed his badge at the attendant and found out that one of the ferries hadn't reached its destination and we put two and two together. Oliver stole a speed boat tethered at the marina next door and we searched the bay until we found you.

"I had to call Mira because I had no idea how to save you without getting you killed. I'm sorry; it's my fault you are in here." His voice was gravelly and he looked so tortured that Azar's hand moved out to touch his face instinctively. She looked into his eyes and she could see so much pain there. "I thought I was too slow. I thought you were going to die."

"You're the reason I'm still alive. I'd say we are square." She kissed his cheek to hide a blush. "Thank you for the oasis also." She still didn't know where they stood, and their time in the oasis had made things more complicated. However, as there was a fairly good chance she wouldn't survive the week, she didn't need to explore her feelings at this moment. She changed the topic. "Where was Keenan? I can remember you shouting orders at Oliver and Donovan, but I don't remember anything about Keenan." She knew she should feel awkward asking one love interest about another, it was probably very poor form, but the crazy love triangle thing they had going on almost felt natural now. Comfortable even.

"I had to get Tao to knock him out and tie him up in the back seat of his car. He threatened to shoot us all if we didn't let him on the boat. I think he would have too. He wanted to be there to save you so badly. But I thought it wouldn't be such a good idea, seeing how I'd called Mira. I didn't want her to conveniently tie up loose ends. He went a little crazy when we found out you'd been abducted." Azar shot straight up. She'd forgotten about Joe.

"Jesus, what about Joe? Is he okay?" She jumped to her feet, feeling awful because she hadn't asked about her best friend until now. The sound of Joe being cracked on the back of the head still echoed in her ears.

"Joe is fine. His helmet took the brunt of the blow. He had a mild concussion and had to stay the night in hospital. He's been calling Keenan every five minutes wanting updates. We told him and your Chief that you'd been abducted by a terrorist group who wanted to use you as a catalyst for a war. We told him that Oliver was an undercover Fed who was trailing you for your protection and that we were FBI. They believed it, but not until Council created some fake documentation for them to see."

Azar wasn't surprised the Council had people who could manipulate the human FBI databases. Bast pulled her back down onto his lap. "We have a lot to thank Joe for. He got a partial number plate before he lost consciousness. It allowed us to pick up Fareet's trail quicker." Bast lifted her hand to his mouth and kissed the tip of every finger in a gesture so loving that she felt tears well behind her eyes.

"And before you ask, Aaron is also fine. We saw him fall into the water but Mira and her partner Joia arrived just in time to fish him out. He had some broken bones, and that knife was still lodged in his chest, but Tao got him back to a Pack doctor as quickly as he could. Oliver said he's mending. He wakes up with night terrors every night, and some of the things that Ellis Fareet did to him make me want to kill that scum all over again, but all in all, Aaron is getting better. He refused to let them treat the hand shaped burn on his side where you sealed up that wound. He said he wanted to keep it as a reminder that you saved his life and that he owes you. I think seeing you would help a lot." A sad smile curled his lips. "It would help Oliver a lot too. He blames himself for your abduction, even though he couldn't have possibly scented Aaron or Fareet over the smoke from the fire."

Poor Oliver. He had such a big heart underneath all that flashy bravado. She wanted to be curled around his giant jaguar right now, safe and warm and not about to get her head chopped off.

They sat in silence for a little while. Bast just rocked her on his lap, one hand holding her tight and the other stroked her hair. At least her friends would be safe from Balraka, and the Djinn would remain hidden for a little while longer.

"If things go bad, can you please make sure Keenan gets away safely?" It was a lot to ask, but Azar needed reassurance that no one would die because of her, especially not Keenan.

Bast nodded as he shushed her. "I'll do my best, but it won't be necessary. I'm going to represent you at the Council trial, and there is no way I am going to let anything happen to you. You'll be out in a week to protect the human yourself. This is my solemn oath."

Azar smiled, but she was skeptical. Bast was a smooth talker, but she doubted anyone could get her out of her charges, considering they were both extremely true. The door to her cell opened and Mira stuck her head in to tell them that they had five more minutes. The smile she gave Bast was so warm and loving that Azar's brow knitted.

"What's up with you and Mira? You look at each other like long lost lovers." Azar really liked the tiny Marid woman but it was obvious that she had a lot of feelings for Bast.

"Mira and I were close friends a very long time ago. We spent a lot of time together, but we were never lovers. That was how I met Moselle. The affection I hold for Mira is different for the affection I hold for you, so you have no need to worry on that front."

There was a haunted look in his eyes, and Azar knew there was more to that story than he was letting on, but she let it go. The next time she saw him would probably be her trial, and she didn't want to spend her last moments with him talking about Mira.

Besides, she shouldn't be jealous. If she was going to serve one hundred years of servitude, she didn't expect Bast to wait around for her. He should be happy with someone, and the petite blond Marid would be a good match for him. At least he would be happy. She didn't dare think about what would happen to Keenan. The best case scenario would be that he would move on, maybe eventually find a nice girl and get married and have children, before dying of old age. This would all happen before she had finished her servitude. The worst case scenario would be that she got her head chopped off in front of the Djinn Council and so did Keenan. She shook off the melancholy thought.

She didn't want to spend her last hours in the depths of self-pity and depression either.

Azar turned on Bast's lap so she was facing him and wrapped her legs around his waist. She kissed him passionately, her arms looping around his neck. She needed to feel the warmth of another person, to get lost in a kiss until nothing and no one mattered. This was the memory that she needed to get her through a hundred years of servitude; one of love and warmth. Bast returned her kiss, his arms wrapped tightly around her waist so her body was pressed flush against his. She let all her emotions pour out of her body and onto his lips.

They stayed that way, devouring each other until her cell door slid open and there was an uncomfortable clearing of a throat. Azar turned to see Mira, standing in the doorway awkwardly.

"It's time to go Bast. I'm sorry," Mira said sympathetically.

Bast looked at the door sadly, and Azar knew how he felt. The kiss had felt like her last meal, like the end of something important. She wiggled off his lap and stood up with her back to the door, straightening her slave uniform. Bast stood also, but wrapped her in his arms again and pulled her close.

"Don't worry, Little Fire. We will get you out of this. The trial is the day after tomorrow and I will give it everything I have. Keep your chin up," he murmured into her ear. He gave her one last kiss on the lips, and followed Mira to the door.

"Bast?" She felt a desperate compulsion to finalize this one last thing, if only she could find the words. "I... I hope that one day we can explore this thing between us. But if not, thank you."

Bast sent her a sad smile, and his eyes told her just how much she meant to him too, even if he didn't verbalize the words. There was a lot of emotion on his face for once, but deep down she'd already known the depth of his feelings. He gave her one last little finger wave and he was gone.

As the door shut behind him, Azar shocked herself again, and cried for a second time that day. But this time there was no Bast to wipe away her tears and the sense of loss just made her cry harder.

CHAPTER 15

The two days until her trial were simultaneously the fastest and slowest of her life. The longest because the days dragged on, like waiting for fireworks to explode. Mostly, she sat and watched the wall. Mira brought her a book on Djinn history, and another on the history of the Adel, but she found it hard to concentrate on the words.

However, she'd rather have stayed in the holding pattern for centuries than go out and face the Djinn Council, and for that reason the steady march of time seemed like it was going too fast for her. Only Mira and her doctor came to visit, and then only briefly. She felt like she was going slowly insane.

So when the morning of her trial came around, Azar found she was relieved. She told herself it was better to face the bad than wait a torturous eternity for the other shoe to drop. An Adel guard brought her freshly pressed white slave uniform and took her to the communal showers to bathe. Even though she was under constant guard, the hot water pouring over her skin felt like bliss. She stood under the spray until her fingers pruned and the guard cleared her throat loudly. Azar begrudgingly turned off the hot water. This was obviously a concession to her half blood heritage, and she was sure it was at Mira's request. She had become close to Mira, but Azar was uncertain if it was a genuine friendship or some kind of demented camaraderie due to Stockholm syndrome.

When Azar got back to her cell, she swallowed down the repulsion and dressed in the slave uniform. The simple wrap shirt was made from a light gauzy material, like an opaque gossamer. She had never seen the material in the human world, and she had a feeling it was something made by the Djinn themselves. The harem pants were made from the same material, and they billowed out like fluffy clouds from her waist before ending in a gold brocade cuff that tightly hugged her ankle. She slipped her feet into the little silk slippers that had been laid out for her.

A light knock at the door heralded another slave, in identical garb to her own, with orders to cut her hair. The woman dried her long hair with towels, cut it, brushed it until it shone like polished mahogany and then braided it into an ornate braid that twisted down her back. The slave, who wouldn't speak to Azar except to give directions, buffed Azar's nails until she could almost see her reflection in them. She felt like she was being groomed to go on display. If they did cut off her head, at least she'd make a pretty corpse.

Eventually, Mira came to retrieve her. She was dressed in her Adel uniform rather than her blue leathers. The Adel uniform was a black silk tunic and loose fitting black pants, similar to that of the slave uniform but tailored for fighting. A thick leather belt studded with gems cinched Mira's waist and from it hung a sword. The gems were in different colors, each one signifying a different Djinn race; Sapphires for the Marid, Emeralds for the Ghul, Rubies for the Ifrit, Lapis Lazuli for the Jann, Diamonds for the Sila and Onyx for the Shaitan. Azar had read in the histories that the Adel wore each color gem on their dress uniform because the members of the order were no longer of their race, but of the Djinn as a whole. Mira looked stunning in the outfit, but Azar assumed she'd look stunning dressed in a garbage bag and standing in the rain.

"It's time to go." Mira's voice was gentle, as if she were coaxing an easily startled bird. Azar looked down and realized her hands were shaking, and her facial muscles ached from the tension in her jaw. Mira came over and threaded a fine gold chain between the slave cuffs that Fareet had shackled to her wrists. They hadn't bothered to take them off, but now they were imbued with the Council ward that suppressed all her Ifrit power.

Azar's knees shook as she followed Mira out beyond her cell door. Joia the Sila immediately stood to her left and Mira was on her right. A serious looking man she didn't know was flanking them and she could only see the back of the man in front, as he led the little ensemble through the hallways. She didn't remember anything of the surrounding hallways and rooms from the trip to her cell; her body had shut down from the hypothermia that Mira had inflicted.

She really wasn't even sure where the Djinn Council was, or if it was even in New York. The halls seemed old; the walls were made out of sandstone, and the floor was slate. It was cold and draughty, but obviously that made little difference to the Djinn.

Shiny metal doors gleamed at the end of the hall, and they seemed so out of place with the rustic feel of the rest of the hall. They'd obviously been added in far later, and no one had bothered to try and make them blend in better with the surroundings. Azar thought they should fire their interior designer. Maybe she'd make it her last request.

"Are we still in New York?" Azar asked, not really expecting a response, so she was surprised when Joia answered.

"We are still in New York. It is the Djinn Councils North American base of operations." Azar couldn't believe that not only were there all sorts of Djinn running around New York, but she had chosen to live in the very city where the Djinn Council had set up shop. Irony really could be a bitch.

They all piled into the elevator, Azar pressed in between all four shoulders, as if she was about to make a mad dash for the doors. It was highly unlikely, considering she was surrounded by four full blooded, trained Adel warriors. The elevator slowly rose up the floors. There was no indicator panel to tell her what floor they were on, or even how many floors they had done, but it felt like a lot. The elevator finally shuddered to a stop and Azar took a deep ragged breath. Her heart was racing and her body felt as if it wanted to burst into flames. She probably would have if it wasn't for the cuffs. Azar's knees buckled and she went down, but was caught midair by the Adel warrior flanking her rear. He held her up with a firm grasp under her upper arm until she steadied. Azar turned and smiled at the man, and he nodded solemnly in return.

Mira squeezed her forearm reassuringly as the elevator doors slid open and she was led out into the center of a large circular room, then up onto a two foot high circular podium. Her accompanying Adel scattered their way around the podium and two more Adel came from somewhere else. They all stood watching her, and some of them looked as if they would take her head if she even so much as sneezed too loudly.

The room itself was huge and filled with people, all staring at her, and Azar immediately shut her eyes against them. She wasn't ready to feel so many accusing stares, all ready to judge her and decide if she lived or died. She looked up at the ceiling. She wanted to look at anything but the room full of Djinn around her. The roof itself was actually a large dome, and the artwork on the inside rivaled some of the Renaissance masters. She stared at the beauty of the ceiling for a few more seconds and regained her composure.

When she finally lowered her gaze, the view was no less intimidating. On the marble floor was a large black and white inlay of the Djinn emblem. Her podium was at the center of the emblem, and at the end of each of the points was a cluster of seats with one large ornate, high backed chair raised above the others in the center of the section.

Taking a wild guess, she assumed that the people seated in those were the Councilor's for each of the Djinn races. They were in their ceremonial robes of grey, with a medallion tied around their necks from which hung a robin's egg sized gem of their race. At the bottom of the section, separated by a wooden barricade from the rest of the seating, was a single row of seats. Azar guessed they were either for witnesses or guests, probably the latter, as the low wooden wall said very clearly 'not one of us.'

Azar made herself turn and look every one of the Councilor's in the eye, and give them an acknowledging nod. There was no point acting like a petulant child. That would just get her a quicker trip to the hangman's noose.

Directly in front of her was the Ifrit section and the Councilor smiled and nodded back. He was a huge man in height and breadth, even in his human form. His eyes flickered like tiny little flames. Azar was mesmerized by him and had to physically force herself to look away.

She stopped at the Jann section, and her eyes fell on Bast, who stood directly in front of the Jann Councilors podium. Just seeing him was like a balm on her raw nerves. She lifted her eyes and bowed her head. The Councilor didn't acknowledge her back, but his eyes looked approving, and that was a good sign. Bast smiled at her and indicated the guest seating below the Jann section.

Azar let out her first real smile in days. Sitting below the Jann section was Aaron, who was accompanied by Anton himself. Aaron looked good, and her spirits lifted at seeing the boy so healthy. He sat stiffly, as if he was still in a little bit of pain, but he was sitting there instead of laid out in a pine box, and for that Azar would be eternally thankful. The smile stayed in place, because next to them was Jerry from the Onyx, Tao and Oliver. Oliver nodded at her soft white gossamer slave uniform, which was probably see through in this light and gave her a smile and a wink. She grinned back. The man could be wildly inappropriate even at the most somber of settings. He'd probably trawled funerals for dates. Azar felt better knowing that she had a few friends in the room.

She turned again and nodded at the Sila Councilor, continuing around to nod at the Marid Councilor as well. Both were aging women, and for the long lived, that must have meant that they were truly ancient. Each showed absolutely no expression. Azar wouldn't like to be at any of the Councilor poker nights.

She turned to the Ghul section and forced herself not to grimace. She nodded at the Councilor, a younger man in comparison to the Marid and Sila councilors, but his age was indeterminable. Her eyes fell on Lila, who was sitting in the front row in a green silk evening dress, as if she was going to a cocktail party rather than Azar's trial and possible execution. Lila smirked at her, and it took every ounce of her willpower not to sneer back. She quickly turned away to the last section.

The Shaitan section was the most sparsely occupied. There were even a few empty seats. Azar worried that if they continued the natural persecution of the Shaitan, there might not be any left. The only person she recognized was Donovan, his face unreadable. She knew that he would have to testify against her, and she also knew he had little choice. He looked strained, and Azar felt sorry for him. It would be tough to rat on your friends - although she wasn't sure they'd actually be classed as friends- especially when the consequence could be death. She didn't want him to feel bad. She bowed her head to the Shaitan Councilor, whose gaze made her want to wet herself, and then gave Donovan a smile and a nod. Some of the tension went out of his shoulders, but his face remained the same granite mask.

The Sila Councilor cleared her throat, and Azar turned to face her.

"Today we have two trials to be overseen. The first will be that of the deceased, Ellis Fareet of the Ifrit, on the charges of treason, conspiracy to release the Balraka, conspiracy to overthrow the Djinn Council, attempted murder of a Djinn, attempted murder of a member of the supernatural commu- nity, three counts of murder of a human, destruction of Djinn owned property and abandonment of his compulsory servitude. Do any stand in defense of him?" No one stood, not even a whisper was made. Apparently years in hiding, plotting to take over the world using a destructive, ancient Djinn, didn't make you any friends. Not even any of the Ifrit so much as raised an eyebrow. In fact the Ifrit Councilor was shaking his head with exasperation.

"So be it. We have read the witness statements compiled by the Adel Mira; does anyone have any questions for the witnesses before we rule?"

"We of the Shaitan have a question." The Shaitan Councilor was a far scarier version of Donovan. His black eyes looked soulless and his mouth was a thin line of barely contained rage. Azar swallowed hard and turned to face him. Her knees shook ferociously. "We wish to know if the Ifrit Fareet knew the location of the other Great Weapons."

Azar tried not to squeak in fear when she answered. "No, your Graciousness. He insinuated he found Drakhul by accident, and didn't search for the other weapons. He was more focused on releasing Balraka than anything else." The Councilor stared at her a little longer, right into her very soul, until droplets of sweat slid down her back. Then he nodded absently to himself.

"The Shaitan have no further questions."

"As there are no further questions, as a matter of course, we must rule. The Sila find the Ifrit Ellis Fareet guilty of all charges. "

"The Jann find Ellis Fareet guilty of all charges."

"The Ifrit find Ellis Fareet guilty of all charges."

"The Shaitan finds Ellis Fareet guilty of all charges."

"The Ghul find Ellis Fareet guilty of all charges."

"The Marid find Ellis Fareet guilty of all charges."

There was a small smattering of applause as the verdict was laid down, but the Sila Councilor called for silence with only a look. "Under the ancient laws of the Djinn, Ellis Fareet shall be sentenced to death by beheading. Conveniently, he has already been beheaded, so we can move on.

"Azar Nazemi of the Ifrit, you are charged with unsanctioned disclosure to a human and failure to come forth for your compulsory servitude. Do any stand in defense of this Ifrit?"

Bast stood, and oddly enough looked over to the Ifrit section. Azar didn't know why he thought someone from the Ifrit may stand in defense of her, as she didn't know any of them from Adam. When no one in the Ifrit section stood, Bast stepped down from the Jann section and walked into the empty space between her and the rows of people.

"I, Bast Shafigh of the Jann, stand for Azar Nazemi of the Ifrit." All the Councilor's agreed to his representation and the trial got underway.

The Sila Councilors lip quirked a little at Bast, which could have been a smile, but also could have been an itch. "Alright Bast, let's get the show on the road." There was a familiarity in her tone, and Azar wondered if Bast and the Sila Councilor had met before.

"My Gracious Councilors, we have all read the statement made by Azar Nazemi to the Adel Mira. You are all aware of the events that have shaped Azar's life so far. We are also very aware that she is indeed guilty of the charges of which she is accused." Azar's eyebrows drew together. She was no lawyer, but admitting her guilt in the opening sentence seemed a little unorthodox. But she trusted Bast; he knew the system, the Council and the laws.

"For those of you here that are unaware of the facts, I will give you the abridged version. Azar was born to a human mother, who for reasons unknown, fled from her homeland and went to Spain, where she died when Azar was five. But before she died, she taught Azar to fear her people. The Djinn became the boogeyman of young Azar's life. She was raised in a Spanish orphanage, and then sent out into the world to fend for herself.

"She moved from place to place, careful to avoid interaction with her own kind, as she was taught to do by the only figure in her life she could trust. She did not get the schooling in the ways of the Djinn like the children within our community, and her powers are untested and feared by her. What little she does know of the Djinn society is secondhand urban legends that spread amongst the Supernatural community.

"But did she go rogue or misuse her abilities because she was nothing more than a mere ghost to the Council? No, she became a firefighter, using her abilities in secret, not for selfish gain, but to save the lives of humans. And when a rogue Ifrit threatened to draw attention to us all, did she walk away and let the people she had feared her whole life deal with their own problems? No, she stepped up and searched for the Ifrit herself, to bring him down before he could expose us and kill millions of Djinn, Supes and humans in the city of New York." As Bast spoke, he walked around the inner edge of the sections, addressing every race equally, and met the eyes of the Councilors with deference.

"She did so without thought of reward or power, in fact she would gain nothing for bringing down Fareet. The only reward she received was near death and imprisonment. She may indeed still get death. But she did what she felt was right and necessary, even if it meant disclosing her true nature to a human. This was an unfortunate accident, but one that ultimately worked in the Djinn's favor. Without the help of Detective Keenan Reilly of the NYPD Arson unit, we would have found it far more difficult to track down Ellis Fareet, a Djinn who was supposed to have been dead for centuries." He paused, probably for gravitas. Even she had to admit, he was compelling.

"I have met Detective Reilly. I have spoken to him, and I am assured of his trustworthiness. Indeed, I believe he would be an asset to the Adel's intelligence network, and would suggest that he receive official authorization from the Council." Azar knew that if he didn't get official authorization, he would be dead before the day was out. Bast was trying to keep his promise to her, despite his assurances that it wouldn't be necessary. She lost a little bit more of her heart to her golden eyed Jann.

"In conclusion, Azar Nazemi does not deserve punishment for her transgressions. To punish her for her failure to complete her servitude would be like punishing a child for being scared of the dark. She was unaware of our traditions; unschooled in our way of life. She deserves our empathy, not our wrath. Indeed, I believe that Azar Nazemi deserves praise for her courage, even at the detriment of her own wellbeing. I implore the Council not be the monsters that Azar was brought up to believe you were; I beg you to show her the mercifulness that I, and every other Djinn in our community, know you are capable of. Thank you." Bast made his way back to his seat in the Jann section and sat down, his face pinched and worried.

Azar was beyond worried now; a cold sweat had broken out over her skin and her heart felt as if it was beating a mile a minute in her chest. She looked at her toes and tried to calm down, but it wasn't working. She looked into the faces of her friends, and felt her heart rate slow. Oliver gave her a reassuring smile, even though he had little lines between his eyes that weren't normally there.

The Marid Councilor spoke up. "Thank you Bast for your input. We recognize Azar Nazemi's admission of guilt on both charges. As many of you are aware, the punishment for an unsanctioned disclosure to a human is death. However, we wish to hear from witnesses regarding the events of the last week to get a better understanding of Miss Nazemi's intent. We have obviously heard from you Bast. However, you were not operating within the letter of the law this week either. This Ifrit's transgressions should have been immediately reported to the Council to be dealt with. The Council has a lot of respect for you Bast, and your many years of loyal service within the Adel was taken into account when we chose not to put you on that podium to face charges also. However, it makes your statements in regard to charges biased, to say the least."

Holy crap, Bast had been in the Adel. That was how he knew Mira, how he knew the processes and the Councilors so well. She was stunned, but it explained so much about Bast; his disgruntlement towards the Council, the scars that littered his body and his easy assurance that he wouldn't rat her out. However, the image of her gentle Bast as a cold blooded killer didn't gel well with her. She now understood the shadows behind his eyes when he talked about his past. Azar snapped out of her stunned stupor when she realized the Marid Councilor was speaking again.

"We would like to call Donovan Rixton of the Shaitan forward." Donovan slowly stood and made his way down to the space between her podium and the race sections. The Adel guards all stood a little straighter, and Azar felt sympathy for the persecution that Donovan must suffer merely because he was of a certain Djinn race. "Donovan, please tell us when you became aware that Azar Nazemi had disclosed her true nature to the human."

Donovan looked at the Adel around her podium and then sadly at her. Azar didn't think he was used to showing so much emotion. "I found out after the traitor had burned down my club and I went to Azar's apartment with the Weres in my employ. The human arrived later, as I believe he and Azar had some kind of romantic relationship. When the human was told of threats made to Azar's life, he accidently let it slip that he was aware of our existence."

"And what was Azar Nazemi's response?" The Ifrit Councilor asked.

"She punched him in the face and broke his nose." A small smile quirked at the corners of Donovan's mouth, as he recalled the night. Even the Ifrit Councilor smirked.

The Jann Councilor spoke for the first time. He looked the same age as Bast, but who knew how old that was. "Do you trust the human not to tell others our secrets?"

Donovan was silent, his face pensive as he seriously considered the question. "I believe that he can be trusted not to spread word of our existence to other humans. He accepted the information calmly and seems to acknowledge that telling another soul would mean instant death. He hid the fact that Onyx was part of a serial arson spree. I believe that at the Blue Smoke club he hid the fact that the death of a human girl was the work of supernatural forces. He did these things to the detriment of his own career, and under the threat of death. He strikes me as a man of integrity, and I believe he will keep our secret. I second Bast's request that he be given official authorization from the Council."

"And do you believe that Azar Nazemi of the Ifrit should be punished for breaking such a sacred law?" The Jann Councilor asked. This time there was no hesitation from Donovan.

"No. Azar has unwittingly followed our laws for a century. I do not believe she maliciously told this secret to the human, it was just unfortunate luck. When it was revealed to me that the human knew the forbidden secret, she did not try to convince me to keep her transgression from the Council. All she asked for was time to ensure that the traitor Fareet was stopped. She was prepared to accept her punishment, but not until she had risked her life to save us all."

That was technically not true. She'd had every intention of making a run for it after she'd brought down Fareet. But you know what they say about the best laid plans of mice and Djinn.

The Jann Councilor nodded to the Marid Councilor, indicating he was finished questioning Donovan, and the Marid Councilor allowed Donovan to go back to his seat. His back was ramrod straight as he walked back to his section and she could feel the waves of frustration pouring off him from her podium. Azar wanted to tell him that it was okay, that he did the best he could in a bad situation. She turned her head to look at all the Councilors, but they all had neutral masks for faces.

The Sila Councilor addressed the other Councilors, "Does anyone wish to hear from any other witnesses? We have all read the statement from the Were boy, does anyone wish to question him?" Azar tensed. She hoped they wouldn't be so cruel. She breathed a sigh of relief when the Jann Councilor agreed with her.

"I don't think that would be necessary. He's been through enough at the hands of our people. We do not need to make him live this atrocity again." He looked over at Aaron. "Is there anything that you wish to add to your statement?" Aaron shook his head vigorously, and the Jann Councilor nodded. "Very well. I think we should get on to the deliberation." The Councilors all nodded and turned to the members of their section, everyone talking in hushed whispers.

Mira had told her that they would seek the opinions of their races, and put forth a suggested punishment. Then they had to get a majority of Councilors to agree on the punishment. If it was a deadlocked, everyone in the room would get a vote on the punishment, including the Adel and any guests. Apparently such a scenario hadn't happened in over three thousand years, and Azar doubted it was going to start with her.

The room was buzzing with the low murmurs of the Djinn, and the sound was like white noise. Mira left her post to walk over to the Marid Councilor, and was saying something furiously to the group. Both Bast and Donovan were talking animatedly to their Councilors and the other people in the section. The minutes dragged on for what seemed like hours. Azar felt like she was made of stone as she stood still on her podium, afraid that if she moved she would shatter into a million pieces. Eventually the noise died down and the Ghul Councilor cleared his throat.

"Have we all come to our decisions?" There was a murmur of agreement from the rest of the Councilors. "Good, the Ghul shall go first. The Ghul recommend death by beheading for both the Ifrit and the human to whom she told the forbidden secret. Our laws are in place for a reason, to protect our race from the hordes of humans that infest our world. Although we are far more powerful, we are not so vast in numbers that we could win a war. Therefore, any breach of our laws should be met with swift and final punishment."

Azar let out a little gasp, which was studiously ignored by everyone as if she no longer existed. She should have known what kind of sentence would come from the race that spawned Lila the Hateful!

The Jann Councilor scoffed, "So your answer to a dwindling population is to cut off heads? Even a Ghul should see the flawed logic in that statement." He shook his head with bemusement. "The Jann seek the sentence of a reduced twenty-five years of servitude, which takes into account the services already rendered to the Djinn people. Furthermore, Bast Shafigh of the Jann would like to petition for control of that servitude. We also believe that the human could be of service to the Djinn, and that he be officially sanctioned by the Council and set under the control of Adel Intelligence officers."

Bast wanted to be her Master? Although the thought of being at his beck and call every day for the next twenty-five years was a little irksome, she could see that servitude under Bast would be the best thing she could hope for. She crossed her fingers that more of the Councilors agreed with the Jann.

She whipped around as the Shaitan Councilor spoke. "Whilst the Shaitan agrees that the death sentence is too harsh given the nature of the transgressions, we believe that twenty-five years of servitude is far too lenient. We suggest the full one hundred years of servitude. We don't want more people believing that they can skip their compulsory servitude, a tradition that has benefited the Djinn for millennia, and the Council will be lenient. We rely on the servitude system to ensure our standing in the wider supernatural community and allow the Djinn as a whole to live prosperously. Therefore, we also suggest death for the human. He is a liability that we don't really need." Azar's eyes flew to Donovan, whose face was set in a hard mask of fury. Obviously, the opinion of a half blood didn't matter to the Shaitan Councilor.

There was a murmur of approval amongst the seated Djinn. One hundred years of servitude. Death for Keenan. Little black spots danced in front of her eyes. The Ifrit Councilor stood on his podium.

"One hundred years would essentially be a death sentence for Azar. She is a half blood, thus has a shorter life span than most and she will be in service until the day she dies. To behead her would be more humane." She sucked in air like she'd been punched. They were going to suggest beheading? He own people?

"However, that is not the Ifrit suggestion. We suggest essentially the same as the Jann. Twenty five years of servitude seems sufficient considering she has practically lived a life of servitude to the humans already. We also suggest she is allowed to continue to work where she is now. A Djinn in the FDNY has already proven useful. Although I hope we never have such a problem again, it is useful to have an authorized person who can maintain our secrecy when things get a little out of control. I think the same applies for the human. The Ifrit would be very grateful if this sentence was agreed upon." The Ifrit Councilor gave a hard look to all of the other Councilors and Azar eyed him. Shocked indignation rippled through the crowd, though no one voiced any real complaint.

Azar could understand their shock, she too realized that if his sentence was accepted, she'd be getting off pretty much punishment free. Was it just race loyalty that made the Ifrit Councilor give her such an indulgent sentence, or was there more going on there? Azar's head started to pound and she didn't think on it any more. The Council was in her life for good now, whether her life was years or only hours long, and there would be plenty of time to figure out the Council intrigues when her life wasn't on the line. Maybe she'd ask Bast, seeing how he was the dark horse in this race.

The Marid Councilor was shaking her head. "To show such favoritism would make a mockery of this Council, and the Councilor for the Ifrit should know better. We are unbiased towards every Djinn who stands on the accused podium, regardless of their heritage or their relation to anyone in power. This is not a corrupt court of the human world. Azar will have a fitting sentence for her crimes. The Marid suggest one hundred years of servitude, under the Adel in their intelligence network. Whilst we agree with the Ifrit Councilor that she should remain in her position as a member of the FDNY for now, she should be at the disposal of the Adel should the need arise. One hundred years of servitude is what is requested of all Djinn and the Marid don't believe that anyone should be exempt from that. The human should also be put to use by the Adel. We don't have enough resources in the human world, and I believe that having someone under our control within the NYPD is an opportunity too good to pass up."

There was so much inference in the Marid Councilors sentence that Azar didn't understand. Was she referring to Bast? And by her heritage was she referring to being an Ifrit? So many questions crowded her mind, and the answers seemed just out of reach. Her nerves were now so shot that she was barely hanging on to her emotions. She wanted to scream or weep. This process seemed unnecessarily cruel. Each sentence that was given out could be the one that was chosen. It was like being presented with six different versions of your life, and the choice was in the hands of six complete strangers.

Azar turned to face the Sila Councilor, the last to give her sentence. The Sila Councilor had the most sway within the group. She was old, and the Sila were known for their wisdom and negotiation skills. To Azar, that made her more fearful than the Shaitan Councilor. She knew in her gut that the sentence she would give would be the one that was agreed upon by the Council. However, the Sila Councilor was not looking at her, but rather at the Jann section and at Bast in particular. She pursed her lips and then turned back to Azar.

"The Marid are correct in stating that one hundred years of servitude is what's requested of all Djinn people, and therefore it must be served. However, the Ifrit are also correct in that giving you one hundred years of servitude would be inhumane, as you would work until the day of your death. So here we have a quandary, do we not? We have one hundred years of service that needs to be fulfilled, but only one of you. So the Sila suggest giving you one hundred years of servitude, unless someone else will complete half of the servitude for you. Then you would get fifty years of servitude each. The Sila suggest the Bast Shafigh of the Jann, who seems to have such a compelling interest in your welfare, completes the other half of your servitude." The Sila Councilor turned to Bast. "We have yet to fill your role in the Adel after all these years Bast. Indeed, your loss to the Adel has been sorely felt by all. It has created a black hole amongst the ranks that refuses to be filled. Fifty years of your service would ensure that the Ifrit Azar does not work until she dies."

Blood roared in her ears as the rage and flames boiled beneath her skin. They were trying to blackmail him, using her. That wasn't right.

"No!" she yelled out from the podium. "I refuse to allow Bast to be forced back into the Adel. I will take the one hundred years of servitude." She looked at Bast, and could see the resignation on his face. He was going to agree.

She thought of the tortured look on his face when he spoke of the Council and Mira's comment about the senseless killing on Council orders not being for everyone. Azar just knew she was talking about Bast. It all made sense now that she knew he was a former Adel. She would not inflict fifty more years of killing onto him.

The Sila Councilor frowned at Azar. "You, as the accused, do not get a say in your sentencing. Bast, would you accept the terms of this agreement, if it is voted through?" Bast looked at Azar for a long minute. She shook her head, mouthed the word no and did everything short of jumping off the podium and slapping some sense into him. But he just gazed back at her, like he was mentally cataloging every kiss, every word, and every interaction between them. He slowly nodded his head, and all the air left her lungs for a second time. He was going to do it.

"I would accept." He gave a hard look to the Sila Councilor. She had backed him into a corner, and everyone in the room knew it. The Sila Councilor had just made her way onto Azar's shit list.

The Sila Councilor gave a nod of satisfaction,

obviously knowing the answer from the outset. "Then let's get the voting underway, shall we? In order of presentation and by a show of hands, all those in favor of the Ghul sentence?" Only the Ghul Councilor raised his hand and Azar breathed a sigh of relief. She knew it was a long shot, but she was glad death was off the table. "The Ghul sentence fails. All those in favor of the Jann sentence?" Both the Jann and the Ifrit Councilors raised their hands. "The Jann sentence fails. All those in favor of the Shaitan sentence." This time only the Ghul and Shaitan Councilors raised their hands. "The Shaitan sentence fails. All those in favor of the Ifrit sentence?" The Ifrit and Jann Councilors again raised their hands and Azar had a dull feeling in the pit of her stomach that she knew where this was heading. "The Ifrit sentence fails. All those in favor of the Marid sentence?" Not even the Marid Councilor raised her hand for this option. Apparently, if they could get two Djinn into servitude for the price of one, they were going to take it. "The Marid sentence fails. All those in favor of the Sila sentence raise your hands?" The Shaitan, Marid, Ifrit and Sila Councilors all raised their hands. Four out of six, that was it. It was done.

"The Sila sentence has passed. Azar Nazemi of

the Ifrit, you are sentenced to fifty years of servitude under the Adel. Bast Shafigh of the Jann shall also serve fifty years of service in the Adel for you. The human has the official validation of the Council. He will be contacted by the Adel and told of his new status. If he refuses, he will be terminated immediately. You are free to go and attend your new duties. Bast, as we cannot bind you with Anadari Bracelets," Anadari Bracelets was the politically correct term for slave cuffs. "We shall have the Scribe write up a contract."

One of the Adel led a pale hunched man over to Bast, and in his hands was a brittle piece of vellum. Both the man and the vellum looked ancient, older than both the Sila and Marid Councilors combined. The man waved his hands over the blank piece of vellum and letters appeared across the sheet in the old tongue. Bast just stared at it for a time, his face unreadable, before he took the quill pen from the Scribe, jabbed his finger and signed in blood. Azar vaulted over the rail of the podium and up to the Jann section of the room.

"What the hell have you done, Bast!? You had no right to offer yourself up like some sacrificial lamb. I could have served the hundred years. Now I am forever indebted to your Jann ass!" She was poking him in the center of the chest as she spoke, and his face got stormier and stormier.

"You're goddamn welcome, you ungrateful wench. I'm sorry if the thought of you toiling away under the Adel until you're old and grey horrified me. Or worse, the plaything of some rich old troll king. Trust me, there are plenty on the waiting list. Or even worse, with your head rolling across this very floor! This is done now, so live with it." He raised his bleeding finger as he yelled back, and then leaned in to kiss her hard on the mouth. "Besides, now you owe me." He smirked at her, and Azar didn't know if she wanted to laugh or kiss him or slap him silly. Maybe all three.

The decision was taken out of her hands as the Were's came over to hug her, unsure whether to congratulate or commiserate. Oliver almost broke her spine when he hugged her tight, and Azar knew that he was thankful that he hadn't caused her death, in one way or another. She'd lecture him on his stupid guilt another time. She hugged Aaron, and he thanked her over and over again. Tears welled in her eyes, and by the time Aaron let go, there were tear stains on the top of his shirt.

Anton shook her hand and seconded Aaron's thanks. She shrugged it off. It had been Aaron who ultimately saved the day, and she made sure everyone knew it. She only realized that someone was standing behind her when Bast bowed his head. She turned to see the Ifrit Councilor standing behind her. She bowed her head also.

"Your Graciousness." Azar hoped that was the correct term. Luckily, it was too late to chop off her head now for bad manners.

"Please, call me Saraf. The Ifrit have searched for you for such a long time. I would like to welcome you into our world, Azar." He bowed. Azar raised an eyebrow.

The man looked familiar, probably because he possessed such strongly Persian features. They were proud and regal, his nose narrow and straight, with a hook at the end, and his face was thin with a solid jawline. He had dark hair and olive skin. He towered over her, and his shoulders were so wide that she couldn't see around him without leaning to the side. He wore a smile, but Azar could feel the barely contained power in the man and it scared the hell out of her. Up close, his eyes were even creepier. It wasn't like there was a little flame instead of a pupil; it was more like little orange strikes of lightning piercing their way through his iris and then disappearing, only to reappear on the opposite side of his pupil. Fareet definitely hadn't had that feature, so it made Azar wonder at just how powerful Saraf was.

"Do the Ifrit search for every bastard child they spawn?" Azar couldn't help that her tone was a little acerbic. A century of distrust wasn't washed away in a day.

"Actually we try to, yes. However, I had a special interest in you. I try to gather all my progeny into Djinn society as soon as possible. Due to their incredible strength, it is unwise to leave them to discover their own nature out in the world. Unfortunately, your mother disappeared with you before I could come and collect you both after your birth. I like to think I am not, uh, what's that term the humans use? A deadbeat Dad?"

"Excuse me?" Azar croaked.

Perhaps she'd actually gone insane in her cell. She could swear that this stranger, this hulking beast of an Ifrit, was saying he was her father. At least now she knew why he looked familiar. Her nose was a smaller version of his, her mouth was his mouth with a feminine twist, the shape of his eyes was exactly like hers. The black dots swam in her vision again, and she collapsed down in the chair beside her. This was too much. She stuck her head between her knees and breathed deep.

She could vaguely hear Bast suggesting that Saraf leave the subject for another day, and Saraf saying goodbye. Her hands were wet, and she realized that it was from the tears pouring down her face. She cried out of relief that she wasn't dead, out of frustration and out of regret.

She was still crying when Bast lifted her up, and walked her out of the room.

CHAPTER 16

Six hours later she was curled up on Bast's couch in his apartment. She didn't know why, but for some reason she thought he actually lived down on Coney Island Boardwalk. In reality, he had a one bedroom apartment on West Fifth street, overlooking a park and the beachfront. If she thought Bast's office was full of plants, it had nothing on his home. Plants literally sat on every surface, and dozens hung from the roof.

Azar could see his Adel sword leaning against a bookcase in a forgotten corner. A picture of Bast and an old man, she assumed it was Moselle, on the Coney Island boardwalk sat on the entertainment unit next to his television. She'd pulled back the curtains so she could watch the water through the double glass doors that led out onto the balcony. Bast had gone out to get her Chinese takeout, and the quiet solitude was almost too much for her. She'd had enough quiet solitude to last for quite a while.

What she really needed to do was go see Keenan, to tell him she was okay. To tell him that he was now forever beholden to a race of people that will kill him if he didn't agree to their terms. That she was tied to another man for the next fifty years, a man she had real feelings for. What she really had to tell him was there would be no future for them. She had to cut contact before she dragged him deeper into a dangerous world that he knew nothing about. Hell, she barely knew anything about it.

All of a sudden, her feet itched. She needed to get this over and done with. She stood up and looked down at herself. She was still in her slave whites from the trial. She tore them off as fast as she could. She went into Bast's room and rummaged through his drawers until she found a pair of jeans and a sweatshirt. The jeans were too long and a little too big, but she belted them up tight and they didn't look too bad. There was some change on Bast's dresser which she borrowed for the cab ride. Who kept fifty dollar bills in their change bowl anyway?

Azar wrote Bast a note, telling him she had gone to see Keenan, that she'd be back and to keep her Chinese food in the fridge for her. She also told him that she owed him some change. She hesitated to write 'Love, Azar' but it felt so right that she wrote it anyway.

Azar put back on the slippers the Council had provided, and walked down the twelve flights of stairs to the street. By a stroke of luck, she got a cab straight away and directed them to her apartment. Azar knew that's where Keenan would be. She didn't know how she knew that, but her gut told her to go straight to her apartment. Besides, she wasn't even sure where Keenan lived.

The cab ride to her apartment seemed to take forever. Azar's notion of time had changed drastically lately. Time could be a balm or a torture. She paid the cabbie as he pulled up in front of her apartment.

She stood there looking at the building that was her former sanctuary. She didn't know if being in the Adel would mean she would have to be housed in the Council compound or if she could keep her apartment. She hadn't stuck around to find out. Tomorrow she would bite the bullet and go back to see Mira. She would begin her fifty years of slavery.

Today she had to tie up loose ends, starting with the one sitting in her apartment.

When Azar reached her front door, she realized she didn't have her keys on her. She'd left them at the station with her other stuff on the night she was abducted. She raised her hand and knocked. It felt weird knocking on her own door, as if she was now a stranger in her own life. She was someone different now. She was no longer Azar, in hiding and on the run. She was Azar, known slave of the Council, Adel member, no longer an orphan.

The door flew open before she could dwell on the latter point, and Keenan filled her vision. He looked like shit. He'd lost weight and hadn't shaved. His shirt was dirty and his hair was scruffy. He had bags under his eyes, and new worry lines between his brows.

"You look like hell." It was the best she could come up with that wouldn't result in her breaking down into a hysterical mess. Keenan didn't answer, just dragged her into his body and squeezed her close until she thought she might run out of breath.

"I thought you were dead. Bast said you'd been stabbed in the heart, that you were being taken care of, but he wouldn't let me go and see you. He said you had to go to trial, that they could give you a death sentence for telling me what you were. This has been the longest day of my life. Oliver sent me a text to tell me you were okay, but he couldn't elaborate." He dragged her into the apartment, his body still pressed close to hers as if he was scared that she would disappear if he let her go.

Azar swallowed the lump in her throat, and moved them both to the couch. He had better be sitting for this. She took a deep breath and explained; about her sentence, about how Bast was going to serve her other fifty years. She even explained about her father being the Ifrit Councilor.

"The problem is Keenan, that they made a judgment about you as well. About whether you were a liability or not." Keenan sat back on the couch, his face going suddenly grey. "They ruled that you were to become an authorized disclosure, but only if you became intelligence for the Adel. If you refuse, they will have you killed." Azar let the news sink in, waiting for the anger and denial that would surely follow.

Instead of rage, Keenan seemed calm. Still very pale, but calm. "What would that entail exactly? Would I be putting people at risk?" Azar couldn't believe how calmly he was contemplating his sentence.

"I don't think so. I'm not really sure, but I think it's basically just fudging some reports when the crime appears to have been done by a Djinn. Maybe reporting anything that looks like a Djinn crime to the Adel. I can't imagine that they would want too much from you. The Djinn don't exactly have a high opinion of the usefulness of the human race."

Keenan was nodding blankly. She felt ashamed. She had been the cause of that expression a lot over the last week or so. Reaching out, she ran her palm over his cheek. The bristly growth on his jaw scraped against her palm, so unlike the clean cut Keenan Reilly of two weeks ago. She rubbed the pad of her thumb over the deep grooves that had suddenly appeared around his eyes, trying to erase them. Keenan pressed his face against her hand, closed his eyes and sighed.

He turned his face and pressed a kiss against her palm. "I don't know what I would have done if I had lost you." His voice was rough and Azar's heart constricted. The next part was going to be painful.

"That's the other thing, Keenan. Like I said, I've been sentenced to fifty years of servitude under the Adel. Bast volunteered to complete the other fifty years of my servitude. I will have to live, sleep and eat at the Council Compound." Keenan moved his face away from her hand and sat back.

"What are you saying?"

Azar swallowed hard. "What I am saying is that there can be no more you and me. I am a slave. You will be in your eighties when I'm released. I am no longer my own person but compelled to meet the every need of my master. It's a physical imperative. I can't disobey a command, because these prevent it." She raised her wrists so he could see her Anadari Bracelets. "If they ordered me to kill you, I would have to do it! So I think it's best if we maintain our distance. It will be safer for us both. They are letting me keep my job for now, until they find something else for me to do, so we will run into each other there. But I'd like to go back to the way things were a month ago." She flinched back as Keenan jumped up off the couch.

"A month ago? A month ago, we could barely say a civil word to one another. A month ago, you weren't a slave, and I didn't have a noose around my neck that could be tightened if I somehow displease a race of people I had no idea existed. So, I'm sorry Azar, but there is no going back to the way things were a month ago!" She knew he was really angry, his Irish lilt had gotten so thick towards the end that she had to strain to understand. He went over to the kitchen counter and poured himself a scotch. It appeared he'd replenished what had been demolished during the celebrations with the Weres.

She decided to go pack some of the things she'd need and let him calm down. She couldn't imagine being back here anytime soon. She walked into her bedroom and pulled out a duffel bag from the back of the closet. She put in the normal stuff, clothes and toiletries, her phone charger and her laptop. She reached under her bed and pulled out a wooden box that was stuffed full of the mementos of her life; a locket with her mother's picture, a vial of sand from Persia, pictures of her and her workmates from every firestation she had worked at. Little things that say, hey, I've lived and loved. She placed it gently on top of her duffel bag.

She changed out of Bast's stuff, folding it and putting it inside her duffel too, before zipping the bag shut. Everything from her one hundred and twenty five years of life fit in that bag. The rest was just stuff. But she still felt sad at leaving it all behind. They were remnants of a happy life.

Azar picked up her duffel and carried it into the entry hall. She walked over to the kitchen counter and pulled a tumbler from the cupboard. She poured another scotch for Keenan, who was still leaning against the counter, and one for herself. He looked as if someone had just run over his brand new puppy, and it tugged at her gut.

She raised her glass in the air. "To us. It may have been brief, but it meant more to me than you will ever know." She clinked her glass to Keenan's. He looked down at her face and a stubborn look that meant trouble came into his eyes.

"To us. And to the Irish. When we know what we want, we fight tooth and nail to get it." He downed his drink in one gulp, his eyes never leaving hers. Azar should have known he wouldn't just go quietly into the night. She rinsed her glass out and placed it in the drainer, purely out of habit. She shook her head, muttering under her breath about the bloody Irish.

She went to the hall and picked up her bags. She turned back to Keenan and gave him a sad smile. He raised his glass again and nodded. He saw this as a challenge, not a break up, if the look of determination on his face was anything to go by. Nothing with Keenan Reilly ever went smoothly.

Azar opened the door to her apartment, hopefully not for the last time, but quickly realized that the doorway wasn't empty. The big Adel who had caught her when she had collapsed on the way to her trial was blocking the way. He nodded curtly again, and Azar wondered if he was mute. So far he'd done a lot of nodding and not much speaking. In the next second, he proved her wrong.

"Azar, I am Danian. I am the human's handler." Azar could hear Keenan striding over to the door. She pushed Danian back into the hall and shut the door quickly behind her. She glanced up and down the hall to make sure it was empty.

"Look, I know you don't have to, and you probably think it's contemptible, but his name is Keenan. He won't respond well to being called 'the human' or being told you are his handler. He's a smart guy, not a piece of office equipment, so treat him as such and the Adel will have a trustworthy ally for life. He deserves better than the hand he has been dealt, so I beg of you to please treat him with respect, and I promise you he will return it." Her voice dropped to a whisper so Keenan, who was just on the other side of the door, couldn't hear. "He is going to be a bit prickly for a little while, because he doesn't really understand. He's been thrown in the deep end, so just give him time."

Danian stared down at her, and Azar hoped he wouldn't have her punished for being an unruly slave already, not even eight hours into her servitude. But the large man just nodded once. Keenan opened the door and just stared, but Danian ignored him for a second.

"Mira expects you at the compound at 0600 sharp. It wouldn't bode well to be late." He turned to Keenan. "Keenan, my name is Danian. I am to be your contact at the Adel. May I come in?" When Keenan nodded, a little bit dazedly, Danian turned back to her. "You are dismissed." He walked through the door, shutting it firmly behind Keenan and himself.

Azar didn't really remember getting in the elevator and travelling down to the ground floor, but when she stepped out of that large metal box, she felt like she was leaving something behind. It was sad and fearfully wonderful at the same time. She could live out in the open now. She could explore a whole new world filled with people just like her. She was free to love and free to test her own abilities. Apparently there was a silver lining to the dark cloud that was fifty years of slavery.

She pushed through the buildings front door, her arm already raised to hail a cab. She lowered it slowly as her eyes fell on Bast leaning against his car.

"I thought you might need a ride," he said casually as he walked over to take her duffel bag and stow it on the back seat.

She just looked at him, the sun shining down on his golden hair, and her heart leapt in her chest, even as it was breaking for the man she'd left in her apartment. She still felt as if she was down a rabbit's hole like Alice, but she was no longer drowning. Instead she was going to be stuck at the Mad Hatter's tea party for the next fifty years. Except it wasn't her that was crazy, but the rest of the world.

He held the door open for her as she slid into the passenger seat, before walking around to slide behind the wheel. She rested her head on the plush leather and let her mind go blank. The weight of the world, or at least New York City, had been lifted off her shoulders and now she could take this small moment of peace.

When Bast continued past his apartment building, Azar realized he was taking her to Coney Island. Somehow, he just knew that she needed the sand and the surf, and the whirling lights of the amusement rides. She needed to immerse herself in humanity.

He parked in his spot next to the warehouse, and came around to open the door for her. He held her hand as she slid out, and instead of letting go, he maintained a good grasp on it. He reached over to the tiny backseat and pulled out a plastic shopping bag filled with Chinese food.

Still holding her hand, he walked her down to the boardwalk, and led her to an empty bench overlooking the ocean. People bustled around behind them, drifting back and forth from the railing to the food vendors. It was all blissfully normal. These people had no idea how close to death they had come.

Bast handed her a box of kung pow chicken and some chopsticks. A guy on the beach threw a frisbee to his dog, which barked excitedly as it leapt high into the air. The dog reminded her of poor Snookums and her date with Keenan in Central Park. Well, it wasn't actually a date but it wasn't quite work either. It was that stupid grey area that seemed to be where Keenan was most comfortable. Azar sighed, shook off her melancholy and enjoyed the atmosphere.

"You saved these people. Every one of them," Bast murmured.

It was true, she had saved them, with the help of Aaron. No matter how difficult her punishment by the Djinn Council would be, they were worth it. She fed a piece of chicken to a seagull and ten more flew over to stare at her intently.

"I guess I did. What happened with Lila and the Ghul?" Azar was dying to know. Obviously nothing too drastic considering both Lila and the Councilor for the Ghul were perched up at her trial today. Bast shook his head in disgust.

"Nothing. Lila vowed black and blue that she tried to get in touch with Franco -he's the Ghul Councilor- and Franco swears equally as fervently that he never received her calls. They just put it down to miscommunication. It's obviously bullshit, we both know that. However, without evidence of misconduct, there's nothing the Adel can do."

The idea made her blood boil. She had almost died, and thousands of New Yorkers as well, and the blood sucking bimbo got away with sitting back and letting it happen. But she was now on the Adel's radar, and they could make her life very uncomfortable. Azar doubted that any of them had fallen for the he said/she said ploy that the Ghul had produced, especially Mira. Azar really wanted to see Lila burn.

"Is Saraf really my father?" She already knew the answer, felt it in her bones, but she needed to hear confirmation from someone else.

Bast sighed heavily. "Yeah, he is. He came to see you when you were out of it, after we brought you back to the compound. He knew all about you, even before you'd even given your statement to Mira. Apparently, he tracked you to Spain, but lost you when you hopped the ocean to the free world. I didn't want to tell you until it was all over; you had enough problems without throwing a long lost father into the mix. But then Saraf beat me to it." He grimaced. "Sorry you couldn't have found out in a less dramatic setting. Saraf isn't exactly known for his tact. His stubbornness is legendary though. You must get that from him," he teased.

So her father really had looked for her. Azar didn't know if she was happy or upset that he'd failed to find her in Spain. She'd had a lot of hard times, gone to sleep hungry in a lot of cardboard boxes, but she also loved the life she'd eventually created. She loved working as a firefighter and she loved her friends. All that would not exist if Saraf had scooped her up from the orphanage when she was five. Azar struggled to comprehend what her life would have been like if that had happened.

Something finally dawned on her. "He said progeny. At the trial, he said he gathered his progeny together. Does that mean I have siblings?"

Bast laughed. "Yeah, you do. Quite a few actually. Saraf takes procreating for the Ifrit race very seriously." Bast was counting on his fingers. "There's ten that I can think of, but there could be more. He has been around for a very long time." Azar shook her head dazedly. She gone from being alone in the world, to having a father and at least ten half siblings. Her life had finally hit the twilight zone.

Bast wrapped an arm around her shoulders and kissed her cheek. The golden five o'clock shadow that covered his jaw tickled her face.

"So, how did it go with Reilly?" He tried to sound nonchalant but there was a tiny thread of compassion, and maybe hope in his voice.

"He's confused and angry. He is too stubborn to give up without a fight, so I doubt that today will be the last time I see him, regardless of the risk to his safety. I'm not going to lie Bast, it hurt to say goodbye to him." It was Azar's turn to heavy sigh. "He took the news about almost being assassinated rather well actually. Danian arrived just as I left, and I had a few words with him, set him straight about a few things, you know?" Bast raised his eyebrows and laughed.

"Danian is very powerful; he is Jann also. We grew up together in service to the Adel. Behind that strong silent type persona he seems to love so much, he really is a nice guy. He will be good to Keenan." A little bit of the guilt that had constricted around her heart eased at Bast's assurances.

Oh, that reminded her of something. Azar turned and punched Bast in the arm. "That's for not telling me you were in The Adel. I think that is a pretty important thing to tell your friends."

Bast pouted and rubbed his arm. The sun had started to set, and the golden colors of the sky painted the ocean in front of them. Azar was just glad she lived to see another sunset.

"It hadn't been a part of my life for a very long time. I was pretty messed up when I left the Adel, and I wanted to hide in my cave, surrounded by humanity but never having to interact with it, and lick my wounds in peace. And then someone burnt down my warehouse, and a sassy little Ifrit wandered in and turned my peaceful world upside down. But you're right, I should have told you." He kissed her neck and his teeth nipped her earlobe. "Why don't we go back to my office so I can try and make it up to you?" His voice was husky and full of promise.

"Wouldn't that upset your plants?" The last time she was in his office, his pot plants had all curled in on themselves, like she was a hillbilly at the ballet. She had to keep reminding herself that they weren't conscious beings. They didn't have opinions! "Besides, isn't there a memo on inter-slave relations?" Azar joked as he slowly kissed his way along her jaw. The crowd on the boardwalk had thinned out as the day visitors went home and the night visitors were yet to arrive.

"Probably, but I won't tell if you don't. How about we go back to my apartment and I really make it up to you. Maybe we can pick up where we left off in the oasis?" Her skin flushed as she remembered him lying her down in the sand. But her heart wasn't in it. She'd been through the emotional ringer today, and the last thing she wanted to do was to start something new. She wanted to take stock of her life, look at the cards in her hands and the chips on the table, and decide where she went from here.

She ran a hand through Bast's hair and then gently pushed him away. "I don't want to do this right now, Bast. I'm not saying never, because we both know that would be a lie, but I need to figure out who I am and where I stand in this new and frightening world before I involve myself with someone else. Does that make sense?"

Bast leaned back against the backrest of the

bench theatrically, but he kept his arm around her shoulders. She felt sorry for him, and maybe a little guilty. He'd committed himself to fifty years of servitude and he still couldn't get into her pants. But she didn't want meaningless sex with Bast.

He had been right when they had first met; there was a pull between them, and she desperately wanted to explore it too. However, she wanted to start her exploration under the right circumstances.

The sun had set on the worst day of her life, but it had brought with it some positive things to counteract the negative and because of that, she couldn't find it in herself to wish that the Rogue had never started his fire pledge. She had lost a lot, her freedom and nearly her life, but she had gained a lot in the process.

Azar took a deep breath, and let her new life begin.

A NOTE FROM THE AUTHOR

Thank you for reading. It was a wild ride, but I hope you are ready for Book 2 in The Azar Trilogy, Burn and Blaze!

I love hearing from readers, so you can find me at any of these places below:

Facebook Author Page: https://www.facebook.com/GraceMcGintyAuthor/

Instagram: @gracemcgintyauthor

Website: www.gracemcginty.com

Twitter: @McgintyGrace

Email: gracemcgintyauthor@gmail.com

And now for the battle cry of all indie authors. If you liked this book, or any book, leave a review, or recommend it to a friend, or write the Amazon link on the wall of a bathroom stall.

Anything helps, and it keeps indie writers creating the stories you love so much.